UNCLE $CROOGE

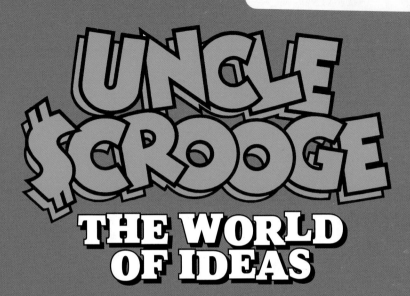

THE WORLD OF IDEAS

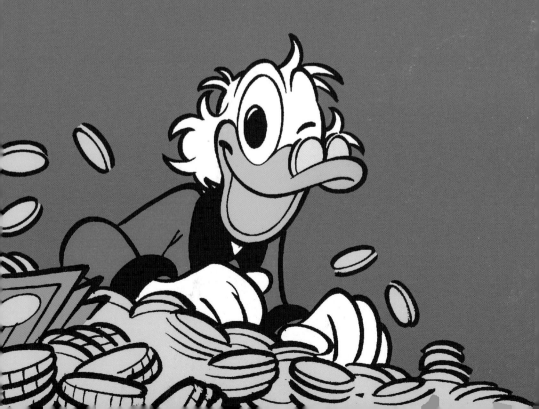

Facebook: **facebook.com/idwpublishing**
Twitter: **@idwpublishing**
YouTube: **youtube.com/idwpublishing**
Tumblr: **tumblr.idwpublishing.com**
Instagram: **instagram.com/idwpublishing**

ISBN: 978-1-68405-572-2   22 21 20 19   1 2 3 4

COVER ART
MARCO MAZZARELLO

COVER COLORS
MARCO COLLETTI

SERIES ASSISTANT EDITOR
ANNI PERHEENTUPA

SERIES EDITOR
CHRIS CERASI

COLLECTION EDITORS
JUSTIN EISINGER
& ALONZO SIMON

COLLECTION DESIGNER
DOM RINALDI

UNCLE SCROOGE: THE WORLD OF IDEAS. NOVEMBER 2019.
FIRST PRINTING. All contents, unless otherwise specified,
copyright © 2019 Disney Enterprises, Inc. All rights reserved.
The IDW logo is registered in the U.S. Patent and Trademark
Office. IDW Publishing, a division of Idea and Design Works,
LLC. Editorial offices: 2765 Truxtun Road, San Diego, CA
92106. Any similarities to persons living or dead are purely
coincidental. With the exception of artwork used for review
purposes, none of the contents of this publication may be
reprinted without the permission of Idea and Design Works,
LLC. Printed in Korea.
IDW Publishing does not read or accept unsolicited
submissions of ideas, stories, or artwork.

Originally published as UNCLE SCROOGE issues #41–43
(Legacy #445–447).

Chris Ryall, President, Publisher, & CCO

John Barber, Editor-in-Chief

Cara Morrison, Chief Financial Officer

Matt Ruzicka, Chief Accounting Officer

David Hedgecock, Associate Publisher

Jerry Bennington, VP of New Product Development

Lorelei Bunjes, VP of Digital Services

Justin Eisinger, Editorial Director, Graphic Novels & Collections

Eric Moss, Senior Director, Licensing and Business Development

Ted Adams and Robbie Robbins, IDW Founders

Special thanks to Stefano Ambrosio, Stefano Attardi, Julie Dorris, Marco
Ghiglione, Jodi Hammerwold, Behnoosh Khalili, Manny Mederos, Eugene
Paraszczuk, Carlotta Quattrocolo, Roberto Santillo, Christopher Troise,
Camilla Vedove, and David Gerstein.

THE WORLD OF IDEAS

FROM ITALIAN *TOPOLINO* #2138, 1996
WRITER: MANUELA MARINATO
ARTIST: GIORGIO CAVAZZANO
COLORIST: DISNEY ITALIA
LETTERER: TOM B. LONG
TRANSLATION AND DIALOGUE: ERIN BRADY

THE TIME VORTEX

FROM ITALIAN *TOPOLINO* #2715, 2007
WRITER: CARLO PANARO
ARTIST: PAOLO DE LORENZI
COLORIST: DISNEY ITALIA
LETTERER: TOM B. LONG
TRANSLATION AND DIALOGUE: THAD KOMOROWSKI

THE HELPFUL HAMMOCK

FROM ITALIAN *TOPOLINO* #3260, 2018
WRITER: VITO STABILE
ARTIST: FRANCESCO GUERRINI
COLORIST: DISNEY ITALIA
LETTERER: TOM B. LONG
TRANSLATION AND DIALOGUE: ERIN BRADY

BUSY BUTLER: THE MIX-UP

FROM ITALIAN *TOPOLINO* #3222, 2017
WRITER: CARLO PANARO
ARTIST: PAOLO CAMPINOTI
COLORIST: DISNEY ITALIA
LETTERER: TOM B. LONG
TRANSLATION AND DIALOGUE: ERIN BRADY

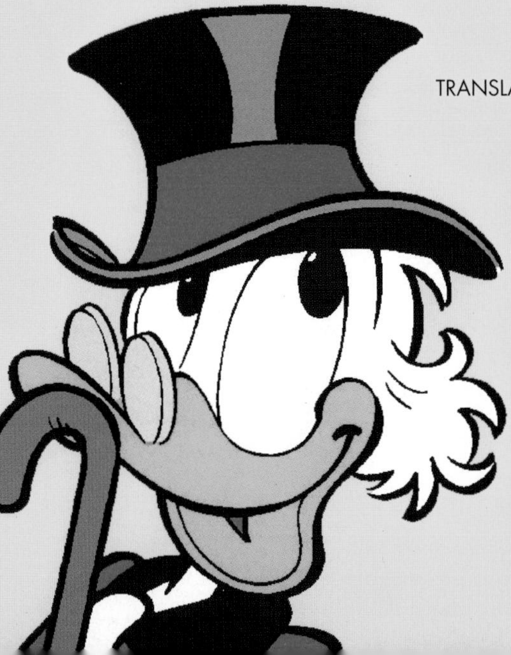

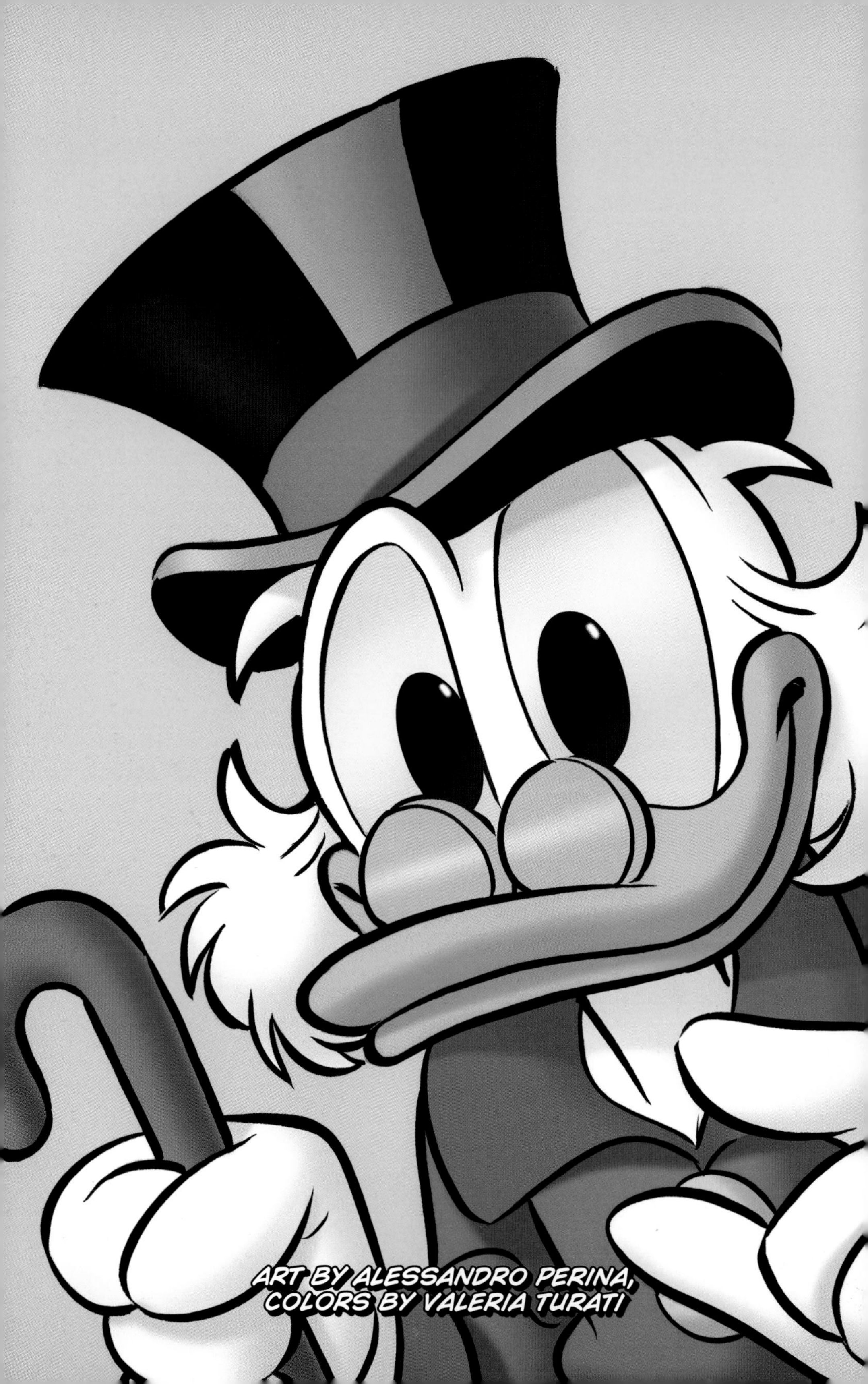

ART BY ALESSANDRO PERINA,
COLORS BY VALERIA TURATI

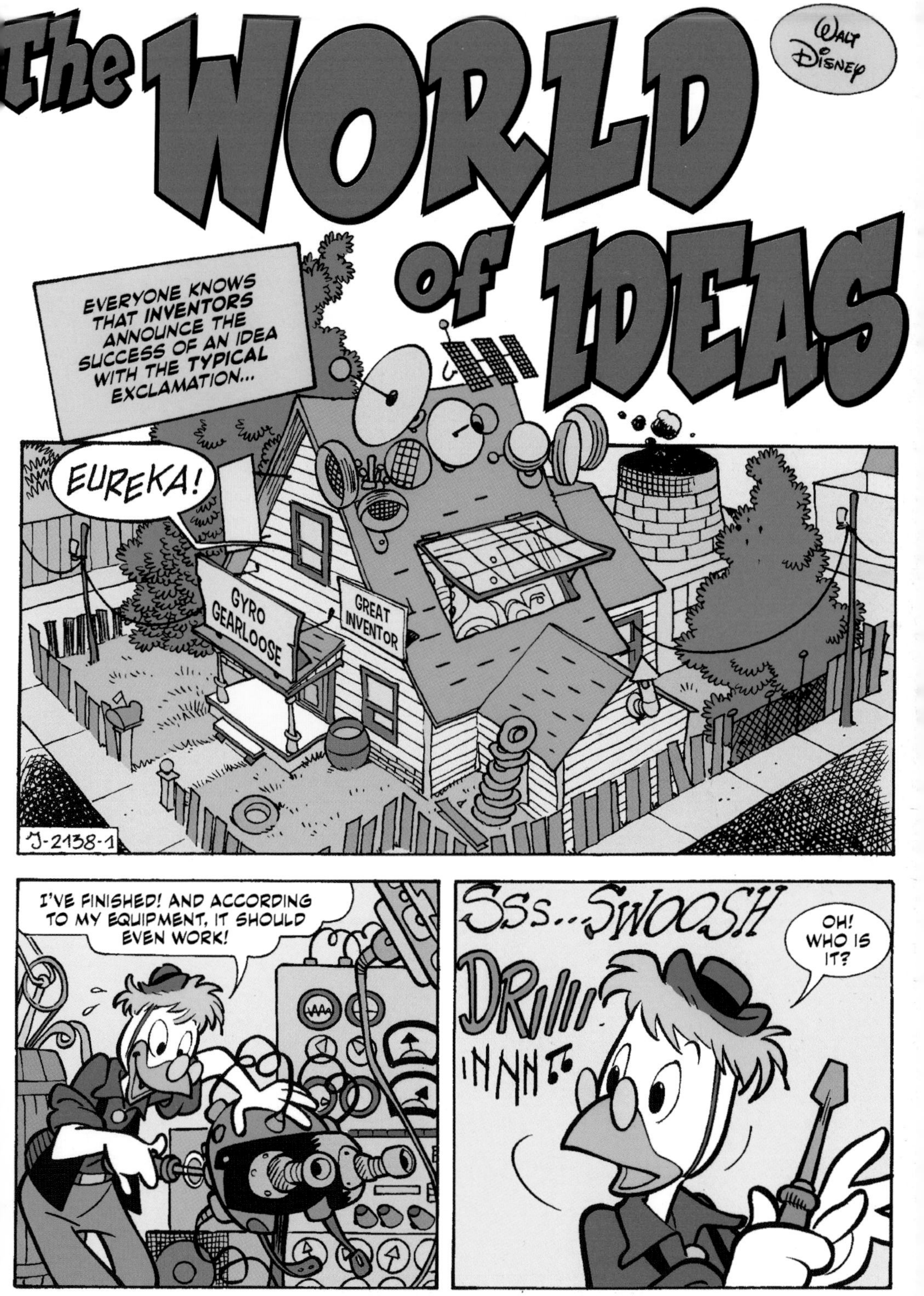
The WORLD of IDEAS
WALT DISNEY
EVERYONE KNOWS THAT INVENTORS ANNOUNCE THE SUCCESS OF AN IDEA WITH THE TYPICAL EXCLAMATION...
EUREKA!
GYRO GEARLOOSE
GREAT INVENTOR
T-2138-1
I'VE FINISHED! AND ACCORDING TO MY EQUIPMENT, IT SHOULD EVEN WORK!
SSS...SWOOSH
DRIIIINNN
OH! WHO IS IT?

ORIGINALLY PUBLISHED IN TOPOLINO #2138 (ITALY, 1996) • FIRST USA PUBLICATION

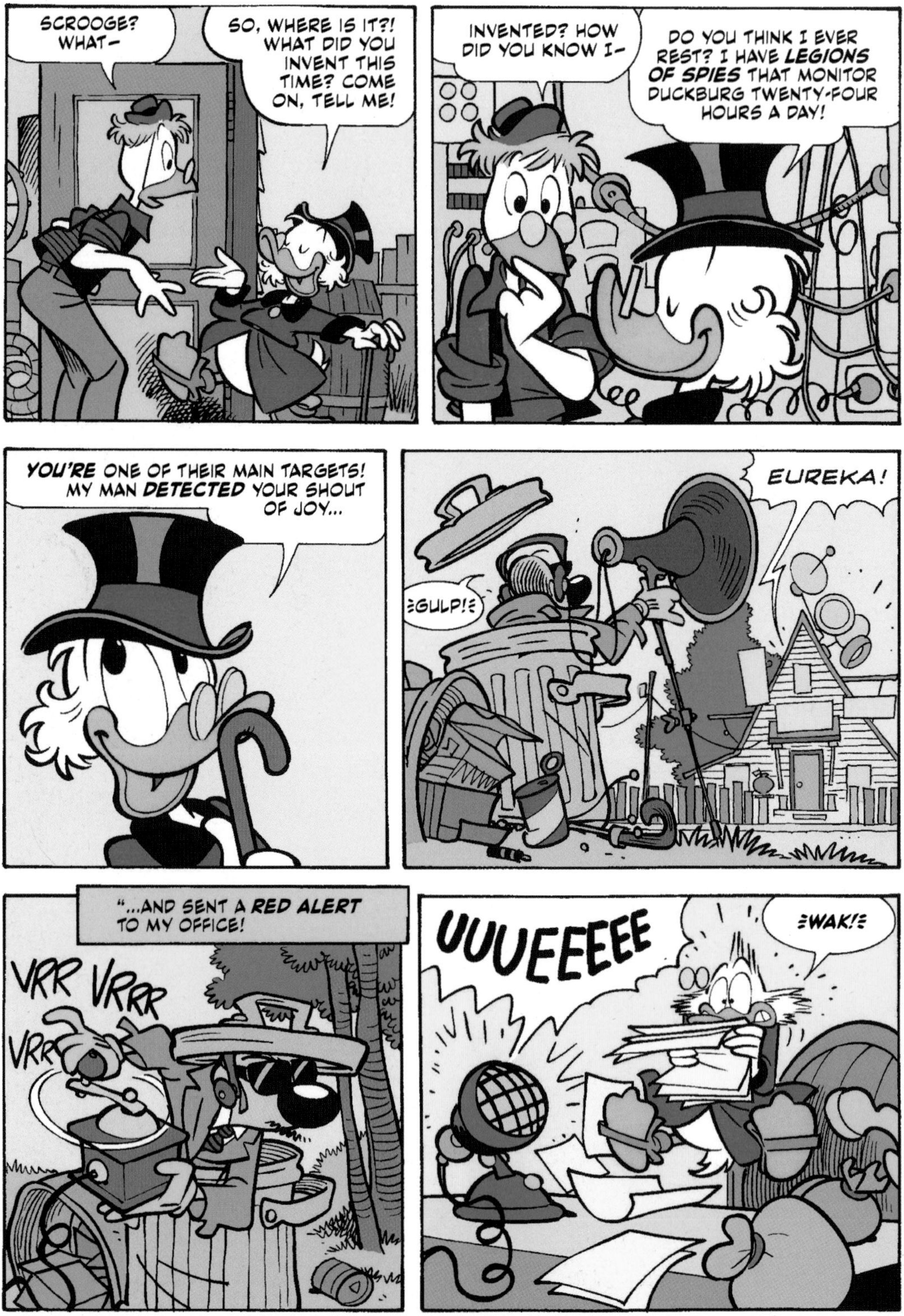
SCROOGE? WHAT–
SO, WHERE IS IT?! WHAT DID YOU INVENT THIS TIME? COME ON, TELL ME!
INVENTED? HOW DID YOU KNOW I–
DO YOU THINK I EVER REST? I HAVE LEGIONS OF SPIES THAT MONITOR DUCKBURG TWENTY-FOUR HOURS A DAY!
YOU'RE ONE OF THEIR MAIN TARGETS! MY MAN DETECTED YOUR SHOUT OF JOY...
EUREKA!
GULP!
"...AND SENT A RED ALERT TO MY OFFICE!
VRR VRRR
VRR
UUUEEEEE
WAK!

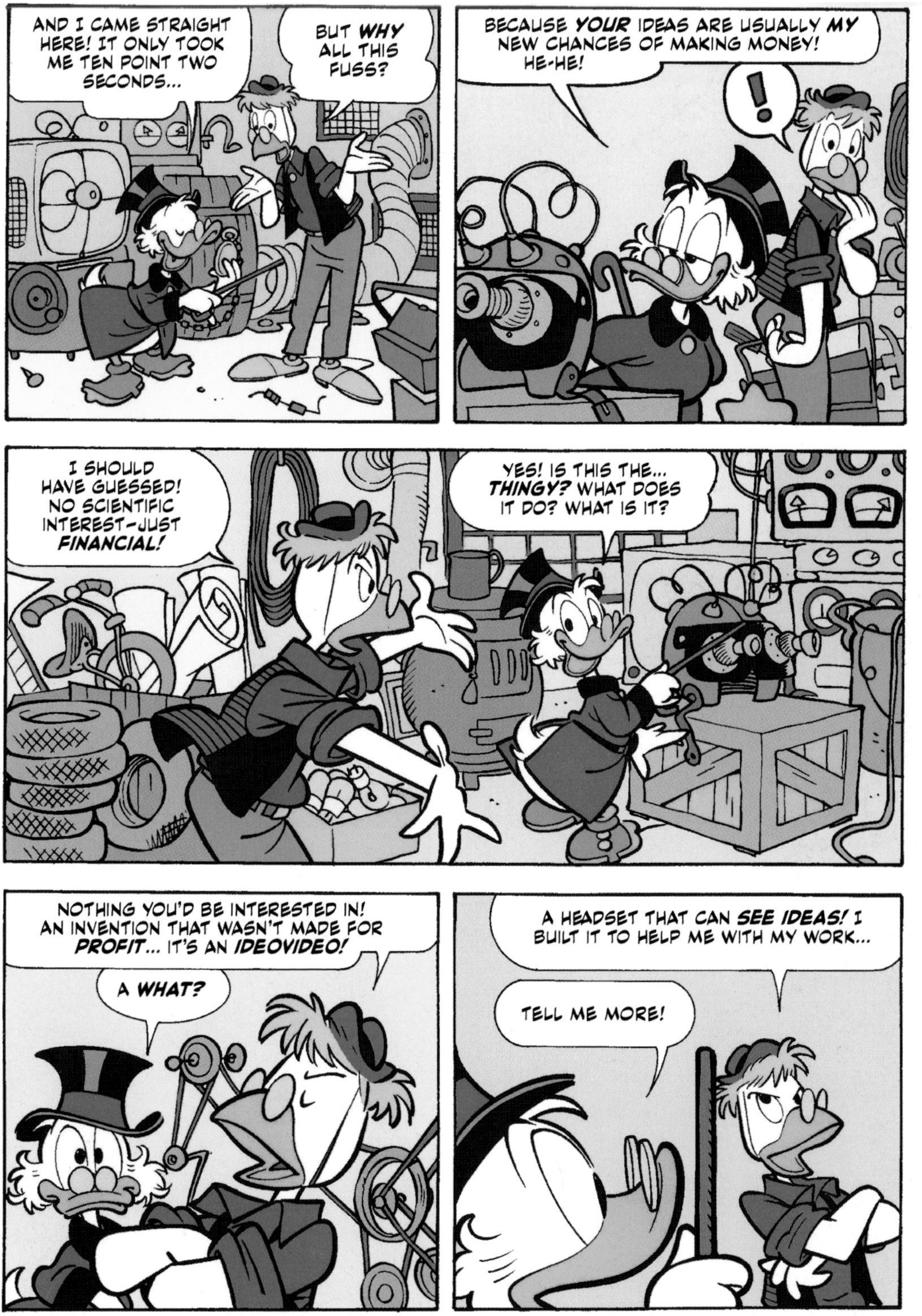
AND I CAME STRAIGHT HERE! IT ONLY TOOK ME TEN POINT TWO SECONDS...
BUT WHY ALL THIS FUSS?
BECAUSE YOUR IDEAS ARE USUALLY MY NEW CHANCES OF MAKING MONEY! HE-HE!
!
I SHOULD HAVE GUESSED! NO SCIENTIFIC INTEREST—JUST FINANCIAL!
YES! IS THIS THE... THINGY? WHAT DOES IT DO? WHAT IS IT?
NOTHING YOU'D BE INTERESTED IN! AN INVENTION THAT WASN'T MADE FOR PROFIT... IT'S AN IDEOVIDEO!
A WHAT?
A HEADSET THAT CAN SEE IDEAS! I BUILT IT TO HELP ME WITH MY WORK...
TELL ME MORE!

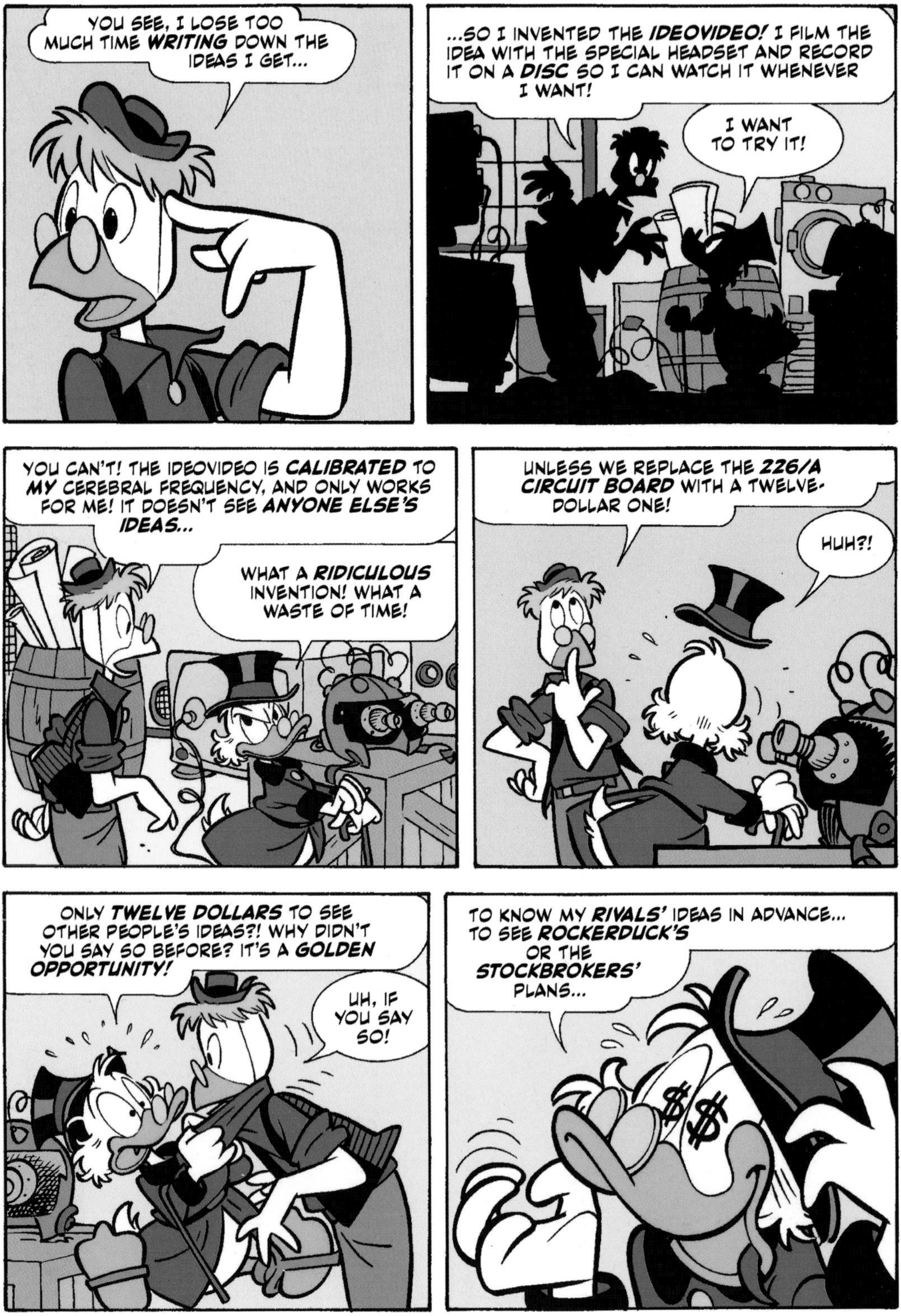
YOU SEE, I LOSE TOO MUCH TIME WRITING DOWN THE IDEAS I GET...
...SO I INVENTED THE IDEOVIDEO! I FILM THE IDEA WITH THE SPECIAL HEADSET AND RECORD IT ON A DISC SO I CAN WATCH IT WHENEVER I WANT!
I WANT TO TRY IT!
YOU CAN'T! THE IDEOVIDEO IS CALIBRATED TO MY CEREBRAL FREQUENCY, AND ONLY WORKS FOR ME! IT DOESN'T SEE ANYONE ELSE'S IDEAS...
WHAT A RIDICULOUS INVENTION! WHAT A WASTE OF TIME!
UNLESS WE REPLACE THE 226/A CIRCUIT BOARD WITH A TWELVE-DOLLAR ONE!
HUH?!
ONLY TWELVE DOLLARS TO SEE OTHER PEOPLE'S IDEAS?! WHY DIDN'T YOU SAY SO BEFORE? IT'S A GOLDEN OPPORTUNITY!
UH, IF YOU SAY SO!
TO KNOW MY RIVALS' IDEAS IN ADVANCE... TO SEE ROCKERDUCK'S OR THE STOCKBROKERS' PLANS...

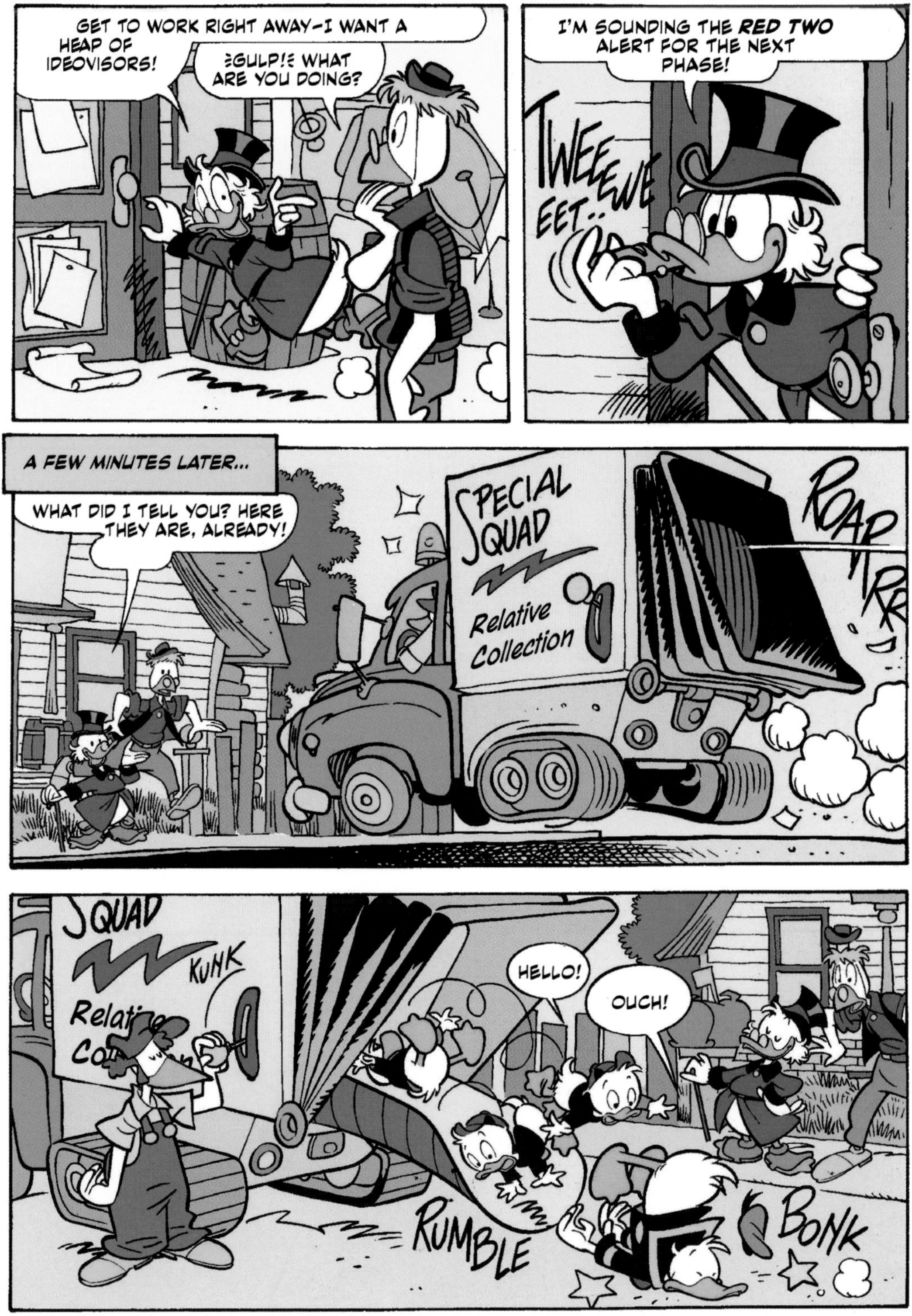
GET TO WORK RIGHT AWAY–I WANT A HEAP OF IDEOVISORS!
GULP! WHAT ARE YOU DOING?
I'M SOUNDING THE RED TWO ALERT FOR THE NEXT PHASE!
TWEEEWEEET...
A FEW MINUTES LATER...
WHAT DID I TELL YOU? HERE THEY ARE, ALREADY!
SPECIAL SQUAD
Relative Collection
ROARRRR
SQUAD
KUNK
HELLO!
OUCH!
RUMBLE
BONK

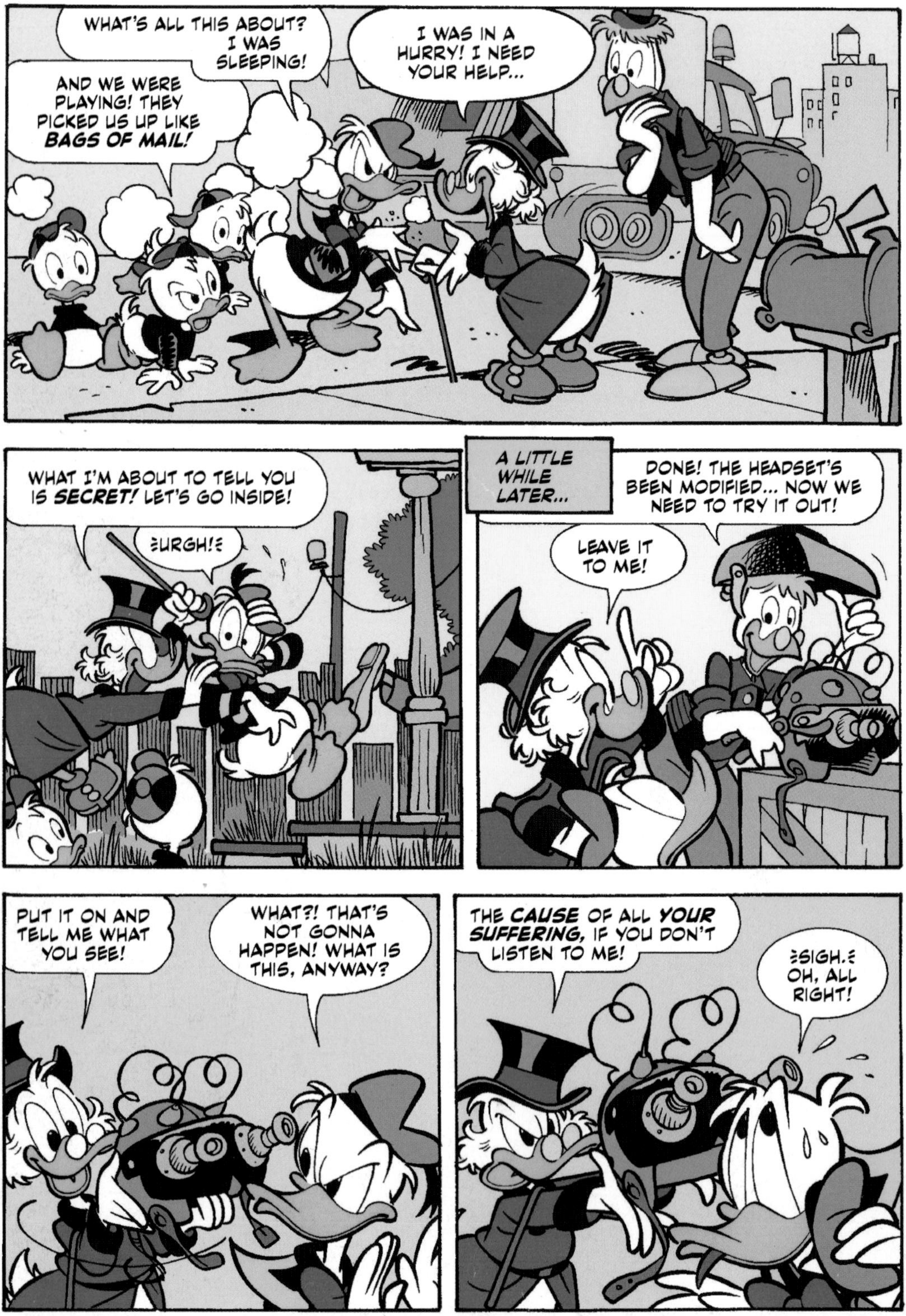
WHAT'S ALL THIS ABOUT? I WAS SLEEPING!
AND WE WERE PLAYING! THEY PICKED US UP LIKE BAGS OF MAIL!
I WAS IN A HURRY! I NEED YOUR HELP...
WHAT I'M ABOUT TO TELL YOU IS SECRET! LET'S GO INSIDE!
URGH!
A LITTLE WHILE LATER...
DONE! THE HEADSET'S BEEN MODIFIED... NOW WE NEED TO TRY IT OUT!
LEAVE IT TO ME!
PUT IT ON AND TELL ME WHAT YOU SEE!
WHAT?! THAT'S NOT GONNA HAPPEN! WHAT IS THIS, ANYWAY?
THE CAUSE OF ALL YOUR SUFFERING, IF YOU DON'T LISTEN TO ME!
SIGH. OH, ALL RIGHT!

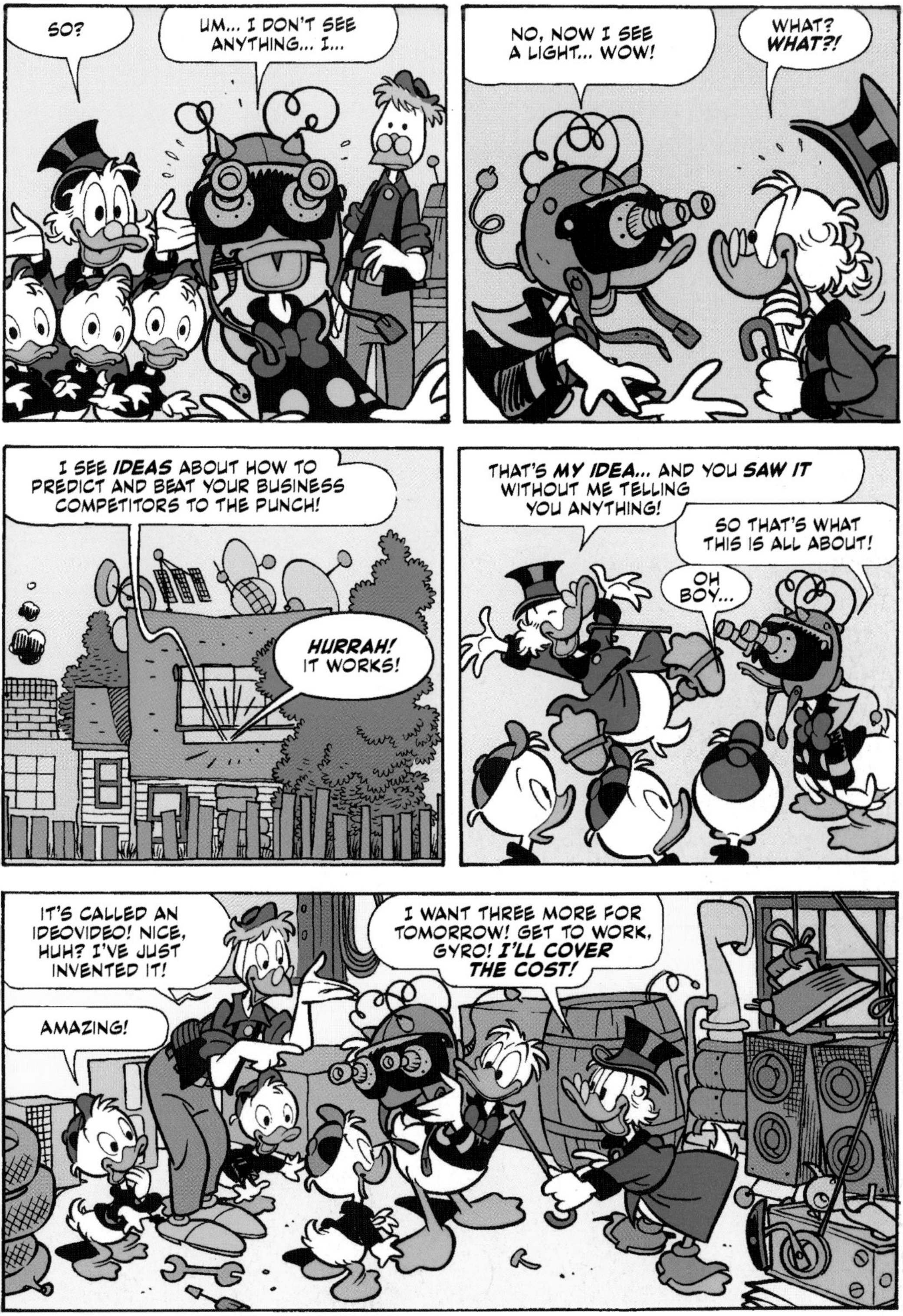
SO?
UM... I DON'T SEE ANYTHING... I...
NO, NOW I SEE A LIGHT... WOW!
WHAT? WHAT?!
I SEE IDEAS ABOUT HOW TO PREDICT AND BEAT YOUR BUSINESS COMPETITORS TO THE PUNCH!
HURRAH! IT WORKS!
THAT'S MY IDEA... AND YOU SAW IT WITHOUT ME TELLING YOU ANYTHING!
SO THAT'S WHAT THIS IS ALL ABOUT!
OH BOY...
IT'S CALLED AN IDEOVIDEO! NICE, HUH? I'VE JUST INVENTED IT!
AMAZING!
I WANT THREE MORE FOR TOMORROW! GET TO WORK, GYRO! I'LL COVER THE COST!

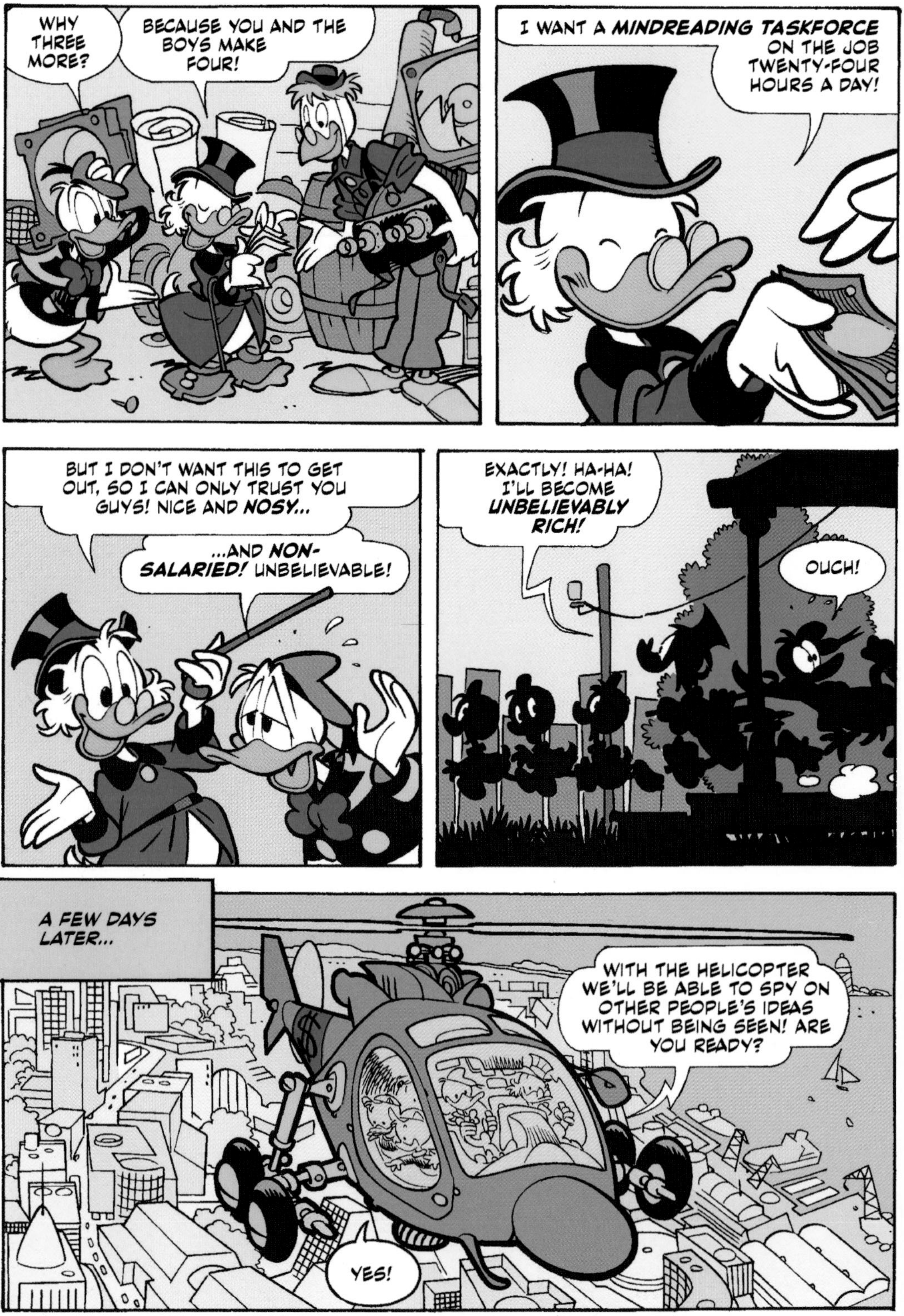
WHY THREE MORE?
BECAUSE YOU AND THE BOYS MAKE FOUR!
I WANT A MINDREADING TASKFORCE ON THE JOB TWENTY-FOUR HOURS A DAY!
BUT I DON'T WANT THIS TO GET OUT, SO I CAN ONLY TRUST YOU GUYS! NICE AND NOSY...
...AND NON-SALARIED! UNBELIEVABLE!
EXACTLY! HA-HA! I'LL BECOME UNBELIEVABLY RICH!
OUCH!
A FEW DAYS LATER...
WITH THE HELICOPTER WE'LL BE ABLE TO SPY ON OTHER PEOPLE'S IDEAS WITHOUT BEING SEEN! ARE YOU READY?
YES!

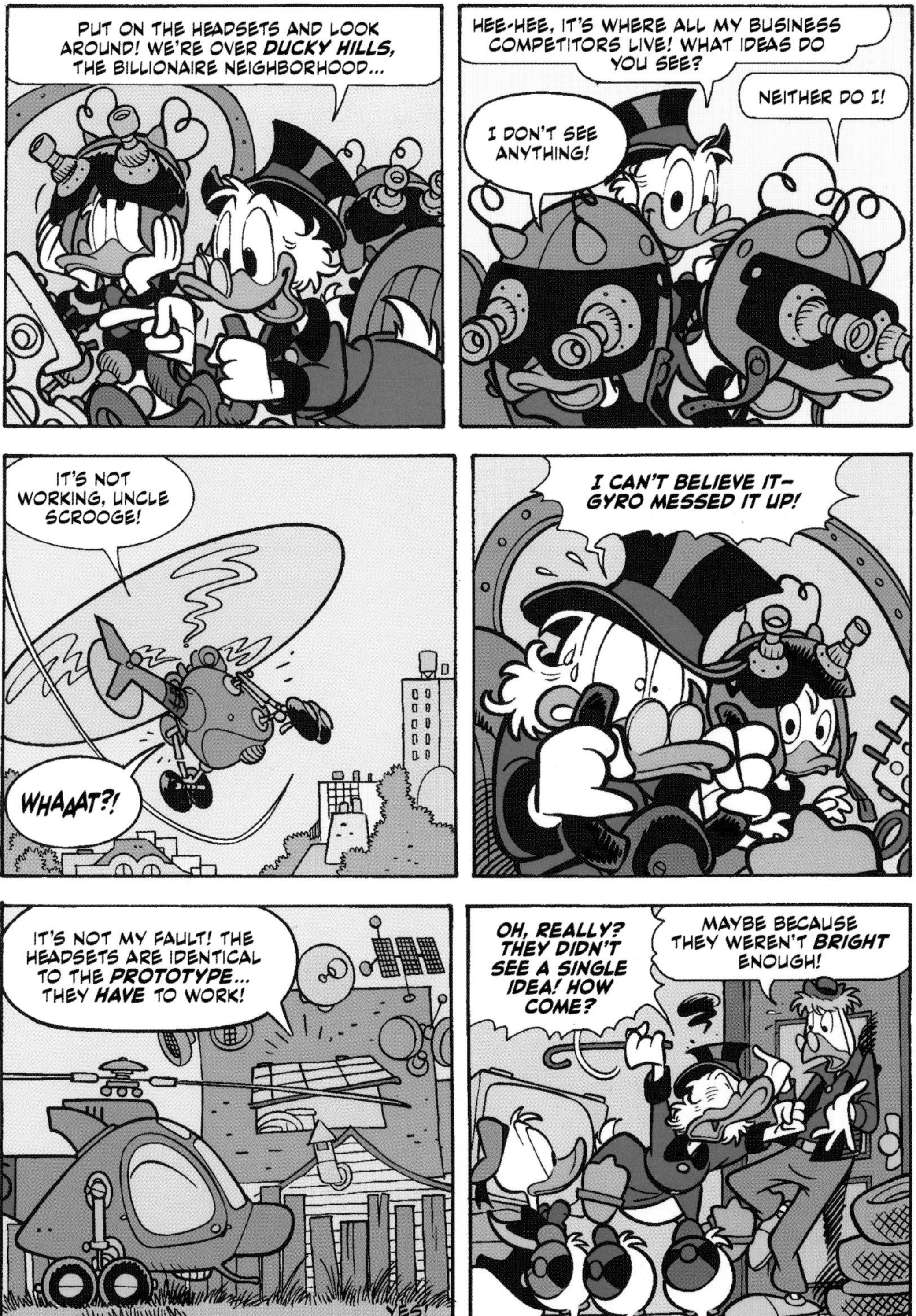
PUT ON THE HEADSETS AND LOOK AROUND! WE'RE OVER *DUCKY HILLS,* THE BILLIONAIRE NEIGHBORHOOD...
HEE-HEE, IT'S WHERE ALL MY BUSINESS COMPETITORS LIVE! WHAT IDEAS DO YOU SEE?
I DON'T SEE ANYTHING!
NEITHER DO I!
IT'S NOT WORKING, UNCLE SCROOGE!
WHAAAT?!
I CAN'T BELIEVE IT– GYRO MESSED IT UP!
IT'S NOT MY FAULT! THE HEADSETS ARE IDENTICAL TO THE *PROTOTYPE*... THEY *HAVE* TO WORK!
YES!
OH, REALLY? THEY DIDN'T SEE A SINGLE IDEA! HOW COME?
MAYBE BECAUSE THEY WEREN'T *BRIGHT* ENOUGH!

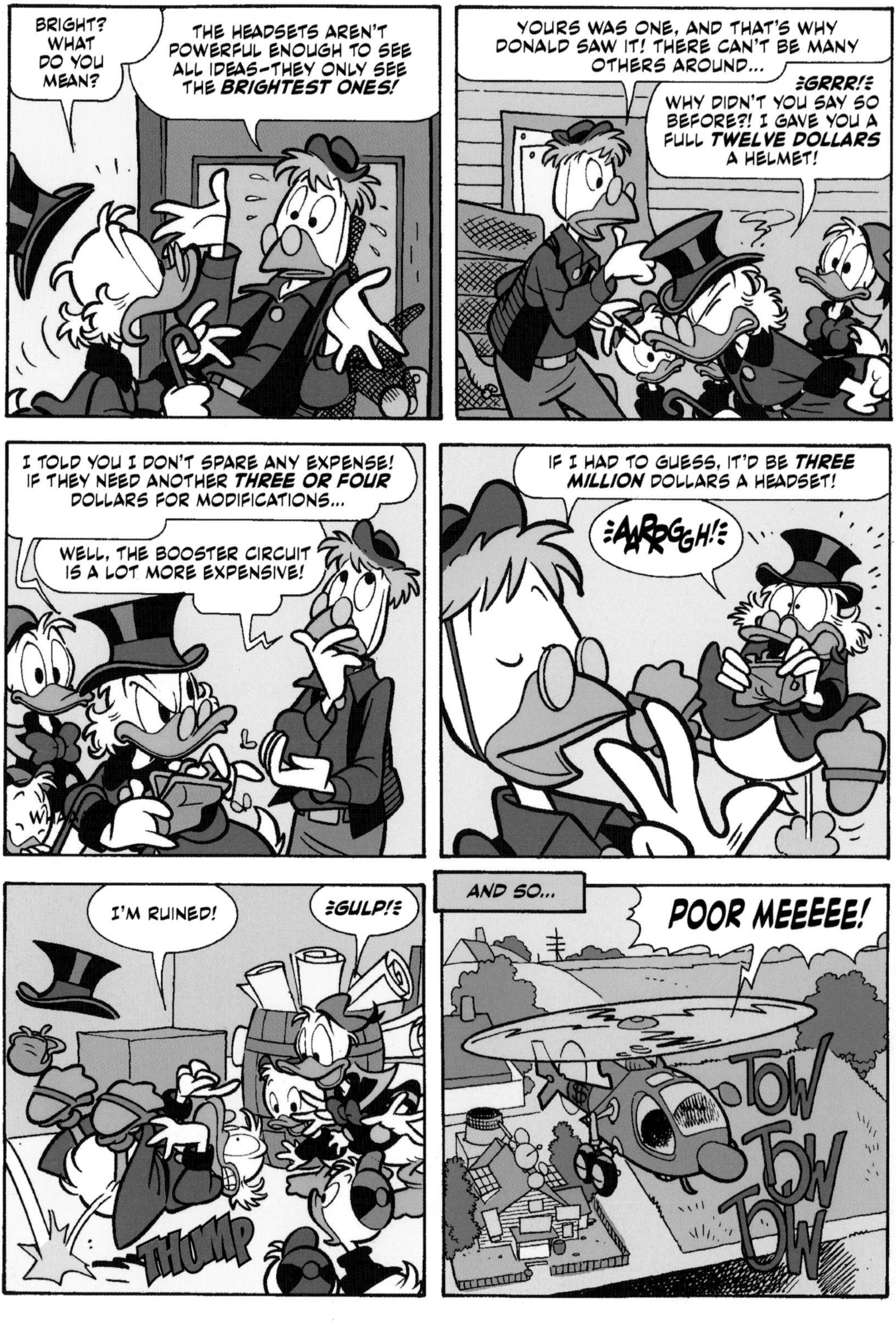
BRIGHT? WHAT DO YOU MEAN?
THE HEADSETS AREN'T POWERFUL ENOUGH TO SEE ALL IDEAS—THEY ONLY SEE THE BRIGHTEST ONES!
YOURS WAS ONE, AND THAT'S WHY DONALD SAW IT! THERE CAN'T BE MANY OTHERS AROUND...
GRRR! WHY DIDN'T YOU SAY SO BEFORE?! I GAVE YOU A FULL TWELVE DOLLARS A HELMET!
I TOLD YOU I DON'T SPARE ANY EXPENSE! IF THEY NEED ANOTHER THREE OR FOUR DOLLARS FOR MODIFICATIONS...
WELL, THE BOOSTER CIRCUIT IS A LOT MORE EXPENSIVE!
IF I HAD TO GUESS, IT'D BE THREE MILLION DOLLARS A HEADSET!
AARRGGH!
I'M RUINED!
GULP!
THUMP
AND SO...
POOR MEEEEE!
TOW TOW TOW

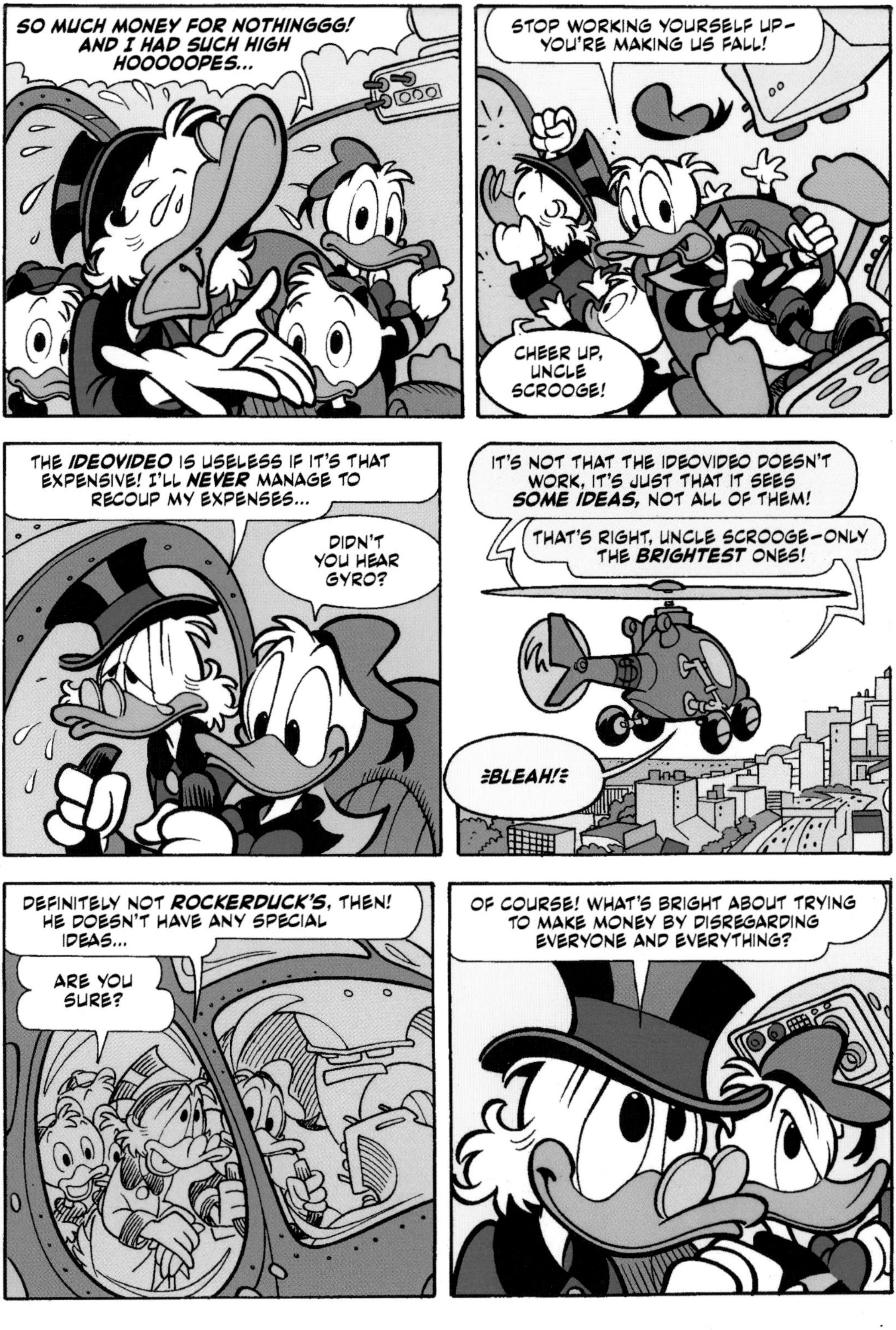
SO MUCH MONEY FOR NOTHINGGG! AND I HAD SUCH HIGH HOOOOOPES...
STOP WORKING YOURSELF UP– YOU'RE MAKING US FALL!
CHEER UP, UNCLE SCROOGE!
THE IDEOVIDEO IS USELESS IF IT'S THAT EXPENSIVE! I'LL NEVER MANAGE TO RECOUP MY EXPENSES...
DIDN'T YOU HEAR GYRO?
IT'S NOT THAT THE IDEOVIDEO DOESN'T WORK, IT'S JUST THAT IT SEES SOME IDEAS, NOT ALL OF THEM!
THAT'S RIGHT, UNCLE SCROOGE–ONLY THE BRIGHTEST ONES!
BLEAH!
DEFINITELY NOT ROCKERDUCK'S, THEN! HE DOESN'T HAVE ANY SPECIAL IDEAS...
ARE YOU SURE?
OF COURSE! WHAT'S BRIGHT ABOUT TRYING TO MAKE MONEY BY DISREGARDING EVERYONE AND EVERYTHING?

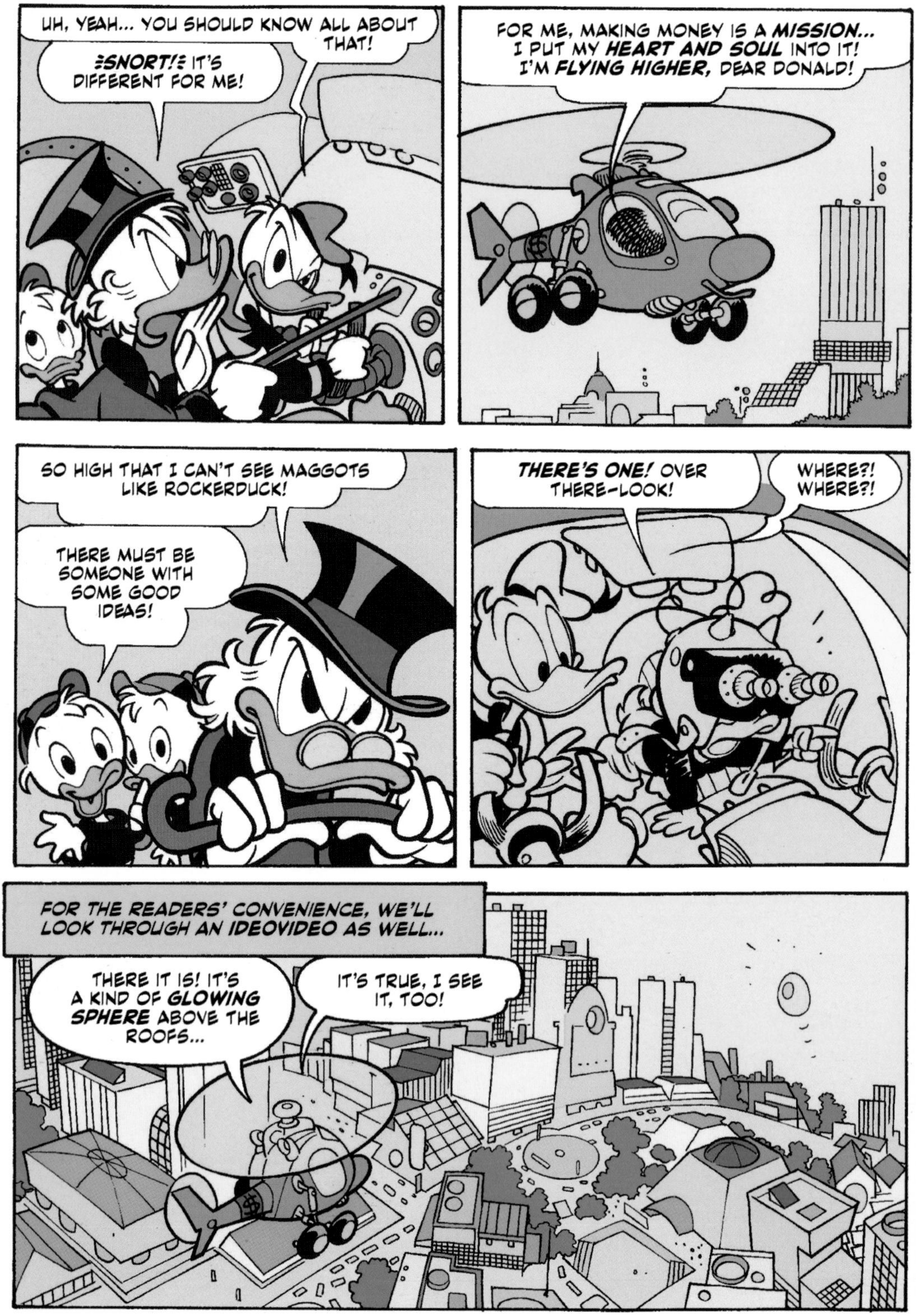
UH, YEAH... YOU SHOULD KNOW ALL ABOUT THAT!
≡SNORT!≡ IT'S DIFFERENT FOR ME!
FOR ME, MAKING MONEY IS A MISSION... I PUT MY HEART AND SOUL INTO IT! I'M FLYING HIGHER, DEAR DONALD!
SO HIGH THAT I CAN'T SEE MAGGOTS LIKE ROCKERDUCK!
THERE MUST BE SOMEONE WITH SOME GOOD IDEAS!
THERE'S ONE! OVER THERE-LOOK!
WHERE?! WHERE?!
FOR THE READERS' CONVENIENCE, WE'LL LOOK THROUGH AN IDEOVIDEO AS WELL...
THERE IT IS! IT'S A KIND OF GLOWING SPHERE ABOVE THE ROOFS...
IT'S TRUE, I SEE IT, TOO!

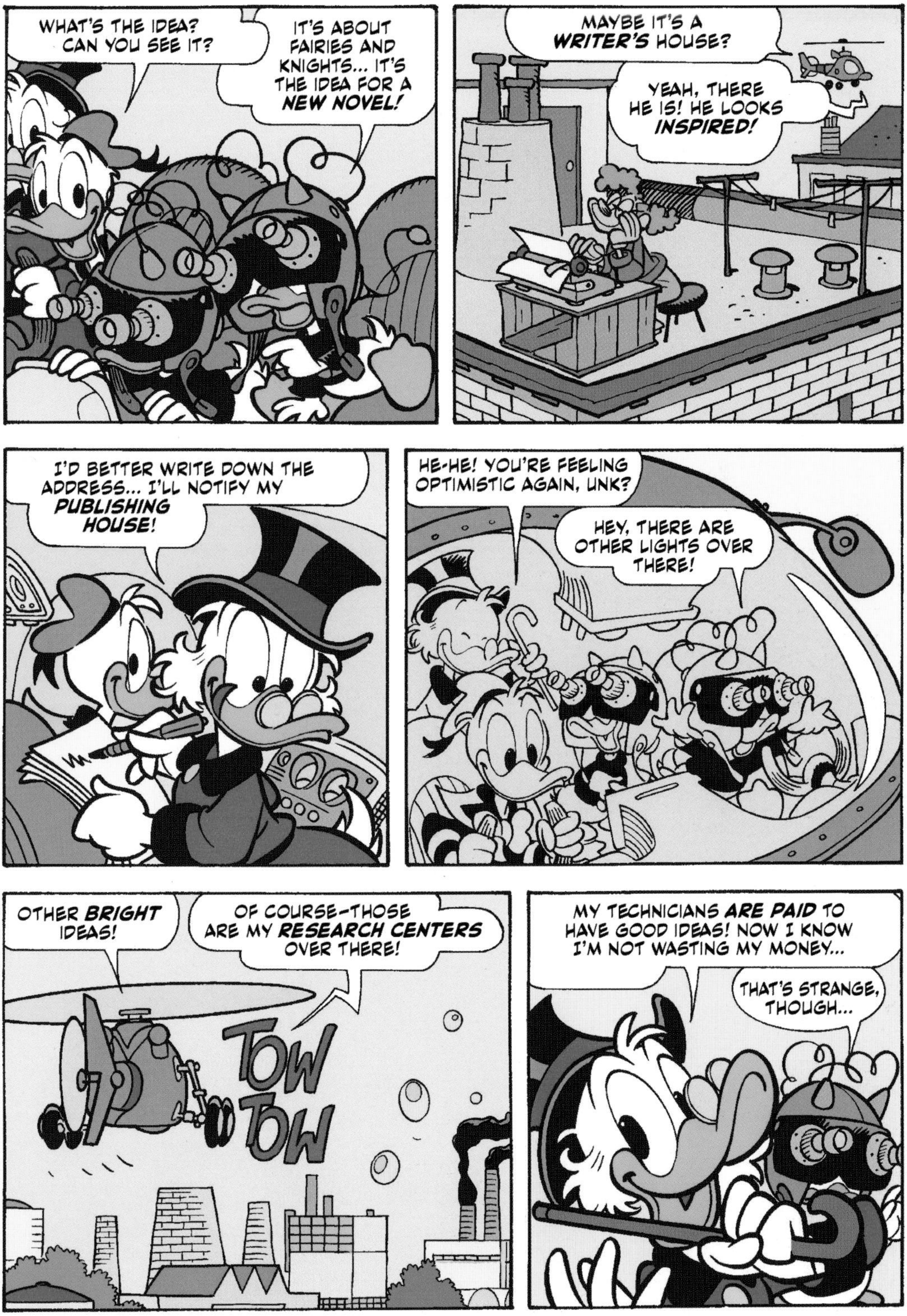
WHAT'S THE IDEA? CAN YOU SEE IT?
IT'S ABOUT FAIRIES AND KNIGHTS... IT'S THE IDEA FOR A *NEW NOVEL!*
MAYBE IT'S A *WRITER'S* HOUSE?
YEAH, THERE HE IS! HE LOOKS *INSPIRED!*
I'D BETTER WRITE DOWN THE ADDRESS... I'LL NOTIFY MY *PUBLISHING HOUSE!*
HE-HE! YOU'RE FEELING OPTIMISTIC AGAIN, UNK?
HEY, THERE ARE OTHER LIGHTS OVER THERE!
OTHER *BRIGHT* IDEAS!
OF COURSE—THOSE ARE MY *RESEARCH CENTERS* OVER THERE!
TOW TOW
MY TECHNICIANS *ARE PAID* TO HAVE GOOD IDEAS! NOW I KNOW I'M NOT WASTING MY MONEY...
THAT'S STRANGE, THOUGH...

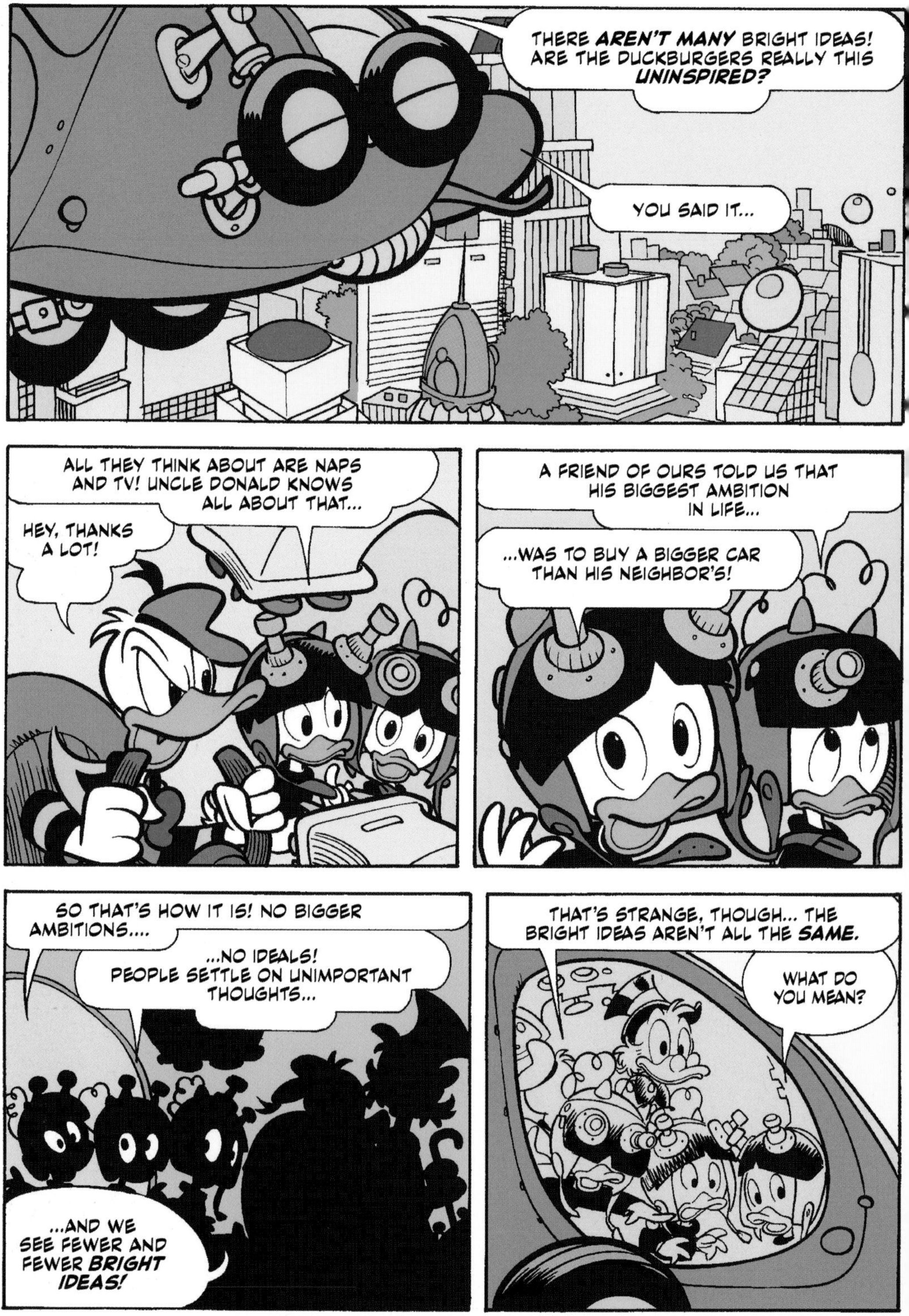
THERE AREN'T MANY BRIGHT IDEAS! ARE THE DUCKBURGERS REALLY THIS UNINSPIRED?
YOU SAID IT...
ALL THEY THINK ABOUT ARE NAPS AND TV! UNCLE DONALD KNOWS ALL ABOUT THAT...
HEY, THANKS A LOT!
A FRIEND OF OURS TOLD US THAT HIS BIGGEST AMBITION IN LIFE...
...WAS TO BUY A BIGGER CAR THAN HIS NEIGHBOR'S!
SO THAT'S HOW IT IS! NO BIGGER AMBITIONS....
...NO IDEALS! PEOPLE SETTLE ON UNIMPORTANT THOUGHTS...
...AND WE SEE FEWER AND FEWER BRIGHT IDEAS!
THAT'S STRANGE, THOUGH... THE BRIGHT IDEAS AREN'T ALL THE SAME.
WHAT DO YOU MEAN?

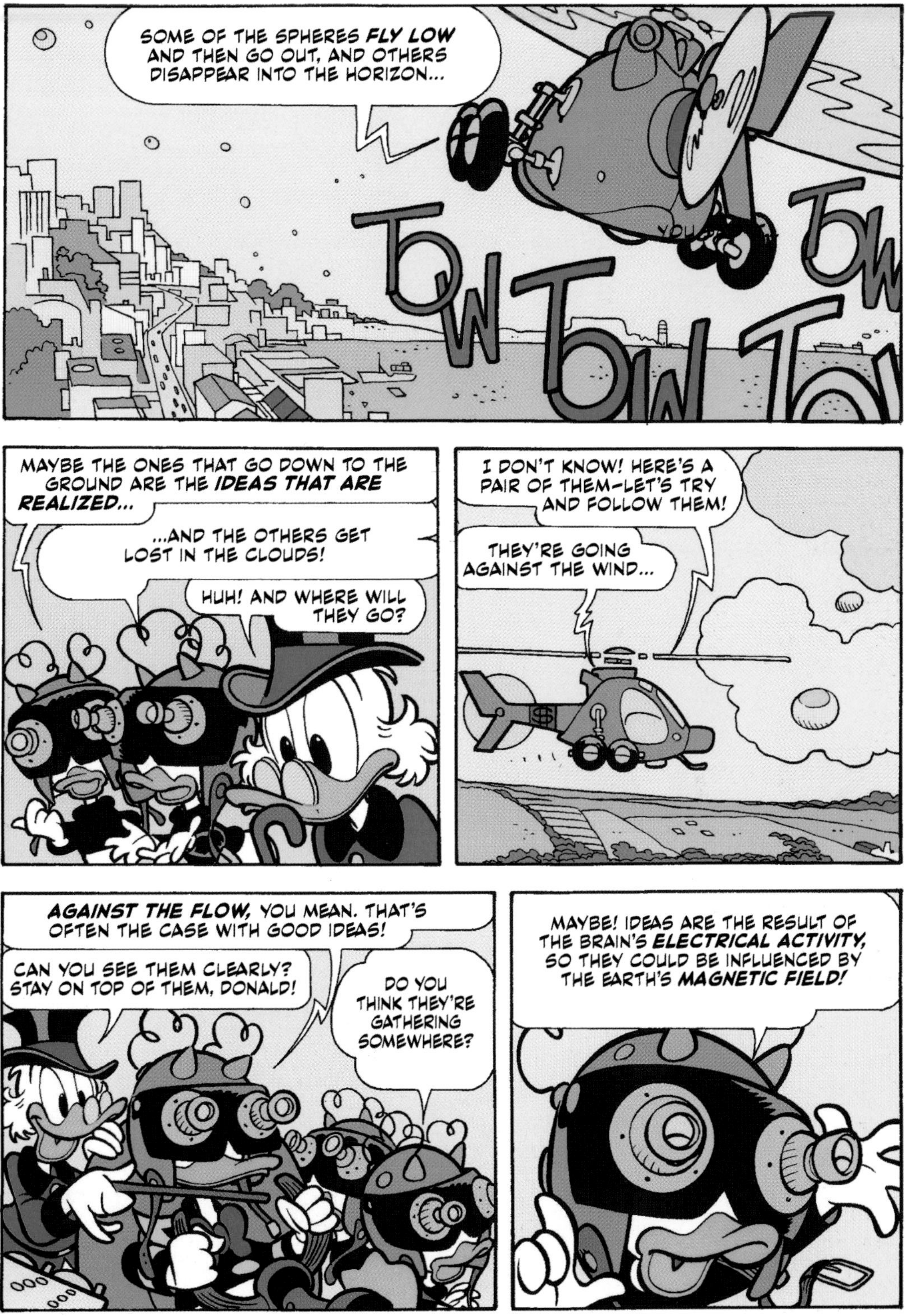
SOME OF THE SPHERES FLY LOW AND THEN GO OUT, AND OTHERS DISAPPEAR INTO THE HORIZON...
TOW TOW TOW TOW TOW
MAYBE THE ONES THAT GO DOWN TO THE GROUND ARE THE IDEAS THAT ARE REALIZED...
...AND THE OTHERS GET LOST IN THE CLOUDS!
HUH! AND WHERE WILL THEY GO?
I DON'T KNOW! HERE'S A PAIR OF THEM—LET'S TRY AND FOLLOW THEM!
THEY'RE GOING AGAINST THE WIND...
AGAINST THE FLOW, YOU MEAN. THAT'S OFTEN THE CASE WITH GOOD IDEAS!
CAN YOU SEE THEM CLEARLY? STAY ON TOP OF THEM, DONALD!
DO YOU THINK THEY'RE GATHERING SOMEWHERE?
MAYBE! IDEAS ARE THE RESULT OF THE BRAIN'S ELECTRICAL ACTIVITY, SO THEY COULD BE INFLUENCED BY THE EARTH'S MAGNETIC FIELD!

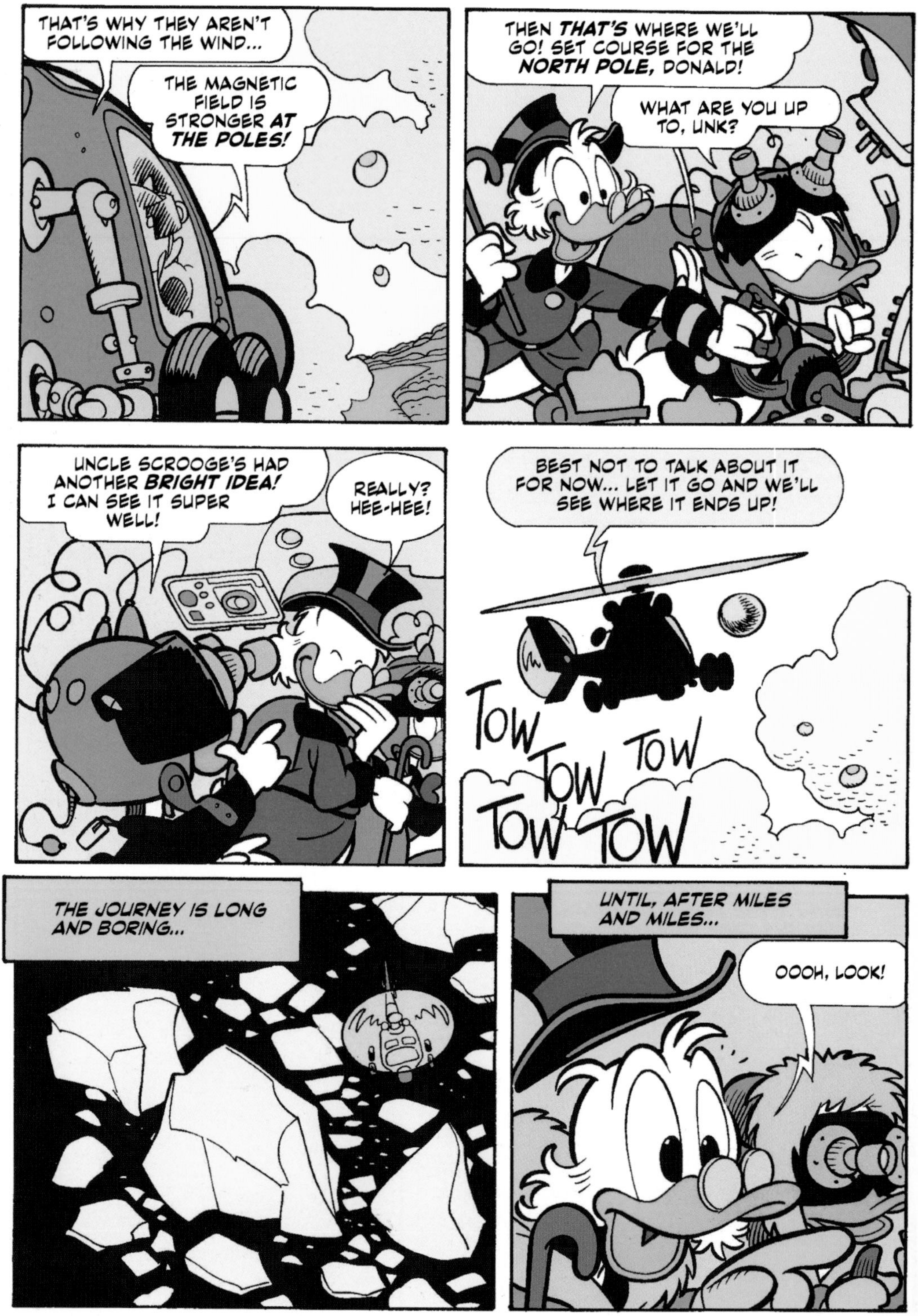
THAT'S WHY THEY AREN'T FOLLOWING THE WIND...
THE MAGNETIC FIELD IS STRONGER AT THE POLES!
THEN THAT'S WHERE WE'LL GO! SET COURSE FOR THE NORTH POLE, DONALD!
WHAT ARE YOU UP TO, UNK?
UNCLE SCROOGE'S HAD ANOTHER BRIGHT IDEA! I CAN SEE IT SUPER WELL!
REALLY? HEE-HEE!
BEST NOT TO TALK ABOUT IT FOR NOW... LET IT GO AND WE'LL SEE WHERE IT ENDS UP!
TOW TOW TOW TOW TOW
THE JOURNEY IS LONG AND BORING...
UNTIL, AFTER MILES AND MILES...
OOOH, LOOK!

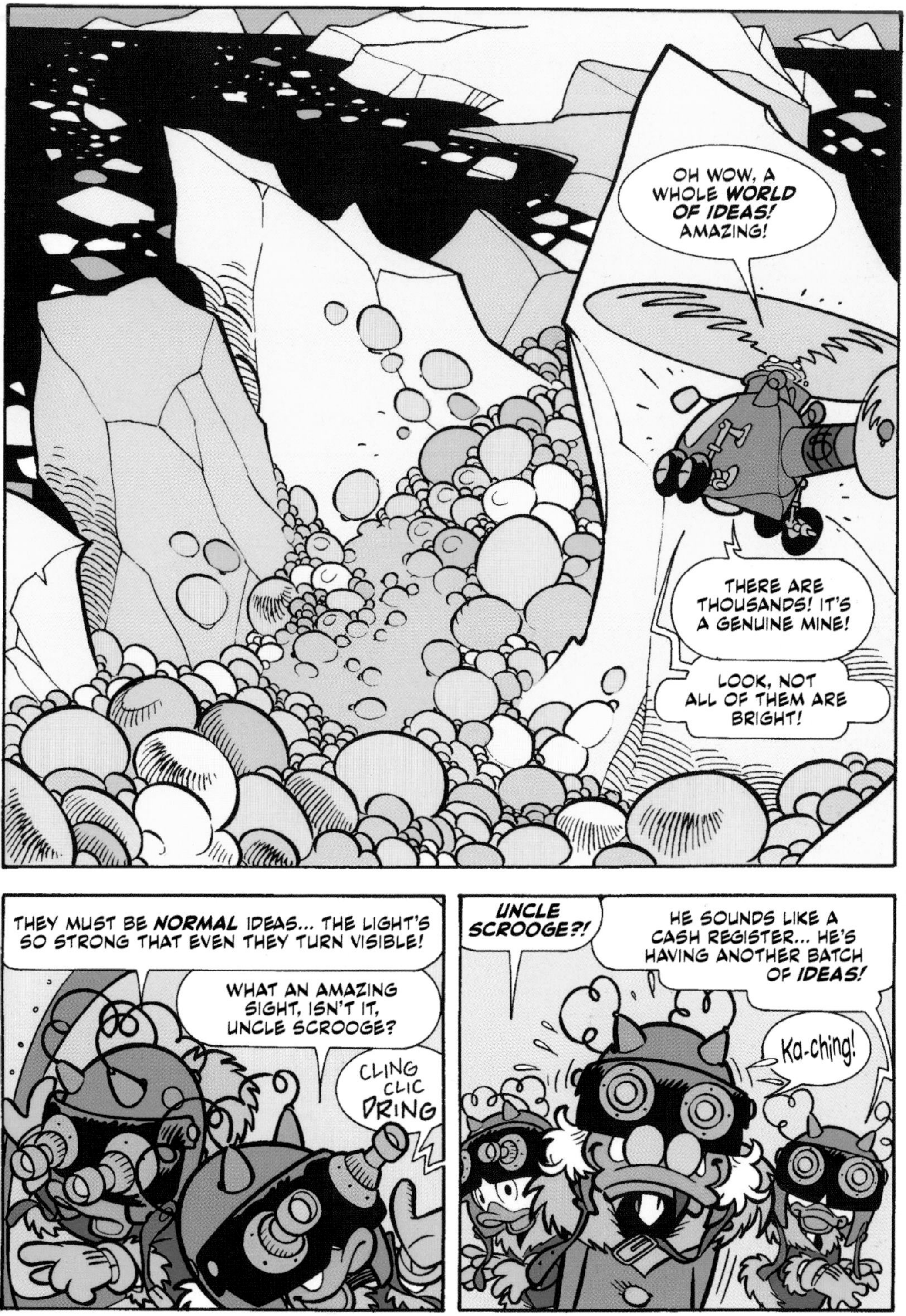
OH WOW, A WHOLE WORLD OF IDEAS! AMAZING!
THERE ARE THOUSANDS! IT'S A GENUINE MINE!
LOOK, NOT ALL OF THEM ARE BRIGHT!
THEY MUST BE NORMAL IDEAS... THE LIGHT'S SO STRONG THAT EVEN THEY TURN VISIBLE!
WHAT AN AMAZING SIGHT, ISN'T IT, UNCLE SCROOGE?
CLING CLIC DRING
UNCLE SCROOGE?!
HE SOUNDS LIKE A CASH REGISTER... HE'S HAVING ANOTHER BATCH OF IDEAS!
Ka-ching!

WHAT'S GOT INTO YOU, UNCLE SCROOGE?

MORE BRILLIANT IDEAS! I SENSE THAT I'M GOING TO BECOME SERIOUSLY *RICH* THIS TIME!

WHAT DO YOU MEAN, *THIS TIME?!* WHAT DO YOU HAVE IN MIND?

SELLING IDEAS TO PEOPLE WHO *DON'T HAVE ANY!* HERE'S WHAT I HAVE IN MIND: I'LL MAKE MILLIONS WITHOUT SPENDING A DIME!

WHAAAT?!

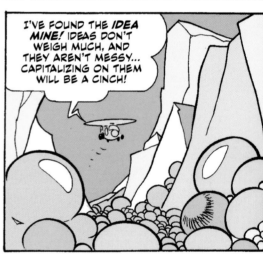

I'VE FOUND THE *IDEA MINE!* IDEAS DON'T WEIGH MUCH, AND THEY AREN'T MESSY... CAPITALIZING ON THEM WILL BE A CINCH!

AND IN ADDITION TO EARNING MILLIONS, I'LL BECOME A *BENEFACTOR* FOR EVERYONE WHO *HAS NO IDEA* WHAT TO DO IN LIFE!

AMAZING!

SELLING IDEAS... WHAT A *GENIUS* IDEA!

HE-HE! I WON'T SELL THEM ALL. I'LL KEEP THE *BEST* ONES FOR MYSELF, OF COURSE!

OF COURSE!

TOW TOW TOW TOW

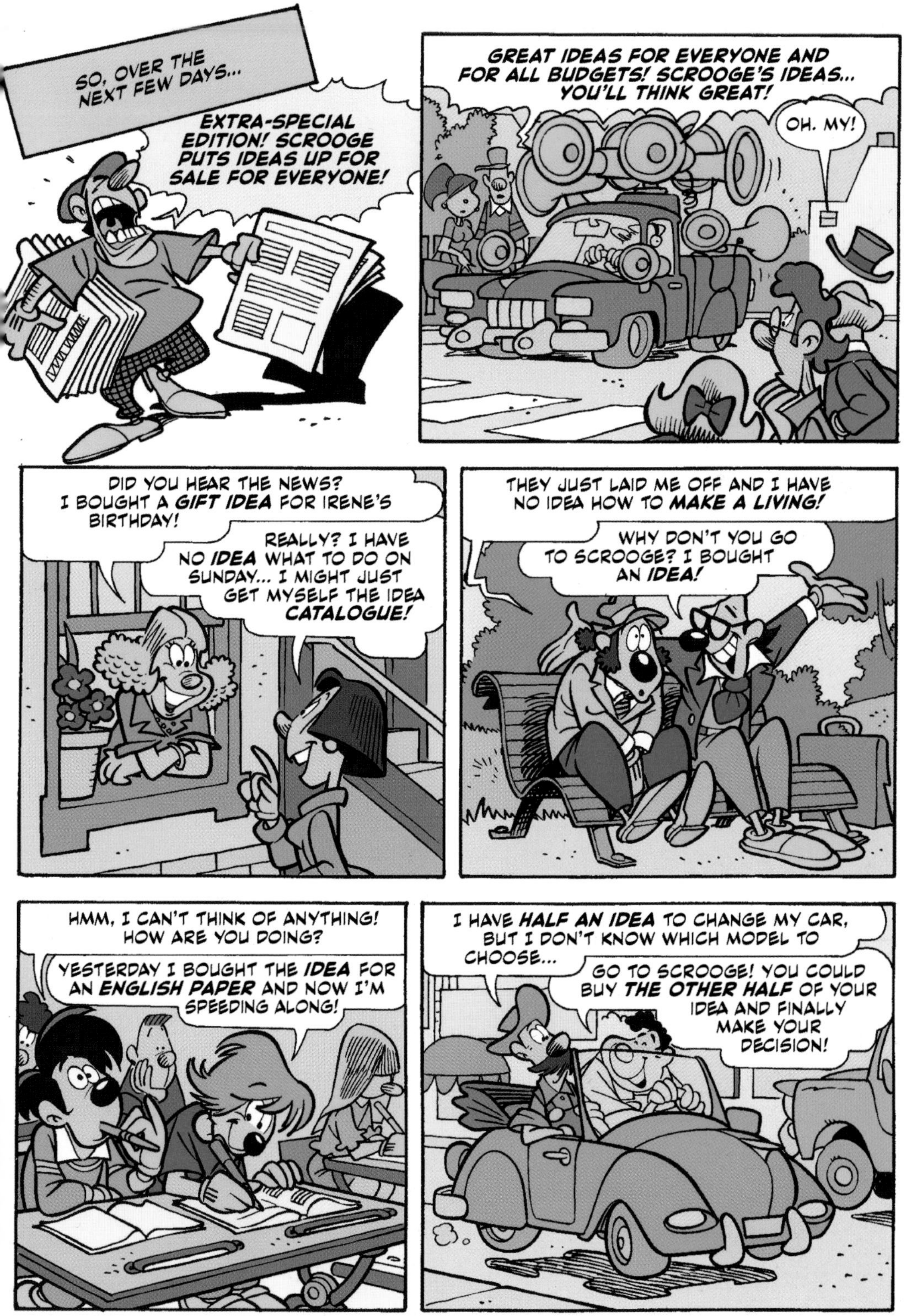
SO, OVER THE NEXT FEW DAYS...
EXTRA-SPECIAL EDITION! SCROOGE PUTS IDEAS UP FOR SALE FOR EVERYONE!
GREAT IDEAS FOR EVERYONE AND FOR ALL BUDGETS! SCROOGE'S IDEAS... YOU'LL THINK GREAT!
OH. MY!
DID YOU HEAR THE NEWS? I BOUGHT A GIFT IDEA FOR IRENE'S BIRTHDAY!
REALLY? I HAVE NO IDEA WHAT TO DO ON SUNDAY... I MIGHT JUST GET MYSELF THE IDEA CATALOGUE!
THEY JUST LAID ME OFF AND I HAVE NO IDEA HOW TO MAKE A LIVING!
WHY DON'T YOU GO TO SCROOGE? I BOUGHT AN IDEA!
HMM, I CAN'T THINK OF ANYTHING! HOW ARE YOU DOING?
YESTERDAY I BOUGHT THE IDEA FOR AN ENGLISH PAPER AND NOW I'M SPEEDING ALONG!
I HAVE HALF AN IDEA TO CHANGE MY CAR, BUT I DON'T KNOW WHICH MODEL TO CHOOSE...
GO TO SCROOGE! YOU COULD BUY THE OTHER HALF OF YOUR IDEA AND FINALLY MAKE YOUR DECISION!

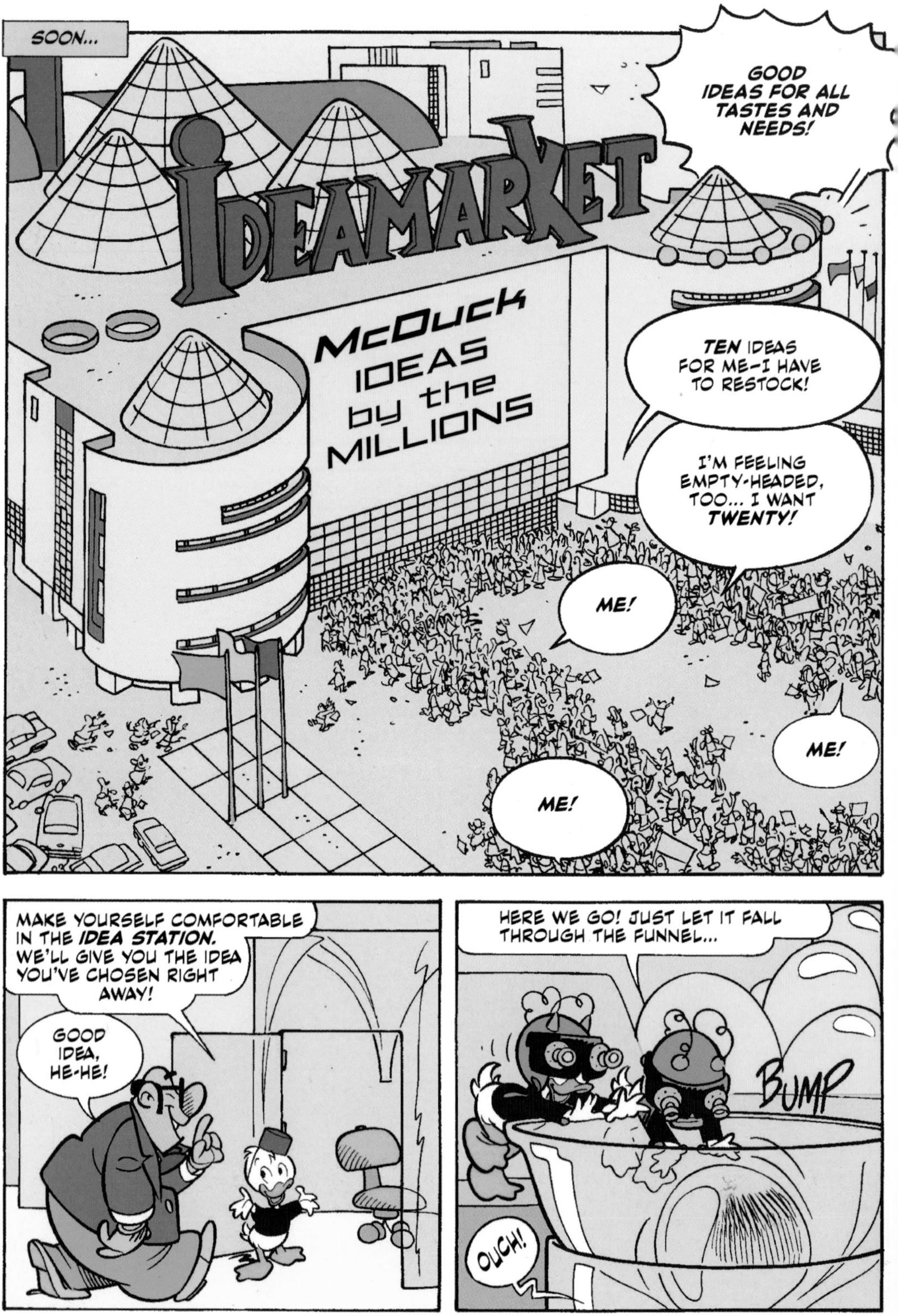
SOON...
IDEAMARKET
GOOD IDEAS FOR ALL TASTES AND NEEDS!
McDuck IDEAS by the MILLIONS
TEN IDEAS FOR ME—I HAVE TO RESTOCK!
I'M FEELING EMPTY-HEADED, TOO... I WANT TWENTY!
ME!
ME!
ME!
MAKE YOURSELF COMFORTABLE IN THE IDEA STATION. WE'LL GIVE YOU THE IDEA YOU'VE CHOSEN RIGHT AWAY!
GOOD IDEA, HE-HE!
HERE WE GO! JUST LET IT FALL THROUGH THE FUNNEL...
BUMP
OUCH!

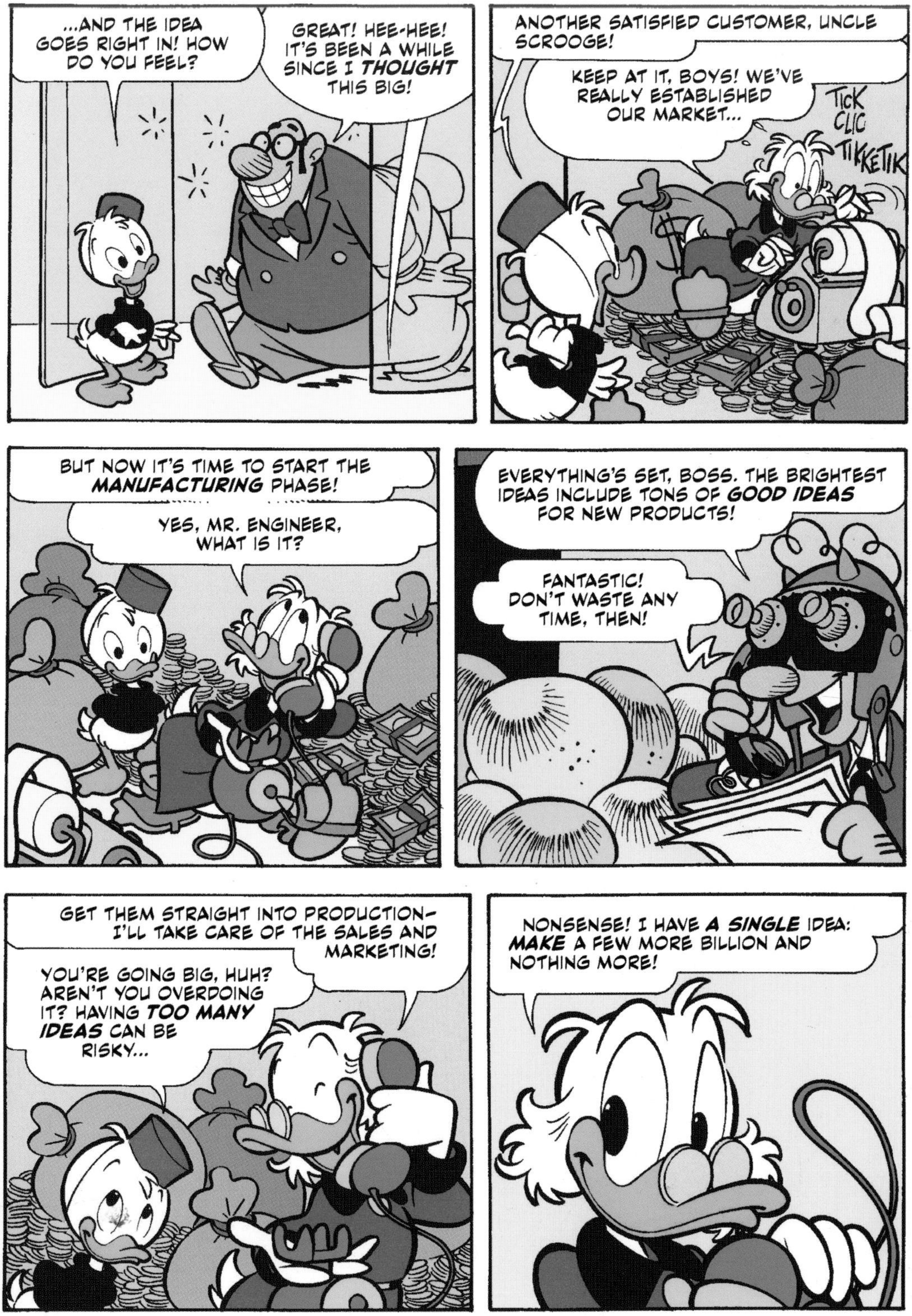
...AND THE IDEA GOES RIGHT IN! HOW DO YOU FEEL?
GREAT! HEE-HEE! IT'S BEEN A WHILE SINCE I THOUGHT THIS BIG!
ANOTHER SATISFIED CUSTOMER, UNCLE SCROOGE!
KEEP AT IT, BOYS! WE'VE REALLY ESTABLISHED OUR MARKET...
TICK CLIC TIKKETIK
BUT NOW IT'S TIME TO START THE MANUFACTURING PHASE!
YES, MR. ENGINEER, WHAT IS IT?
EVERYTHING'S SET, BOSS. THE BRIGHTEST IDEAS INCLUDE TONS OF GOOD IDEAS FOR NEW PRODUCTS!
FANTASTIC! DON'T WASTE ANY TIME, THEN!
GET THEM STRAIGHT INTO PRODUCTION-I'LL TAKE CARE OF THE SALES AND MARKETING!
YOU'RE GOING BIG, HUH? AREN'T YOU OVERDOING IT? HAVING TOO MANY IDEAS CAN BE RISKY...
NONSENSE! I HAVE A SINGLE IDEA: MAKE A FEW MORE BILLION AND NOTHING MORE!

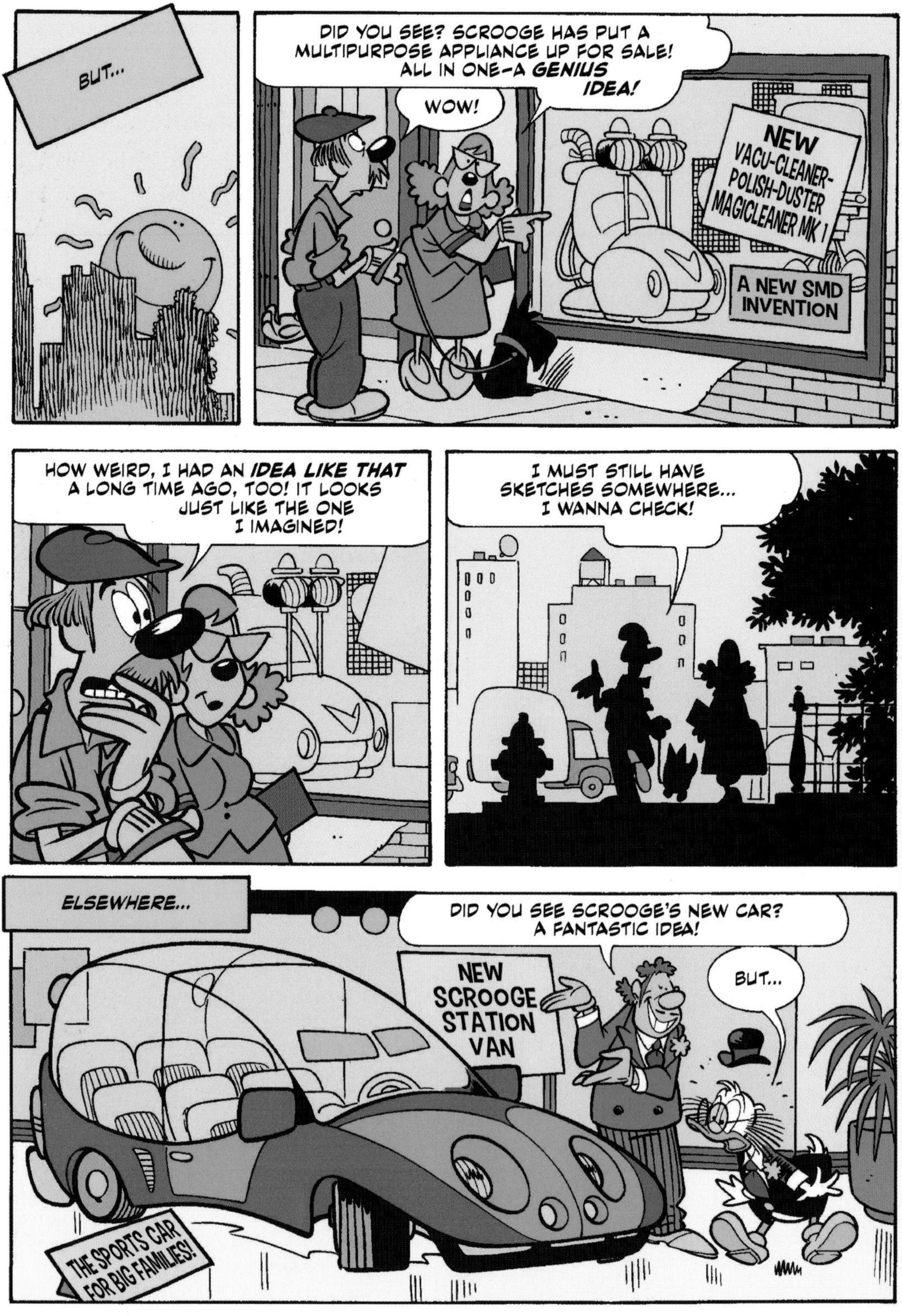
BUT...
DID YOU SEE? SCROOGE HAS PUT A MULTIPURPOSE APPLIANCE UP FOR SALE! ALL IN ONE—A GENIUS IDEA!
WOW!
NEW VACU-CLEANER-POLISH-DUSTER MAGICLEANER MK 1
A NEW SMD INVENTION
HOW WEIRD, I HAD AN IDEA LIKE THAT A LONG TIME AGO, TOO! IT LOOKS JUST LIKE THE ONE I IMAGINED!
I MUST STILL HAVE SKETCHES SOMEWHERE... I WANNA CHECK!
ELSEWHERE...
DID YOU SEE SCROOGE'S NEW CAR? A FANTASTIC IDEA!
NEW SCROOGE STATION VAN
BUT...
THE SPORTS CAR FOR BIG FAMILIES!

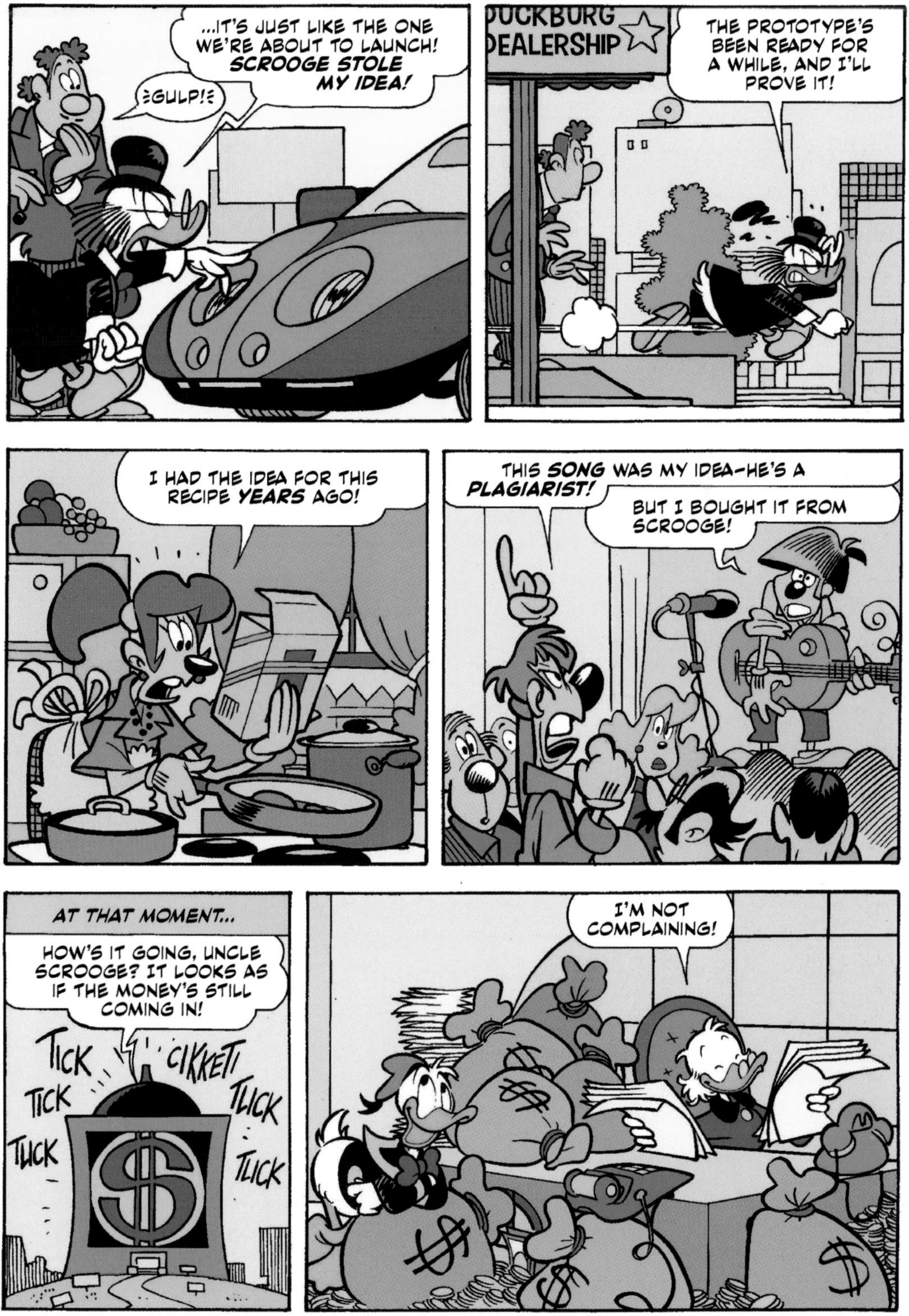
...IT'S JUST LIKE THE ONE WE'RE ABOUT TO LAUNCH! SCROOGE STOLE MY IDEA!
GULP!
DUCKBURG DEALERSHIP
THE PROTOTYPE'S BEEN READY FOR A WHILE, AND I'LL PROVE IT!
I HAD THE IDEA FOR THIS RECIPE YEARS AGO!
THIS SONG WAS MY IDEA—HE'S A PLAGIARIST!
BUT I BOUGHT IT FROM SCROOGE!
AT THAT MOMENT...
HOW'S IT GOING, UNCLE SCROOGE? IT LOOKS AS IF THE MONEY'S STILL COMING IN!
TICK
CIKKETI
TICK
TLICK
TLICK
TLICK
I'M NOT COMPLAINING!

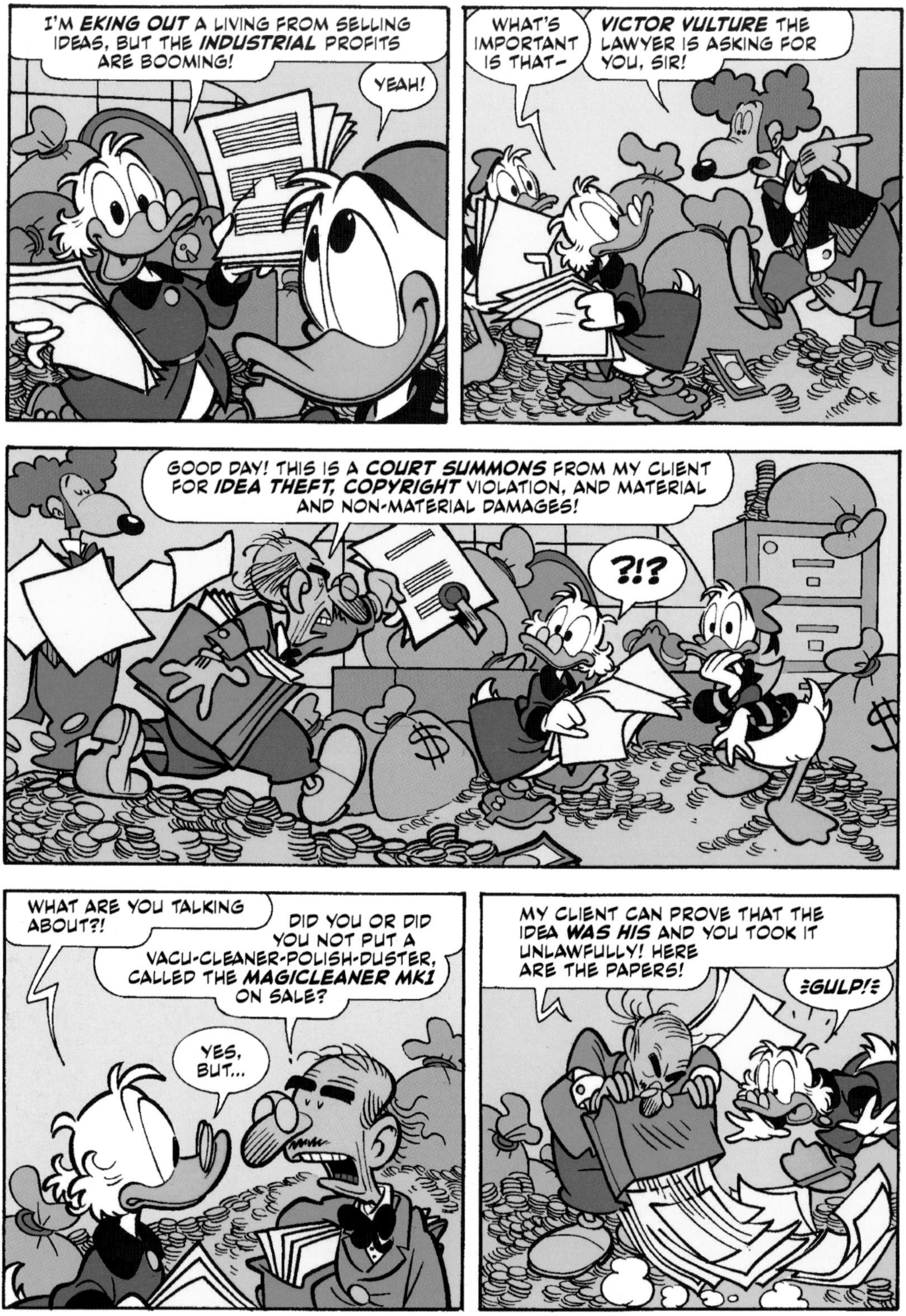
I'M EKING OUT A LIVING FROM SELLING IDEAS, BUT THE INDUSTRIAL PROFITS ARE BOOMING!
YEAH!
WHAT'S IMPORTANT IS THAT–
VICTOR VULTURE THE LAWYER IS ASKING FOR YOU, SIR!
GOOD DAY! THIS IS A COURT SUMMONS FROM MY CLIENT FOR IDEA THEFT, COPYRIGHT VIOLATION, AND MATERIAL AND NON-MATERIAL DAMAGES!
?!?
WHAT ARE YOU TALKING ABOUT?!
DID YOU OR DID YOU NOT PUT A VACU-CLEANER-POLISH-DUSTER, CALLED THE MAGICLEANER MK1 ON SALE?
YES, BUT...
MY CLIENT CAN PROVE THAT THE IDEA WAS HIS AND YOU TOOK IT UNLAWFULLY! HERE ARE THE PAPERS!
GULP!

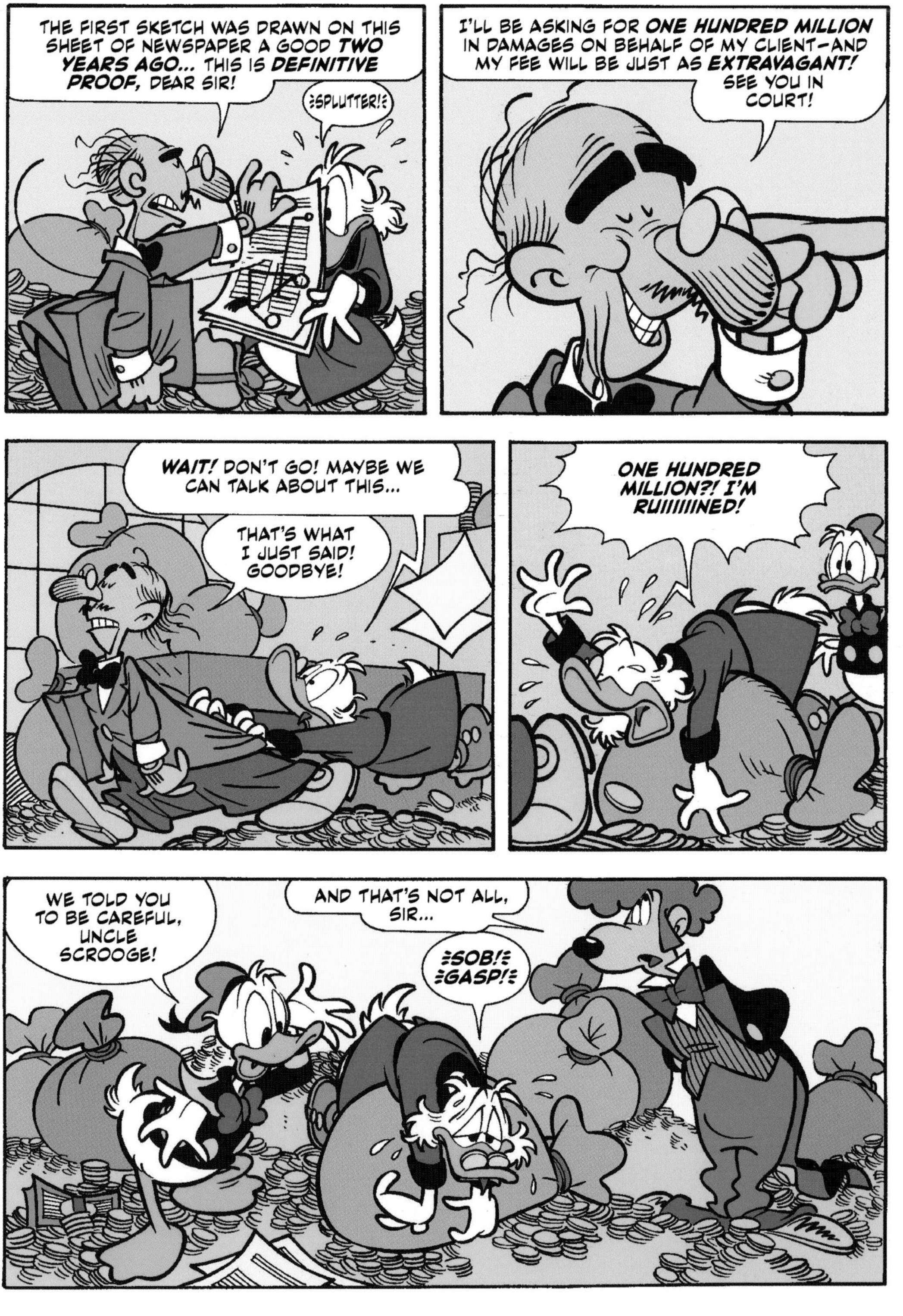
THE FIRST SKETCH WAS DRAWN ON THIS SHEET OF NEWSPAPER A GOOD *TWO YEARS AGO...* THIS IS *DEFINITIVE PROOF,* DEAR SIR!
SPLUTTER!
I'LL BE ASKING FOR *ONE HUNDRED MILLION* IN DAMAGES ON BEHALF OF MY CLIENT—AND MY FEE WILL BE JUST AS *EXTRAVAGANT!*
SEE YOU IN COURT!
WAIT! DON'T GO! MAYBE WE CAN TALK ABOUT THIS...
THAT'S WHAT I JUST SAID! GOODBYE!
ONE HUNDRED MILLION?! I'M RUIIIIIINED!
WE TOLD YOU TO BE CAREFUL, UNCLE SCROOGE!
AND THAT'S NOT ALL, SIR...
SOB! GASP!

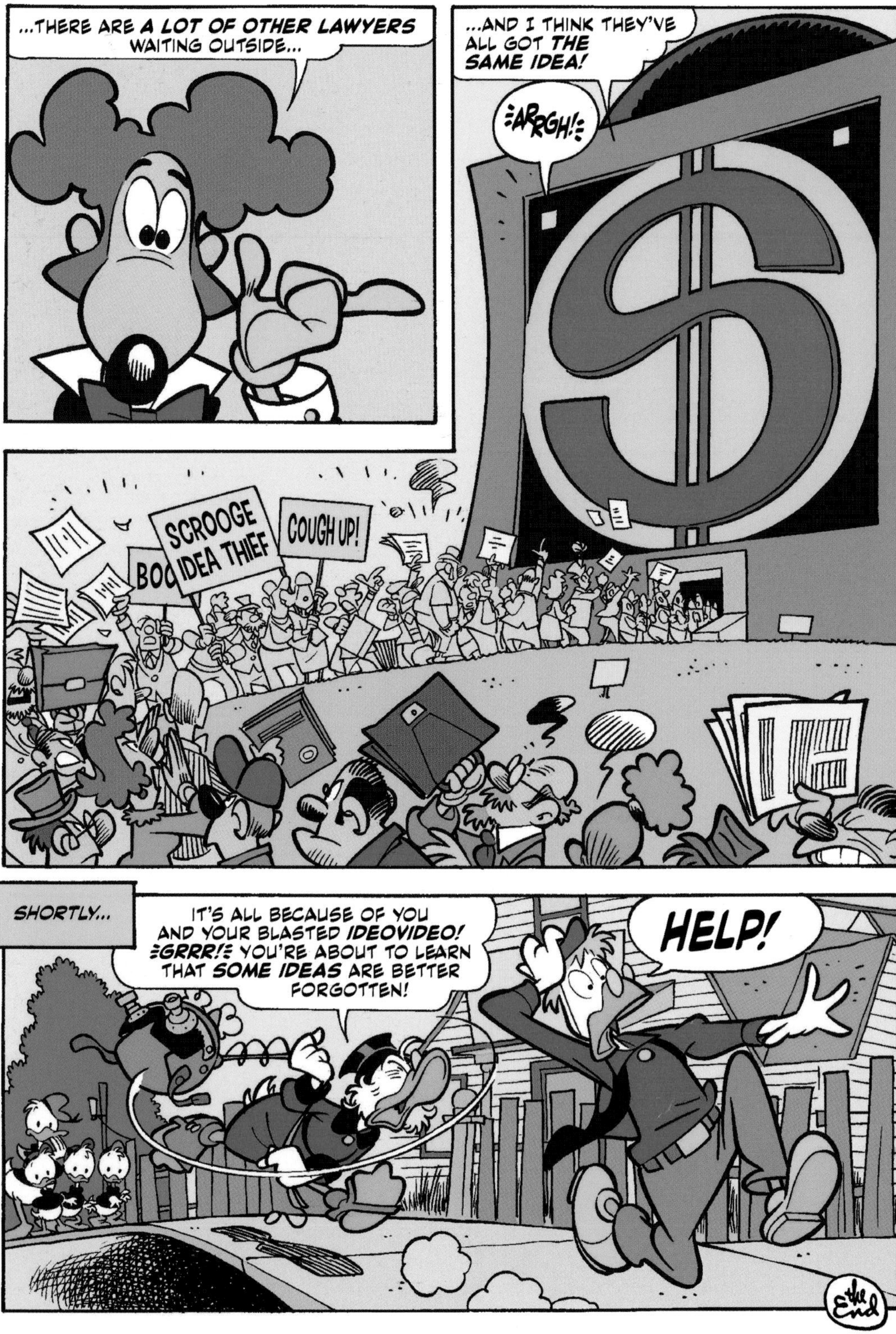

...THERE ARE A LOT OF OTHER LAWYERS WAITING OUTSIDE...
...AND I THINK THEY'VE ALL GOT THE SAME IDEA!
ARRGH!
SCROOGE IDEA THIEF
COUGH UP!
BOO
SHORTLY...
IT'S ALL BECAUSE OF YOU AND YOUR BLASTED IDEOVIDEO! GRRR! YOU'RE ABOUT TO LEARN THAT SOME IDEAS ARE BETTER FORGOTTEN!
HELP!
the End

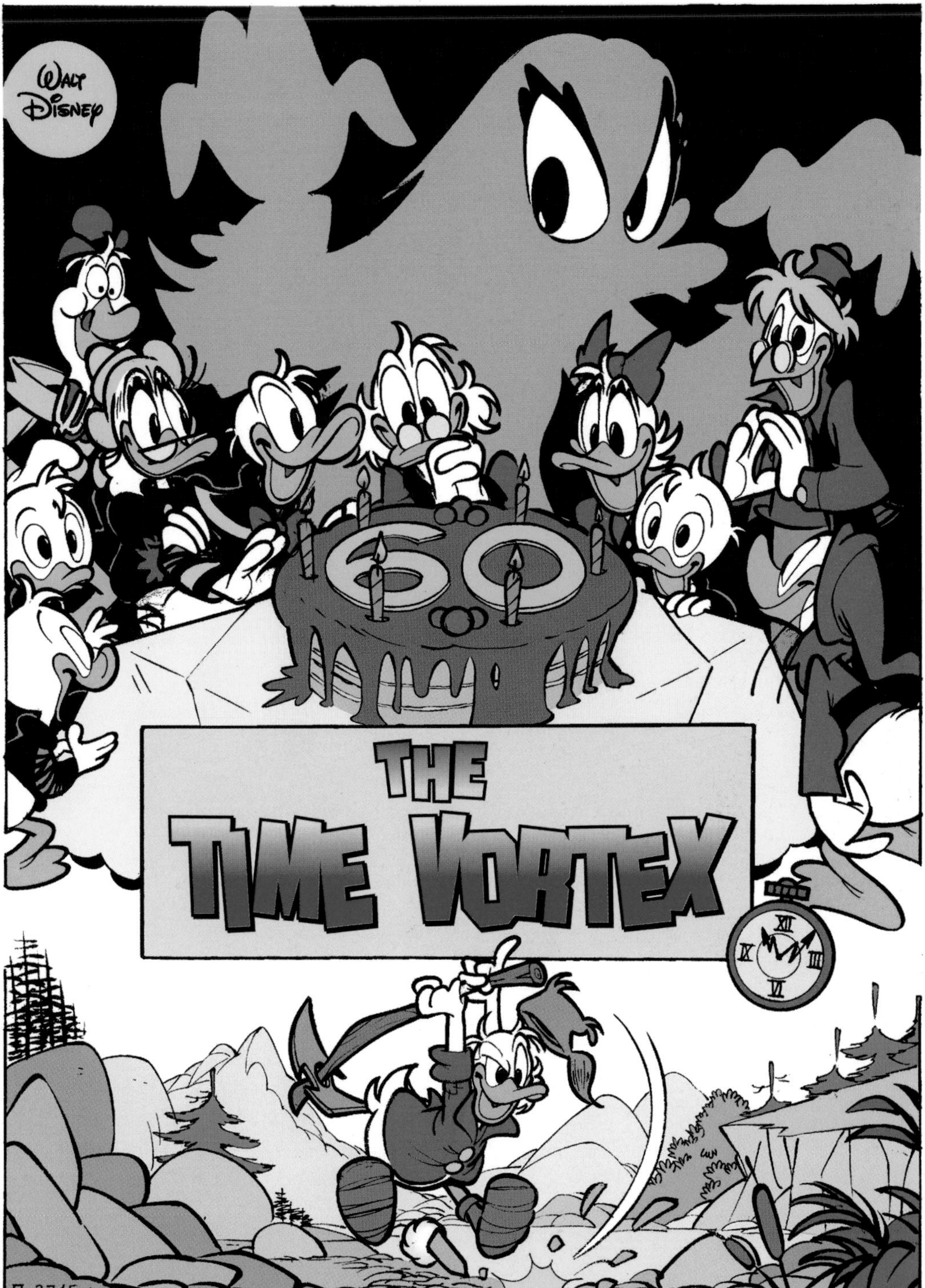
WALT DISNEY
THE TIME VORTEX
J-2715-1

ORIGINALLY PUBLISHED IN TOPOLINO #2715 (ITALY, 2007) • FIRST USA PUBLICATION

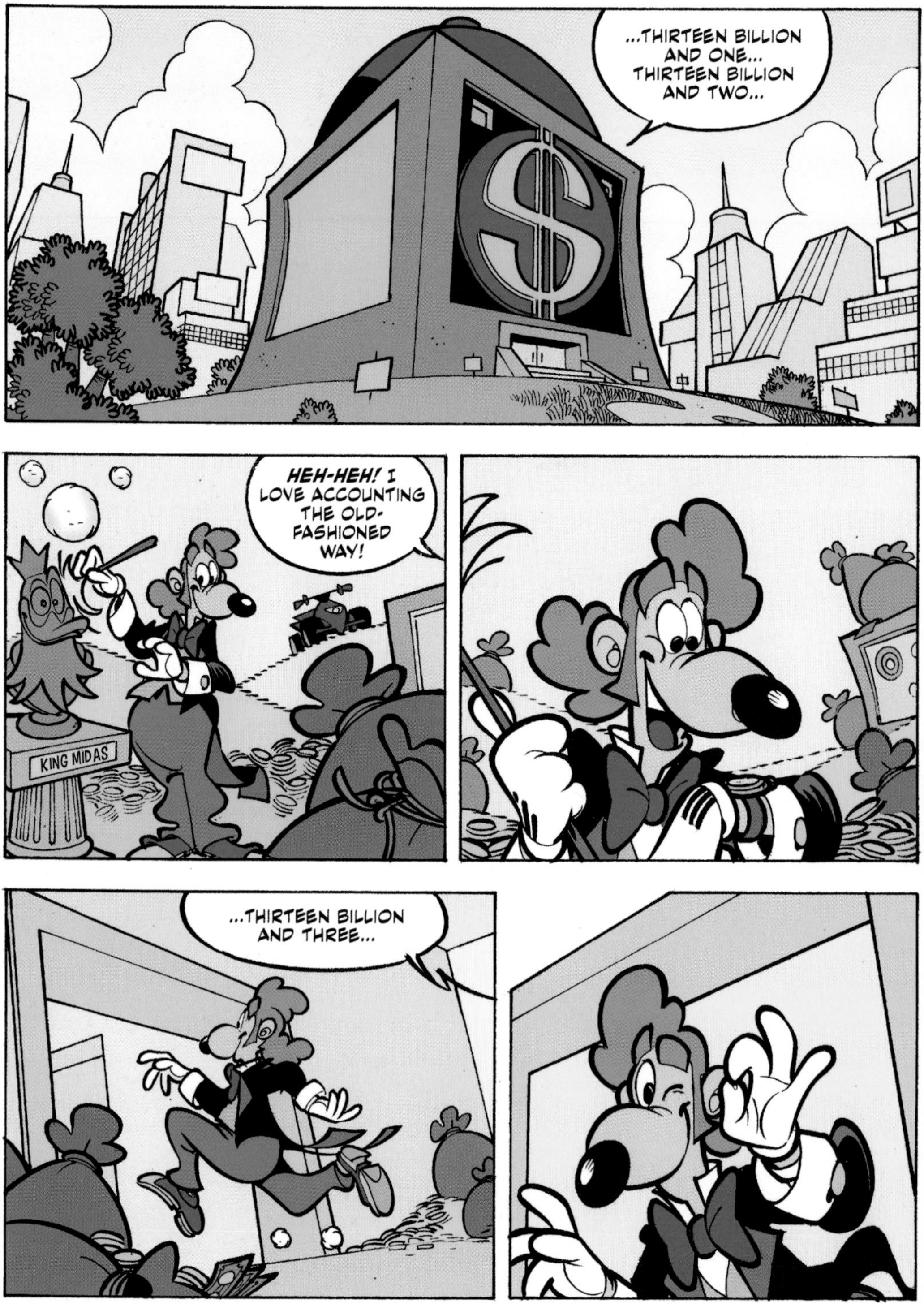
...THIRTEEN BILLION AND ONE... THIRTEEN BILLION AND TWO...
HEH-HEH! I LOVE ACCOUNTING THE OLD-FASHIONED WAY!
KING MIDAS
...THIRTEEN BILLION AND THREE...

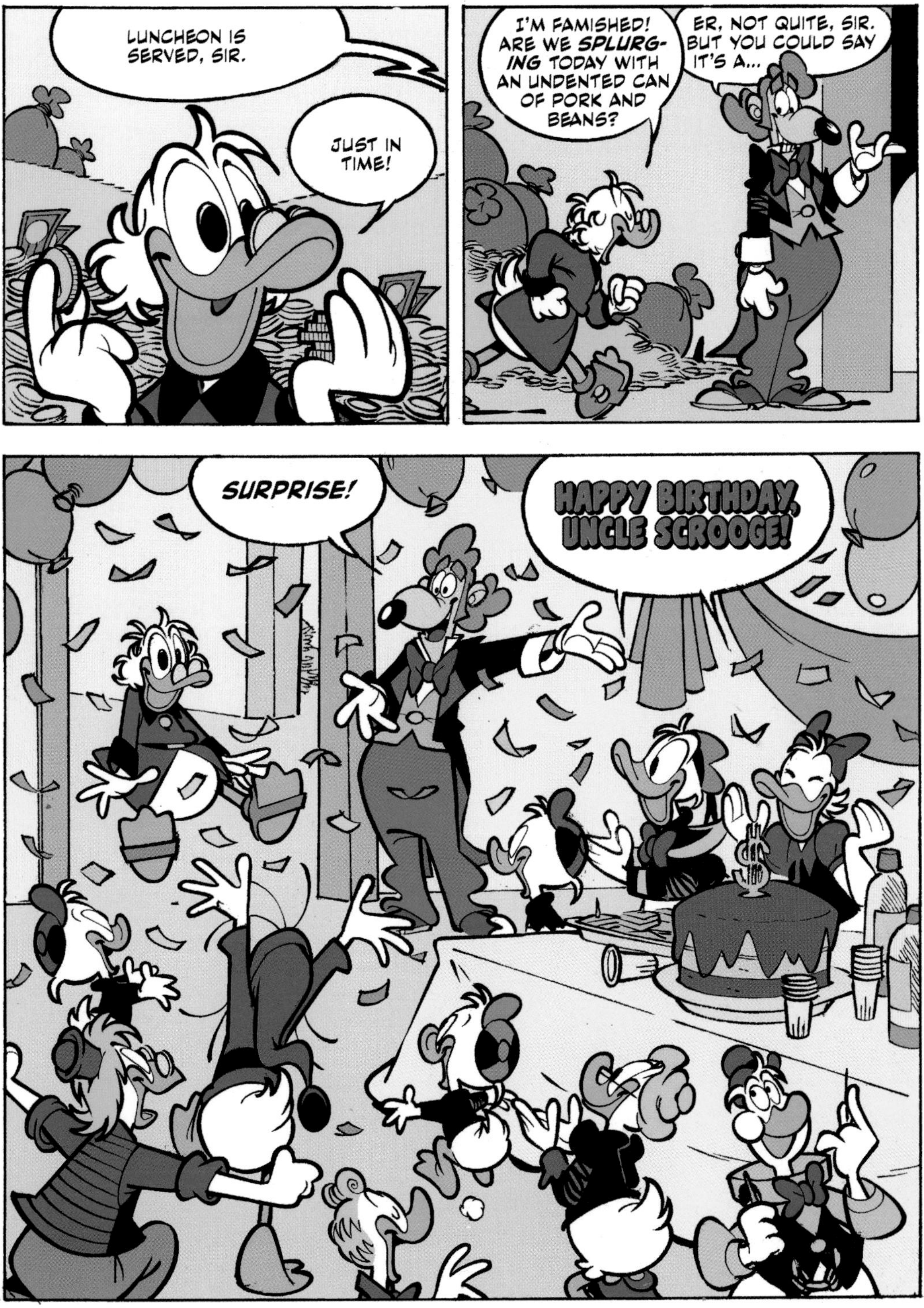
LUNCHEON IS SERVED, SIR.
JUST IN TIME!
I'M FAMISHED! ARE WE *SPLURGING* TODAY WITH AN UNDENTED CAN OF PORK AND BEANS?
ER, NOT QUITE, SIR. BUT YOU COULD SAY IT'S A...
SURPRISE!
HAPPY BIRTHDAY, UNCLE SCROOGE!

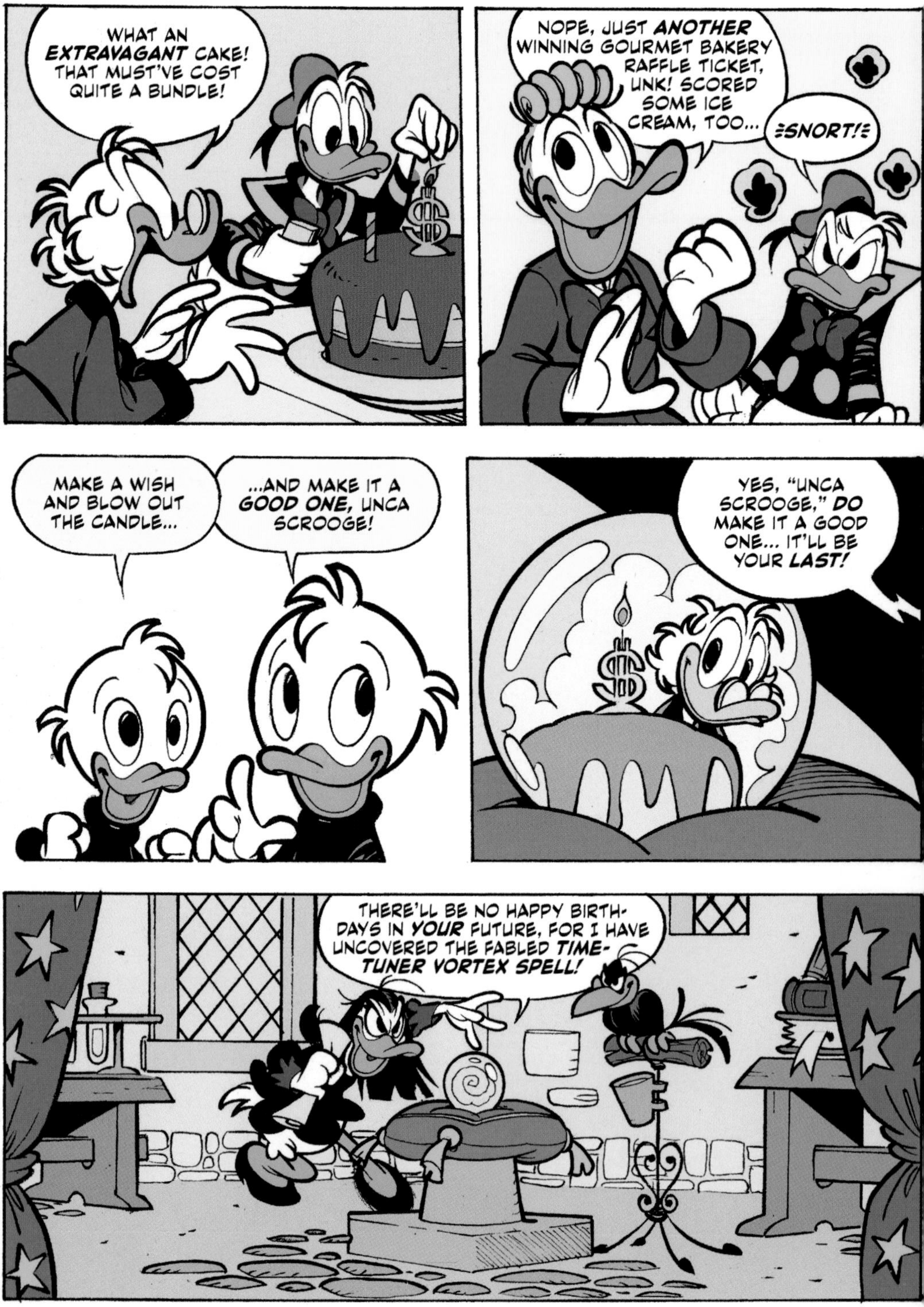
WHAT AN EXTRAVAGANT CAKE! THAT MUST'VE COST QUITE A BUNDLE!
NOPE, JUST ANOTHER WINNING GOURMET BAKERY RAFFLE TICKET, UNK! SCORED SOME ICE CREAM, TOO...
SNORT!
MAKE A WISH AND BLOW OUT THE CANDLE...
...AND MAKE IT A GOOD ONE, UNCA SCROOGE!
YES, "UNCA SCROOGE," DO MAKE IT A GOOD ONE... IT'LL BE YOUR LAST!
THERE'LL BE NO HAPPY BIRTHDAYS IN YOUR FUTURE, FOR I HAVE UNCOVERED THE FABLED TIME-TUNER VORTEX SPELL!

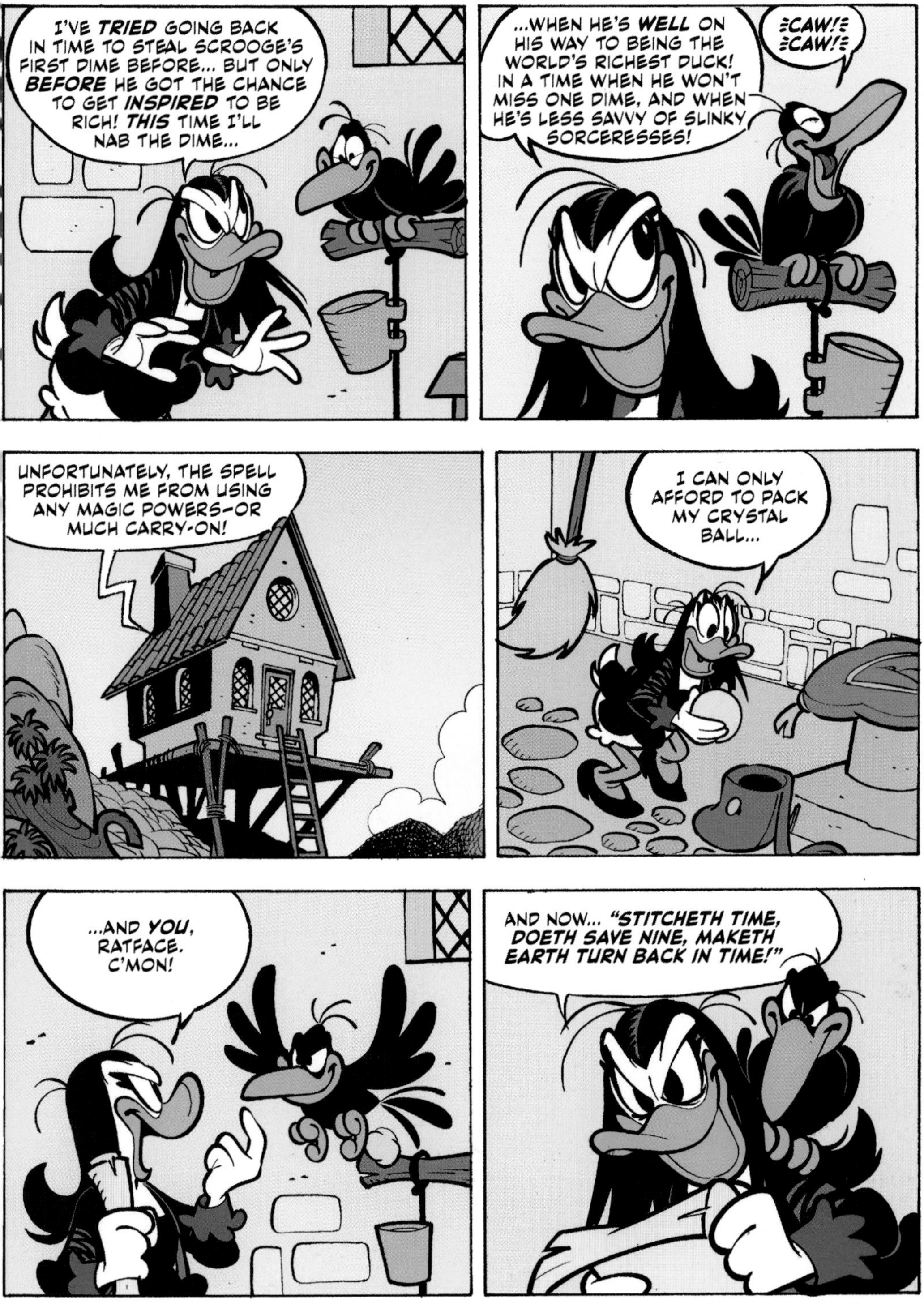
I'VE *TRIED* GOING BACK IN TIME TO STEAL SCROOGE'S FIRST DIME BEFORE... BUT ONLY *BEFORE* HE GOT THE CHANCE TO GET *INSPIRED* TO BE RICH! *THIS* TIME I'LL NAB THE DIME...
...WHEN HE'S *WELL* ON HIS WAY TO BEING THE WORLD'S RICHEST DUCK! IN A TIME WHEN HE WON'T MISS ONE DIME, AND WHEN HE'S LESS SAVVY OF SLINKY SORCERESSES!
CAW! CAW!
UNFORTUNATELY, THE SPELL PROHIBITS ME FROM USING ANY MAGIC POWERS—OR MUCH CARRY-ON!
I CAN ONLY AFFORD TO PACK MY CRYSTAL BALL...
...AND *YOU*, RATFACE. C'MON!
AND NOW... *"STITCHETH TIME, DOETH SAVE NINE, MAKETH EARTH TURN BACK IN TIME!"*

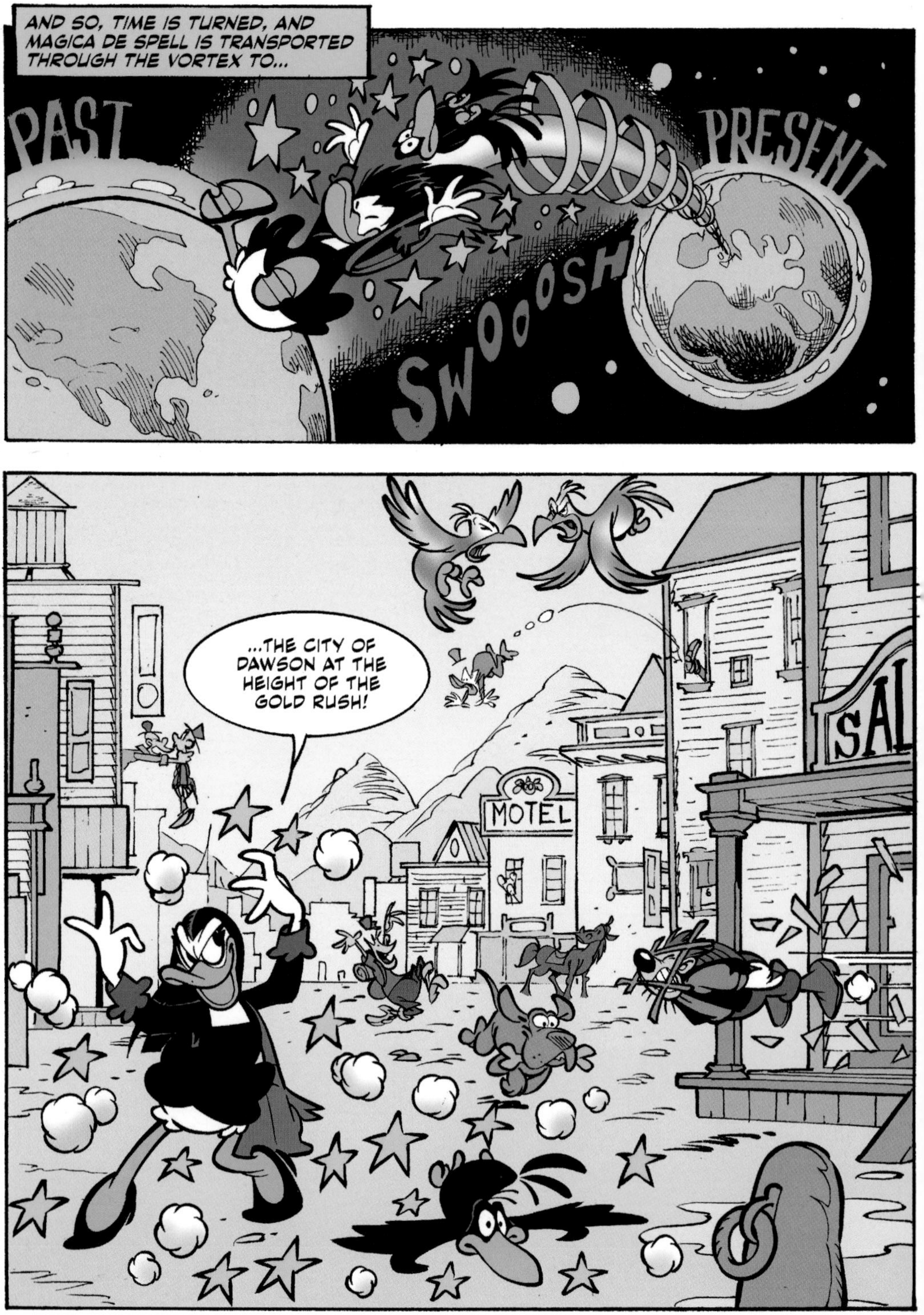
AND SO, TIME IS TURNED, AND MAGICA DE SPELL IS TRANSPORTED THROUGH THE VORTEX TO...
PAST
PRESENT
SWOOOSH
...THE CITY OF DAWSON AT THE HEIGHT OF THE GOLD RUSH!
MOTEL
SAL

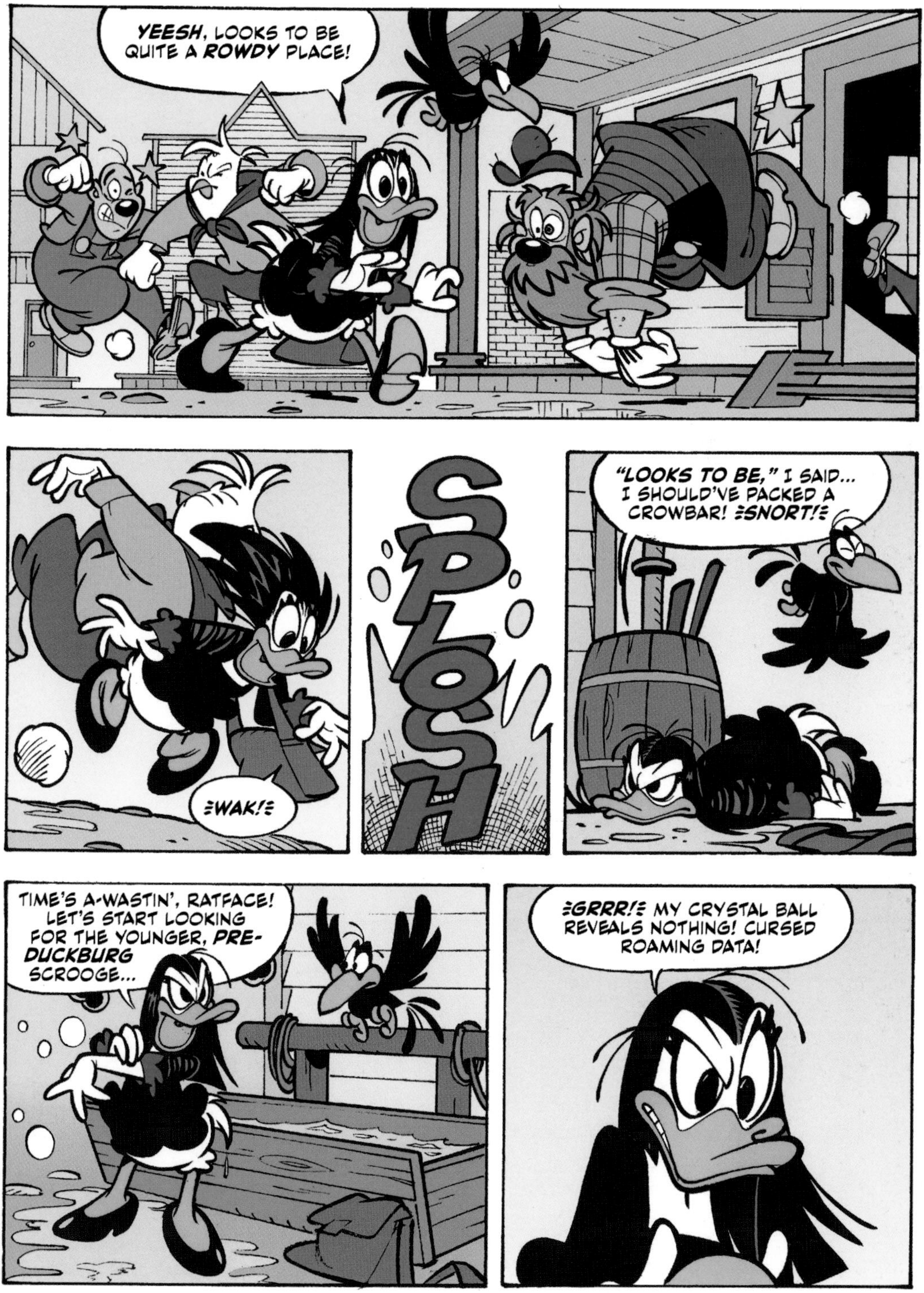
YEESH, LOOKS TO BE QUITE A ROWDY PLACE!
WAK!
SPLOSH
"LOOKS TO BE," I SAID... I SHOULD'VE PACKED A CROWBAR! SNORT!
TIME'S A-WASTIN', RATFACE! LET'S START LOOKING FOR THE YOUNGER, PRE-DUCKBURG SCROOGE...
GRRR! MY CRYSTAL BALL REVEALS NOTHING! CURSED ROAMING DATA!

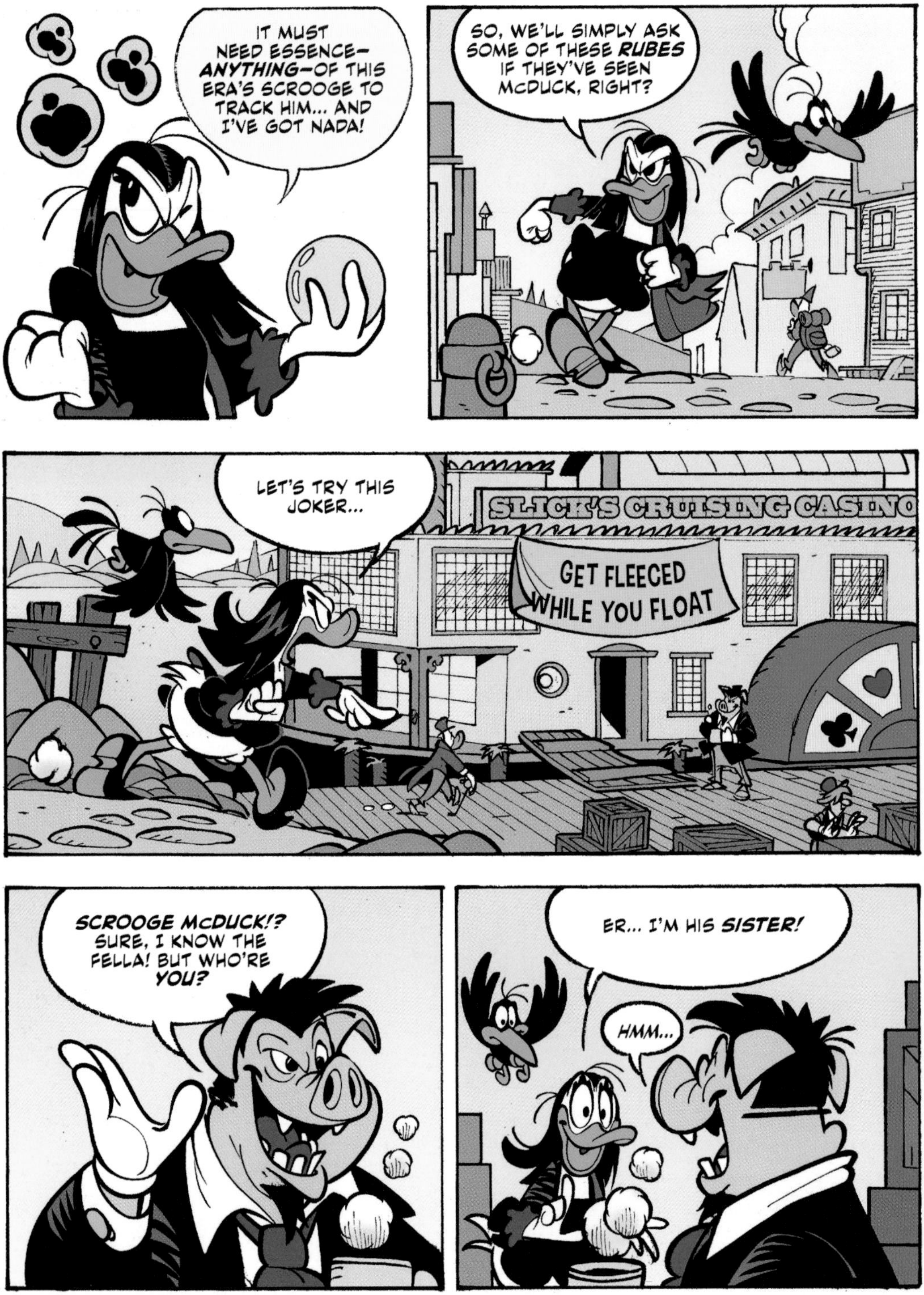
IT MUST NEED ESSENCE—ANYTHING—OF THIS ERA'S SCROOGE TO TRACK HIM... AND I'VE GOT NADA!
SO, WE'LL SIMPLY ASK SOME OF THESE RUBES IF THEY'VE SEEN McDUCK, RIGHT?
LET'S TRY THIS JOKER...
SLICK'S CRUISING CASINO
GET FLEECED WHILE YOU FLOAT
SCROOGE McDUCK!? SURE, I KNOW THE FELLA! BUT WHO'RE YOU?
ER... I'M HIS SISTER!
HMM...

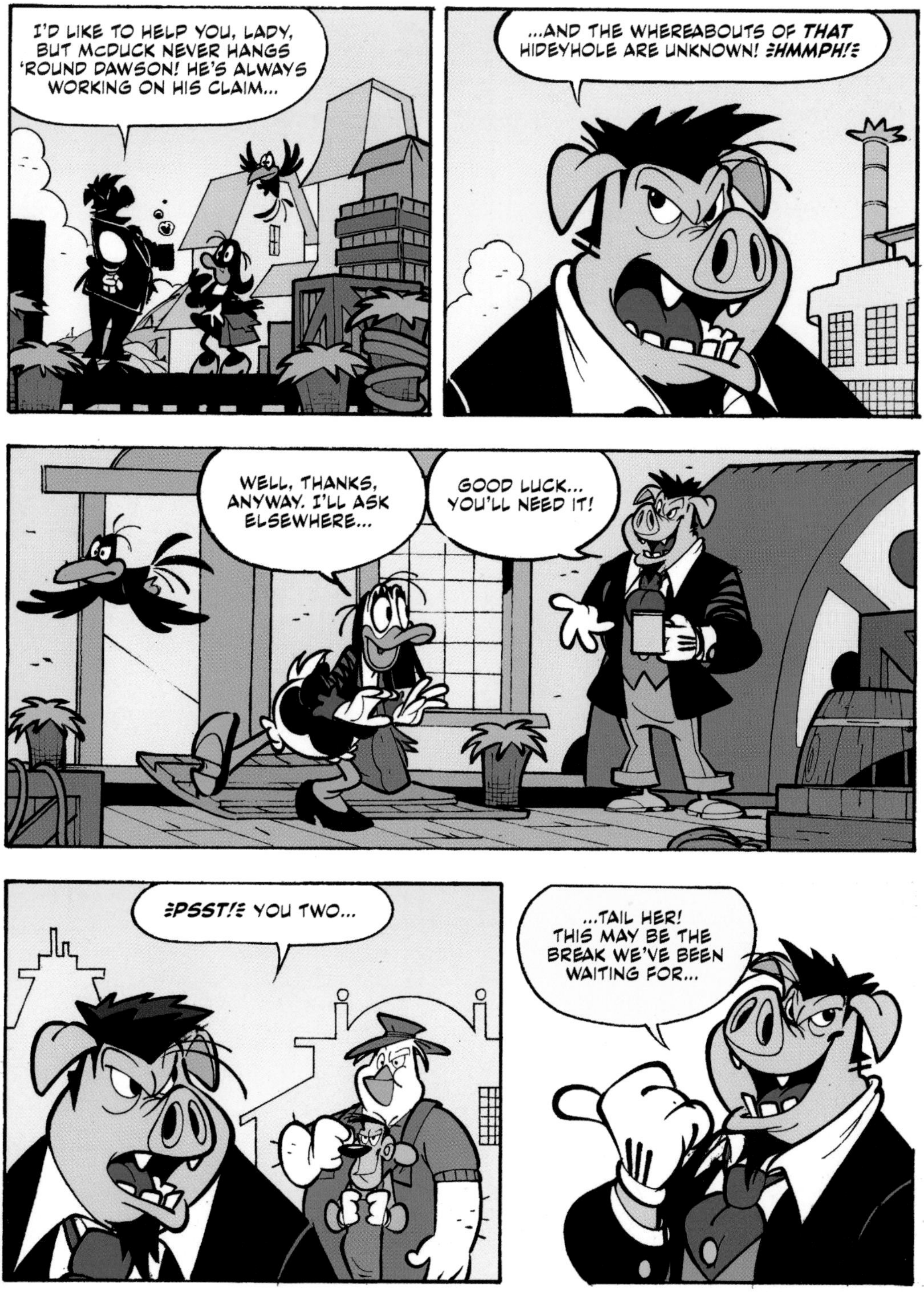
I'D LIKE TO HELP YOU, LADY, BUT McDUCK NEVER HANGS 'ROUND DAWSON! HE'S ALWAYS WORKING ON HIS CLAIM...
...AND THE WHEREABOUTS OF *THAT* HIDEYHOLE ARE UNKNOWN! *HMMPH!*
WELL, THANKS, ANYWAY. I'LL ASK ELSEWHERE...
GOOD LUCK... YOU'LL NEED IT!
PSST! YOU TWO...
...TAIL HER! THIS MAY BE THE BREAK WE'VE BEEN WAITING FOR...

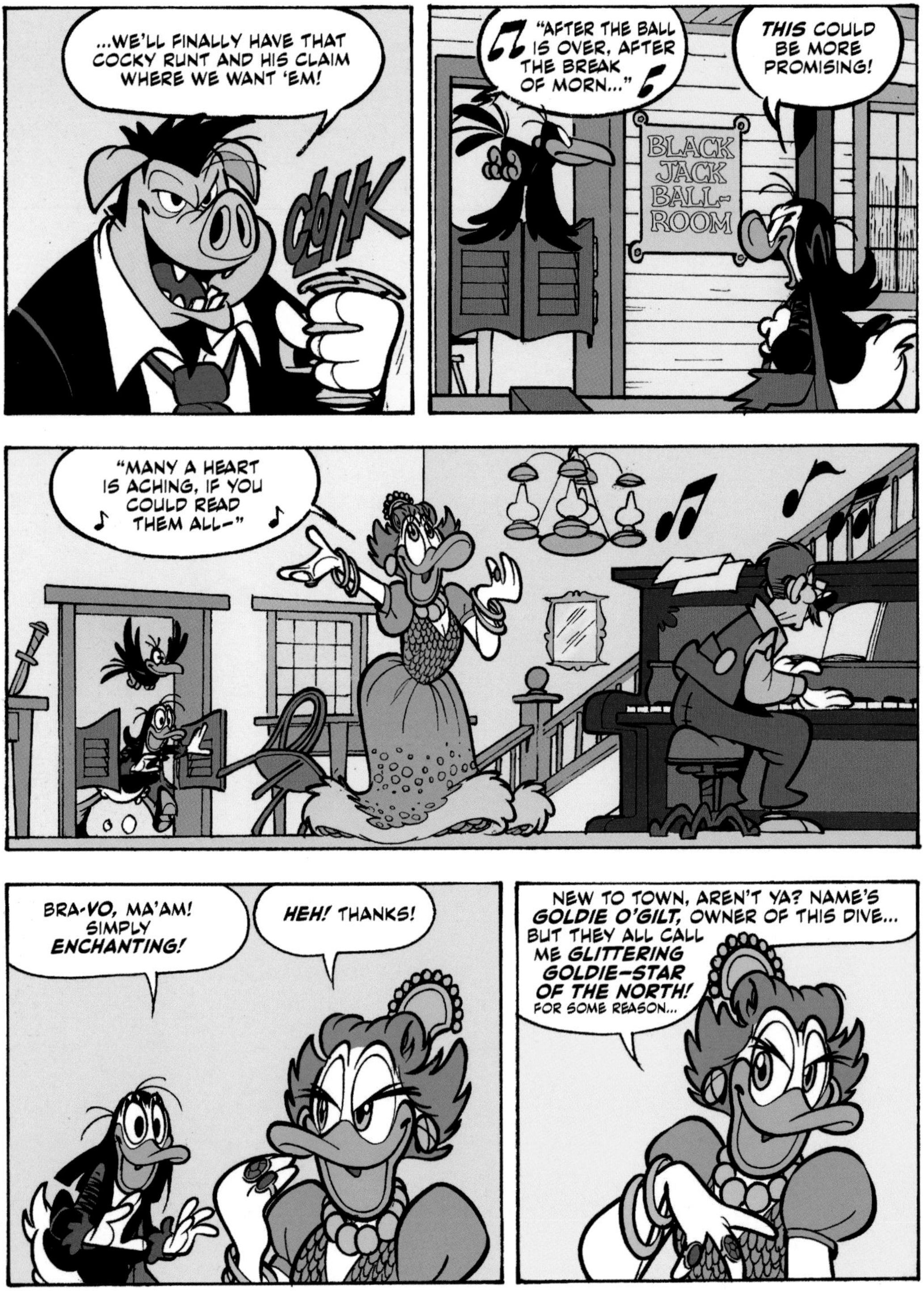
...WE'LL FINALLY HAVE THAT COCKY RUNT AND HIS CLAIM WHERE WE WANT 'EM!
CLONK
"AFTER THE BALL IS OVER, AFTER THE BREAK OF MORN..."
BLACK JACK BALL-ROOM
THIS COULD BE MORE PROMISING!
"MANY A HEART IS ACHING, IF YOU COULD READ THEM ALL–"
BRA-VO, MA'AM! SIMPLY ENCHANTING!
HEH! THANKS!
NEW TO TOWN, AREN'T YA? NAME'S GOLDIE O'GILT, OWNER OF THIS DIVE... BUT THEY ALL CALL ME GLITTERING GOLDIE—STAR OF THE NORTH! FOR SOME REASON...

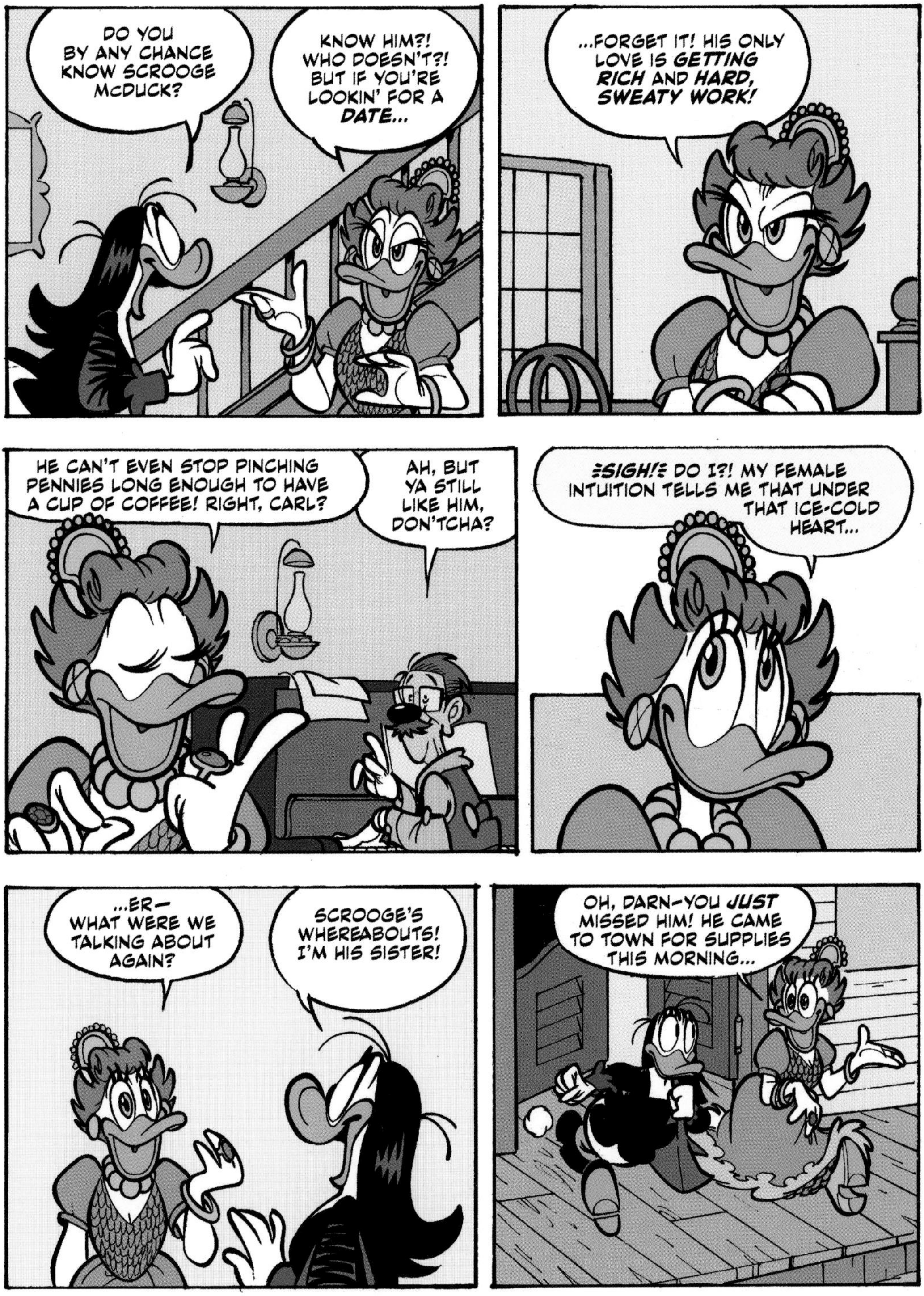
DO YOU BY ANY CHANCE KNOW SCROOGE McDUCK?
KNOW HIM?! WHO DOESN'T?! BUT IF YOU'RE LOOKIN' FOR A *DATE*...
...FORGET IT! HIS ONLY LOVE IS *GETTING RICH* AND *HARD, SWEATY WORK!*
HE CAN'T EVEN STOP PINCHING PENNIES LONG ENOUGH TO HAVE A CUP OF COFFEE! RIGHT, CARL?
AH, BUT YA STILL LIKE HIM, DON'TCHA?
SIGH! DO I?! MY FEMALE INTUITION TELLS ME THAT UNDER THAT ICE-COLD HEART...
...ER— WHAT WERE WE TALKING ABOUT AGAIN?
SCROOGE'S WHEREABOUTS! I'M HIS SISTER!
OH, DARN—YOU *JUST* MISSED HIM! HE CAME TO TOWN FOR SUPPLIES THIS MORNING...

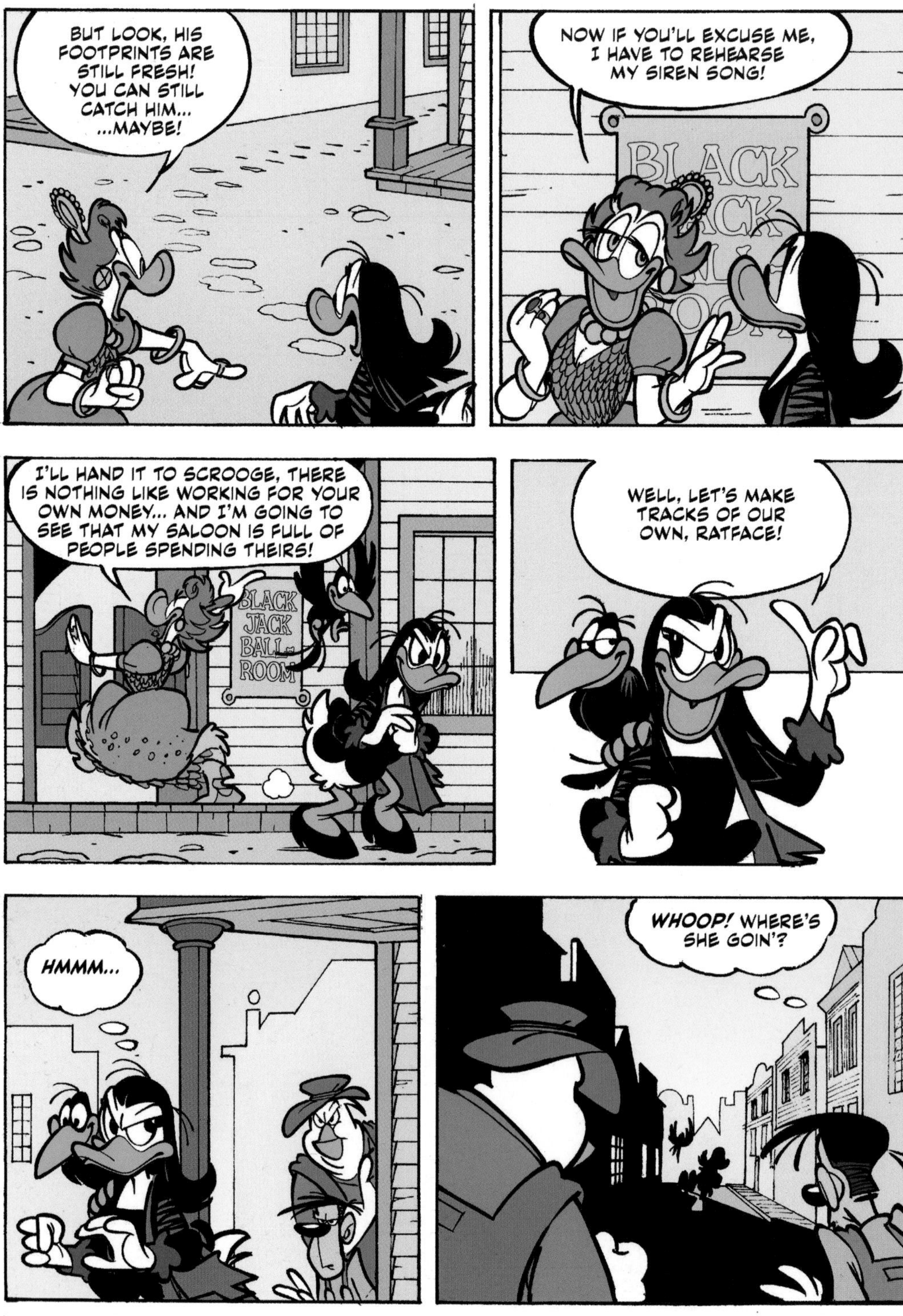
BUT LOOK, HIS FOOTPRINTS ARE STILL FRESH! YOU CAN STILL CATCH HIM... ...MAYBE!
NOW IF YOU'LL EXCUSE ME, I HAVE TO REHEARSE MY SIREN SONG!
BLACK JACK BALL ROOM
I'LL HAND IT TO SCROOGE, THERE IS NOTHING LIKE WORKING FOR YOUR OWN MONEY... AND I'M GOING TO SEE THAT MY SALOON IS FULL OF PEOPLE SPENDING THEIRS!
BLACK JACK BALL ROOM
WELL, LET'S MAKE TRACKS OF OUR OWN, RATFACE!
HMMM...
WHOOP! WHERE'S SHE GOIN'?

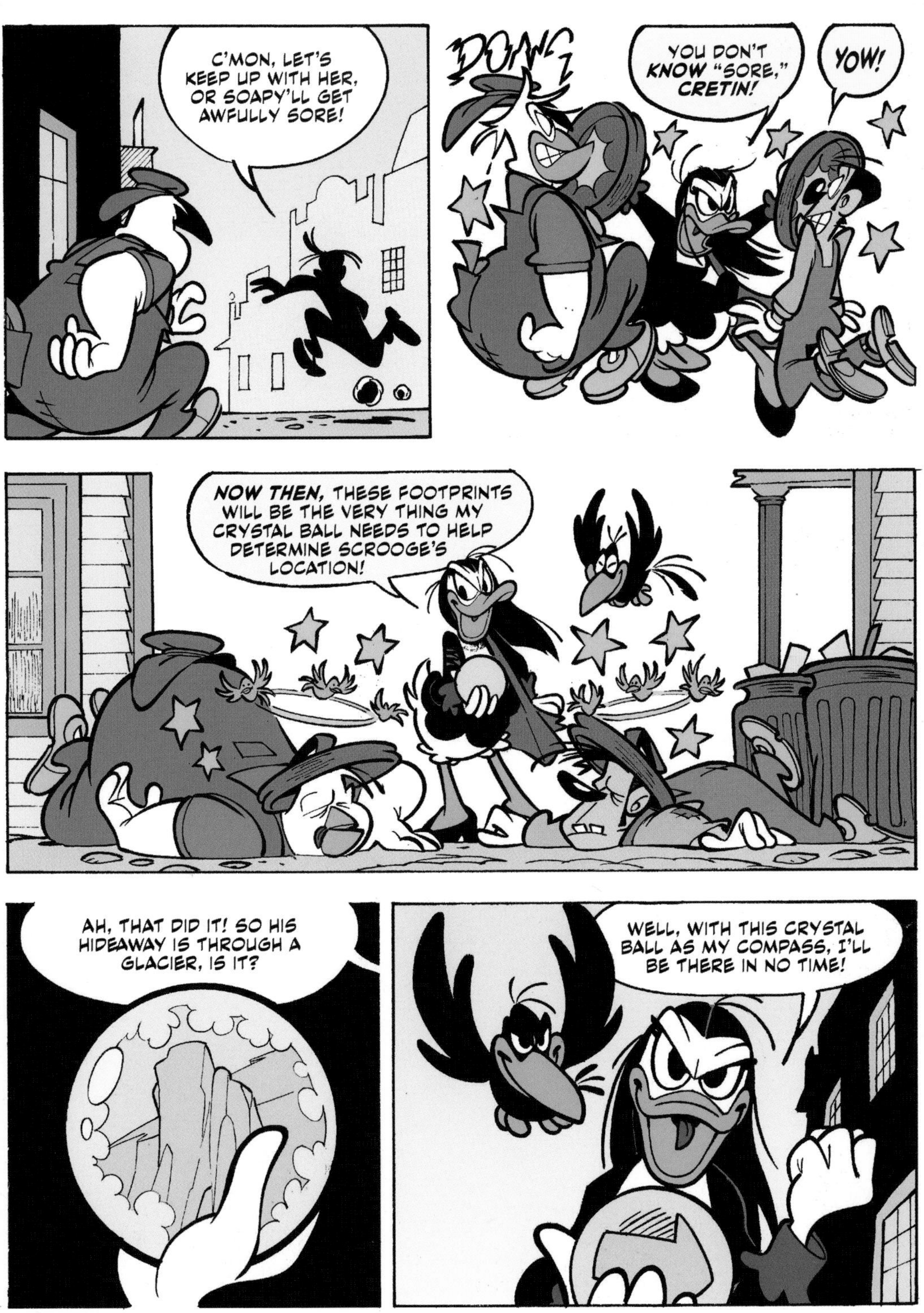
C'MON, LET'S KEEP UP WITH HER, OR SOAPY'LL GET AWFULLY SORE!
DONG
YOU DON'T KNOW "SORE," CRETIN!
YOW!
NOW THEN, THESE FOOTPRINTS WILL BE THE VERY THING MY CRYSTAL BALL NEEDS TO HELP DETERMINE SCROOGE'S LOCATION!
AH, THAT DID IT! SO HIS HIDEAWAY IS THROUGH A GLACIER, IS IT?
WELL, WITH THIS CRYSTAL BALL AS MY COMPASS, I'LL BE THERE IN NO TIME!

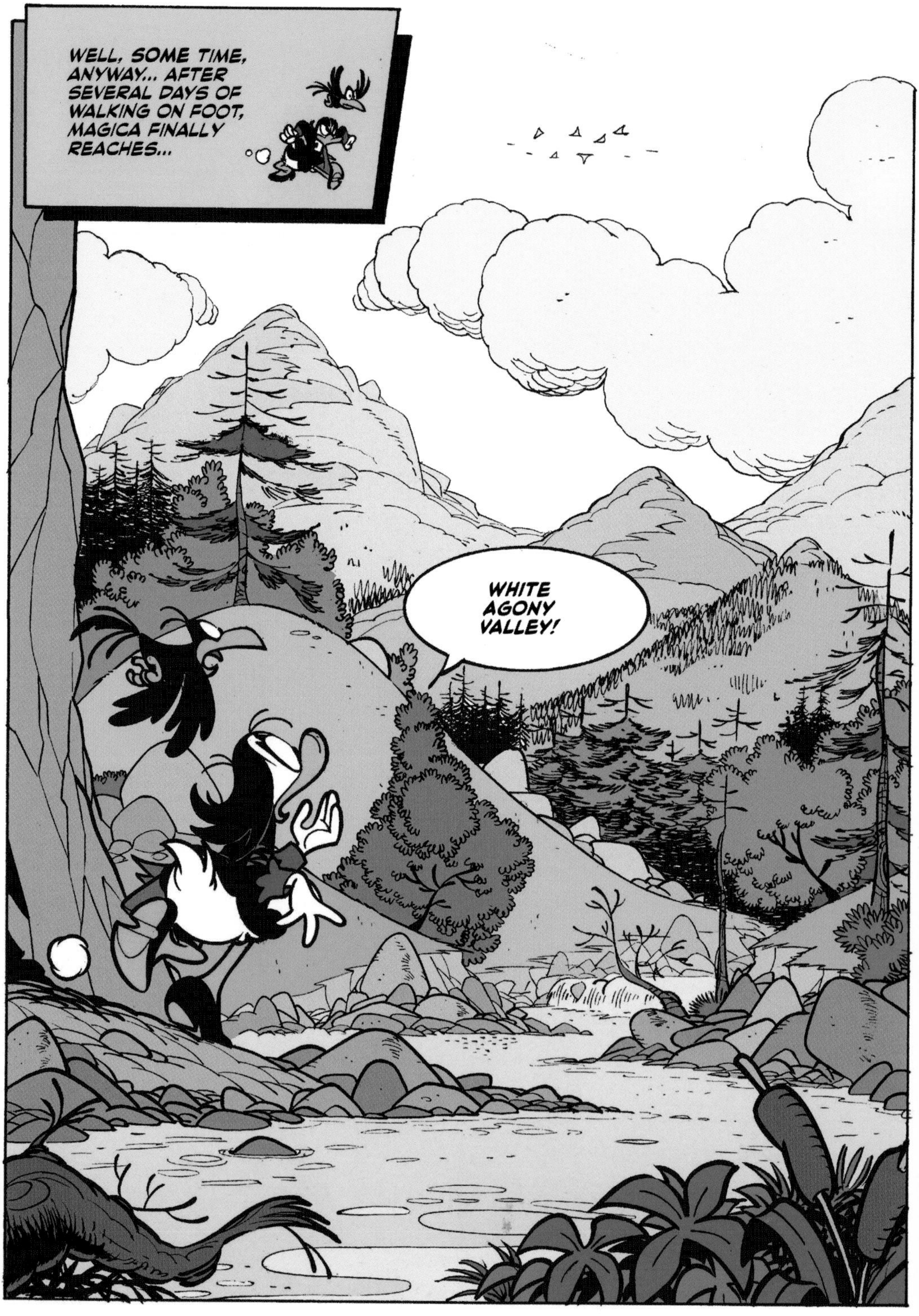
WELL, SOME TIME, ANYWAY... AFTER SEVERAL DAYS OF WALKING ON FOOT, MAGICA FINALLY REACHES...
WHITE AGONY VALLEY!

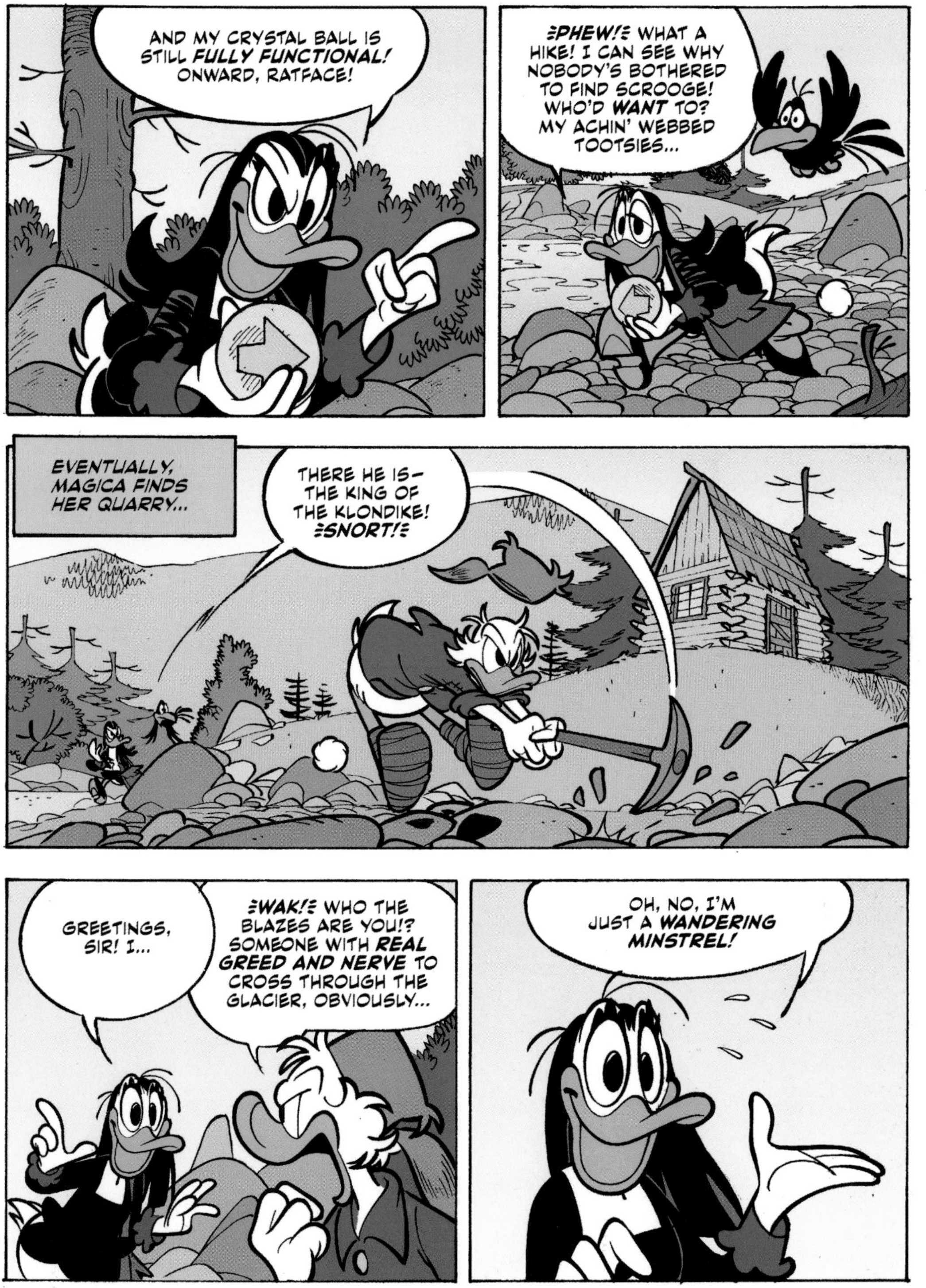
AND MY CRYSTAL BALL IS STILL FULLY FUNCTIONAL! ONWARD, RATFACE!
PHEW! WHAT A HIKE! I CAN SEE WHY NOBODY'S BOTHERED TO FIND SCROOGE! WHO'D WANT TO? MY ACHIN' WEBBED TOOTSIES...
EVENTUALLY, MAGICA FINDS HER QUARRY...
THERE HE IS— THE KING OF THE KLONDIKE! SNORT!
GREETINGS, SIR! I...
WAK! WHO THE BLAZES ARE YOU!? SOMEONE WITH REAL GREED AND NERVE TO CROSS THROUGH THE GLACIER, OBVIOUSLY...
OH, NO, I'M JUST A WANDERING MINSTREL!

AND I'M MARK TWAIN! STATE YOUR PURPOSE, OR *SCAT!*

ʒGULP!ʒ ETERNALLY ORNERY, I SEE...

WITH NO POWERS OR FOOF BOMBS AT HAND, I'LL JUST HAVE TO USE ALL OF MY CUNNING!

CALM YOURSELF, SIR! YOUR CLAIM AND GOLD IS NO INTEREST TO ME...

WHADDAYA TAKE ME FOR, LASS!? GOLD IS OF INTEREST TO *EVERYBODY!*

NO, I *AM* INTERESTED IN OLD COINS! I'M A COLLECTOR, AND IF YOU HAVE ANY...

YOU EXPECT ME TO BELIEVE YOU WENT ON THAT *GOD-FORSAKEN TRAIL* FOR *SPARE CHANGE?!*

SPARE ME!

I KNOW IT *SOUNDS* INSANE, BUT I...

ʒGRUNT!ʒ

FLIIIIII

?

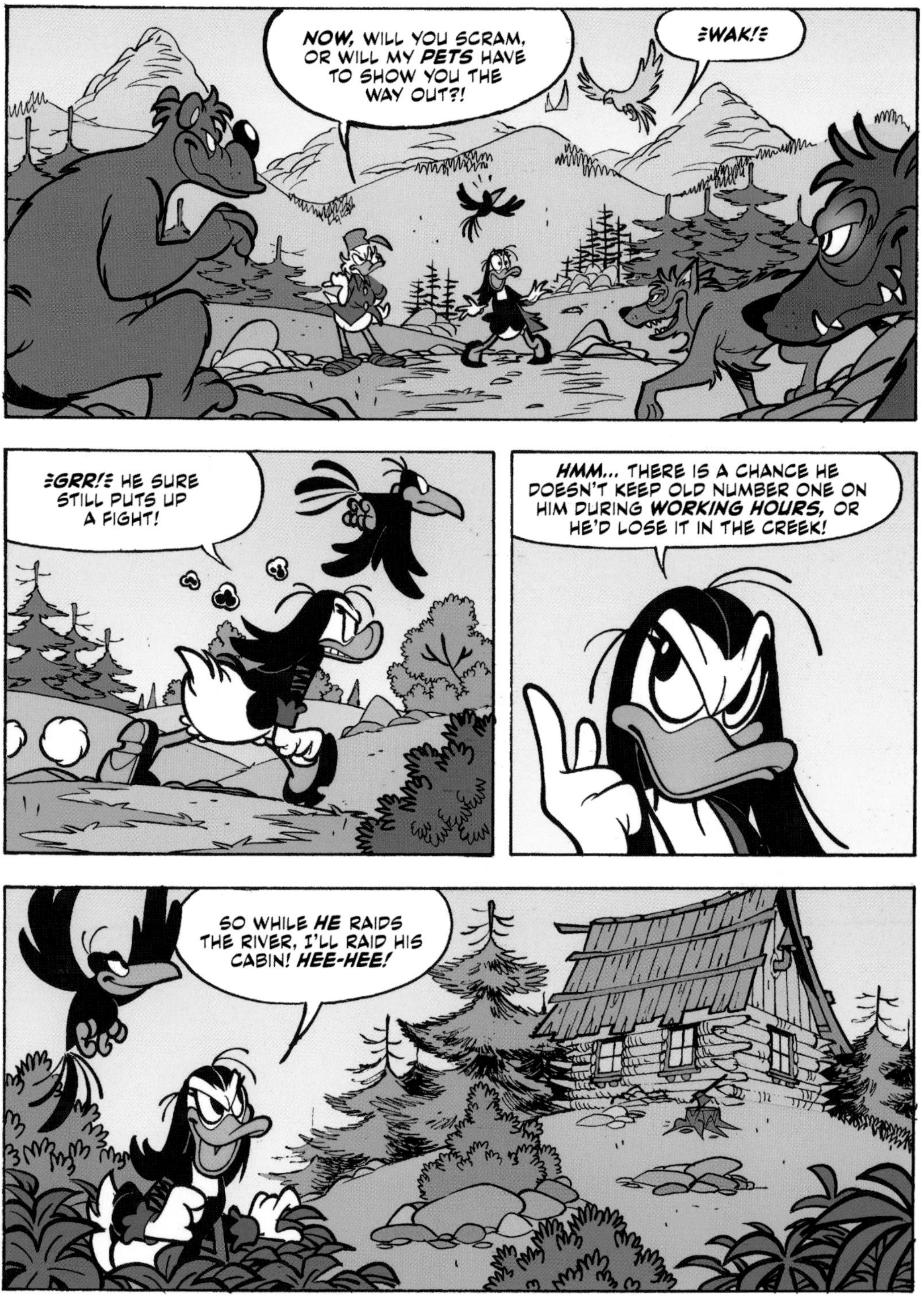
NOW, WILL YOU SCRAM, OR WILL MY PETS HAVE TO SHOW YOU THE WAY OUT?!
WAK!
GRR! HE SURE STILL PUTS UP A FIGHT!
HMM... THERE IS A CHANCE HE DOESN'T KEEP OLD NUMBER ONE ON HIM DURING WORKING HOURS, OR HE'D LOSE IT IN THE CREEK!
SO WHILE HE RAIDS THE RIVER, I'LL RAID HIS CABIN! HEE-HEE!

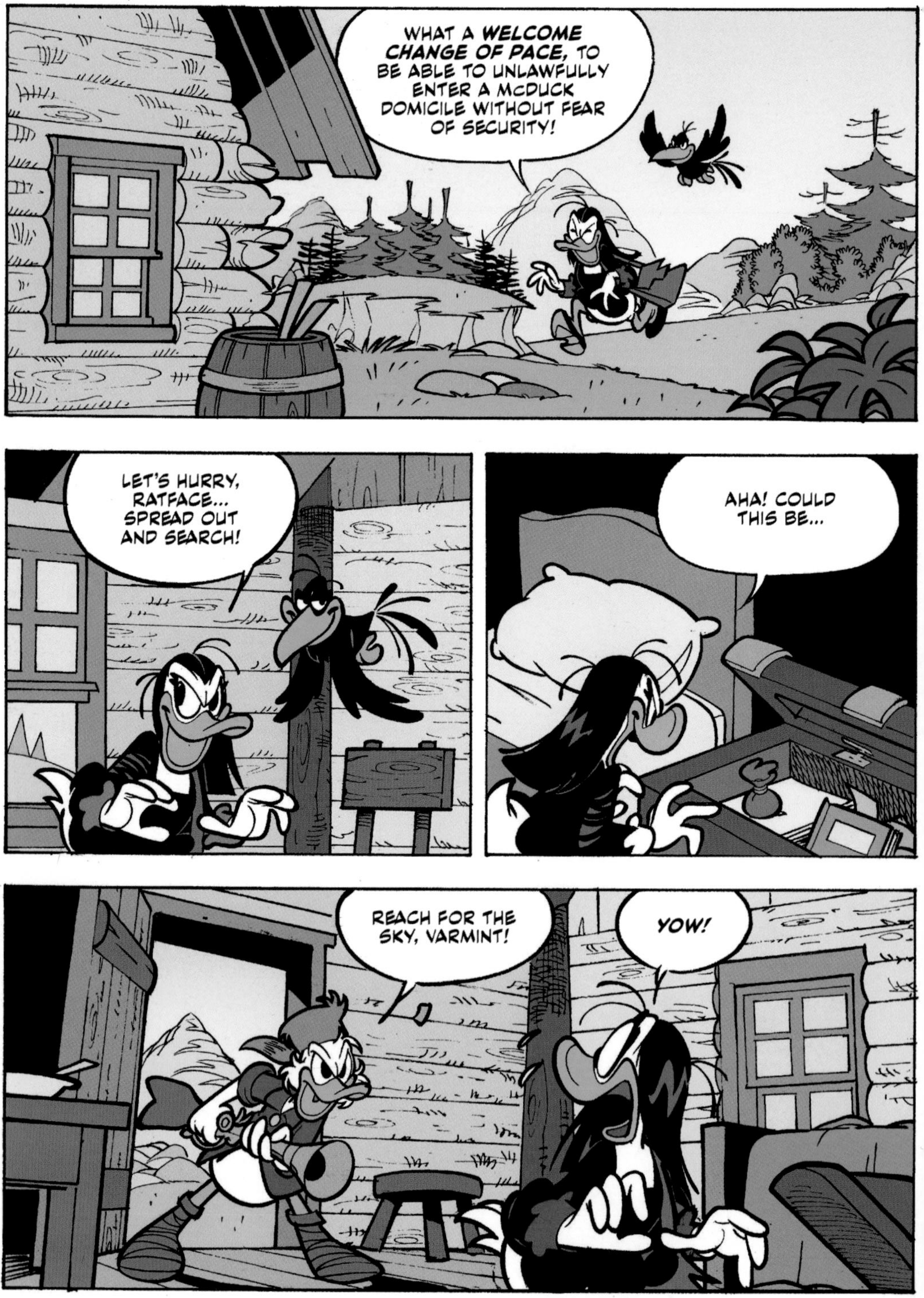
WHAT A ***WELCOME CHANGE OF PACE,*** TO BE ABLE TO UNLAWFULLY ENTER A McDUCK DOMICILE WITHOUT FEAR OF SECURITY!
LET'S HURRY, RATFACE... SPREAD OUT AND SEARCH!
AHA! COULD THIS BE...
REACH FOR THE SKY, VARMINT!
YOW!

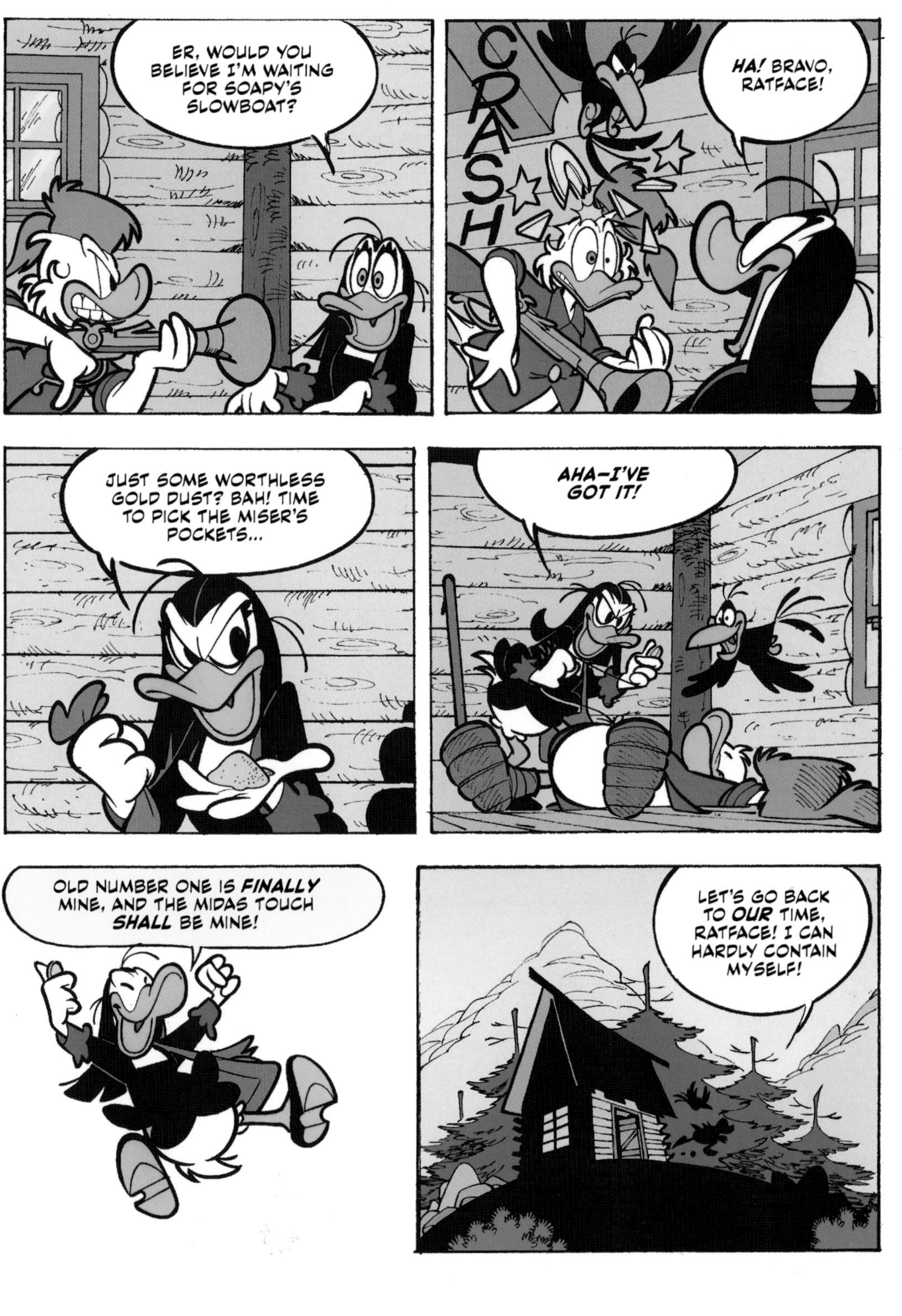
ER, WOULD YOU BELIEVE I'M WAITING FOR SOAPY'S SLOWBOAT?
CRASH
HA! BRAVO, RATFACE!
JUST SOME WORTHLESS GOLD DUST? BAH! TIME TO PICK THE MISER'S POCKETS...
AHA—I'VE GOT IT!
OLD NUMBER ONE IS FINALLY MINE, AND THE MIDAS TOUCH SHALL BE MINE!
LET'S GO BACK TO OUR TIME, RATFACE! I CAN HARDLY CONTAIN MYSELF!

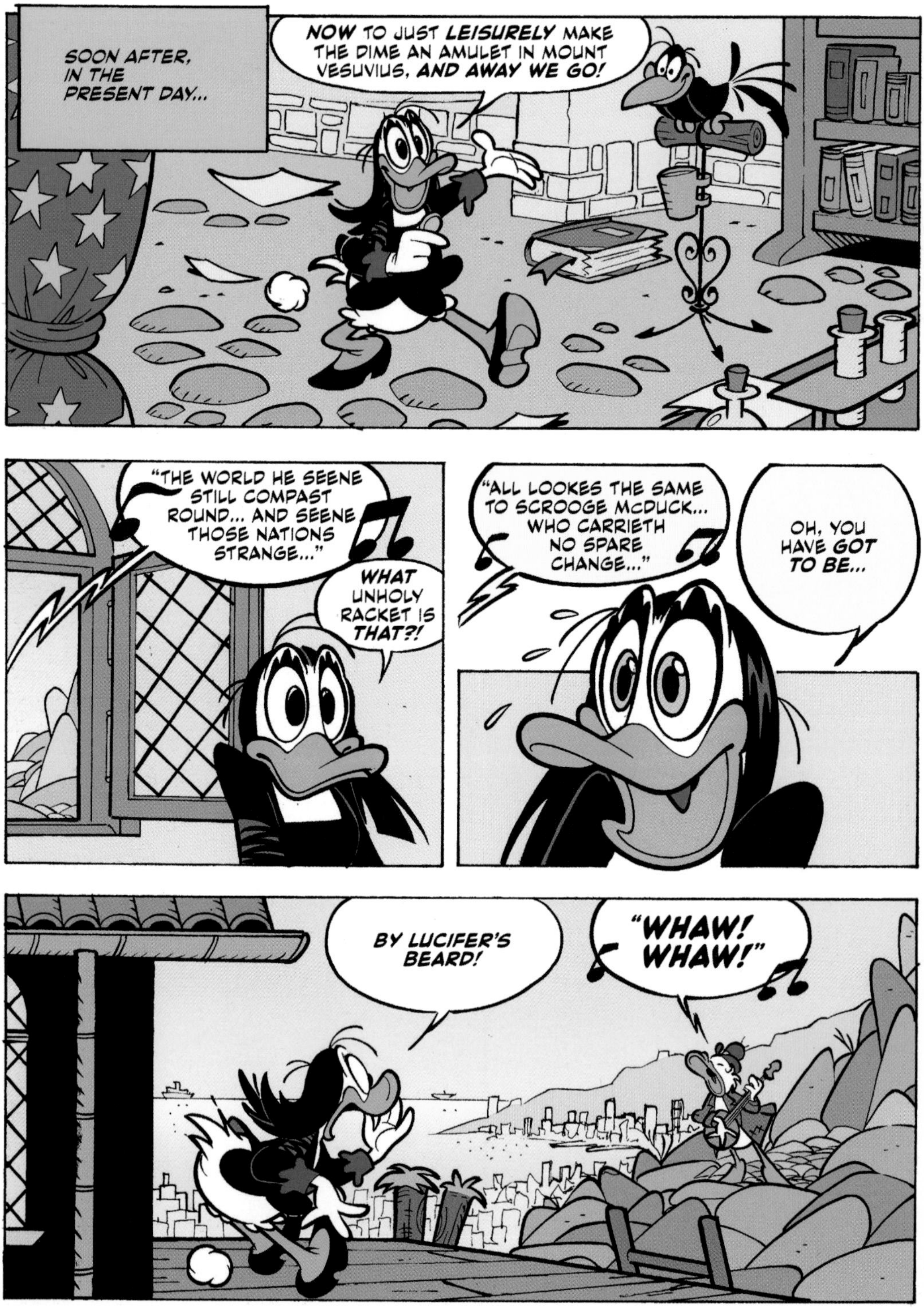
SOON AFTER, IN THE PRESENT DAY...
NOW TO JUST LEISURELY MAKE THE DIME AN AMULET IN MOUNT VESUVIUS, AND AWAY WE GO!
"THE WORLD HE SEENE STILL COMPAST ROUND... AND SEENE THOSE NATIONS STRANGE..."
WHAT UNHOLY RACKET IS THAT?!
"ALL LOOKES THE SAME TO SCROOGE McDUCK... WHO CARRIETH NO SPARE CHANGE..."
OH, YOU HAVE GOT TO BE...
BY LUCIFER'S BEARD!
"WHAW! WHAW!"

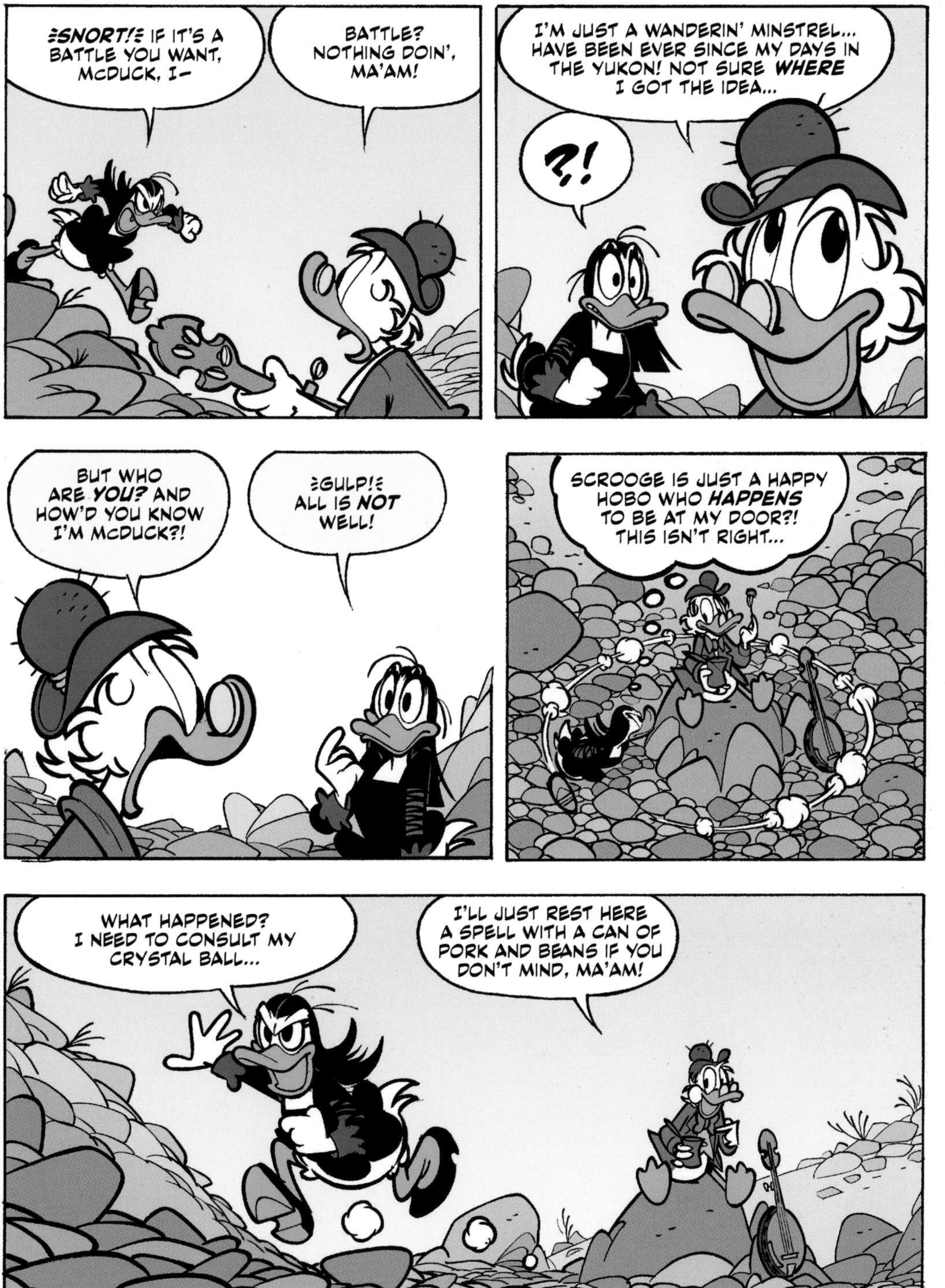

≡SNORT!≡ IF IT'S A BATTLE YOU WANT, McDUCK, I—
BATTLE? NOTHING DOIN', MA'AM!
I'M JUST A WANDERIN' MINSTREL... HAVE BEEN EVER SINCE MY DAYS IN THE YUKON! NOT SURE *WHERE* I GOT THE IDEA...
?!
BUT WHO ARE *YOU?* AND HOW'D YOU KNOW I'M McDUCK?!
≡GULP!≡ ALL IS *NOT* WELL!
SCROOGE IS JUST A HAPPY HOBO WHO *HAPPENS* TO BE AT MY DOOR?! THIS ISN'T RIGHT...
WHAT HAPPENED? I NEED TO CONSULT MY CRYSTAL BALL...
I'LL JUST REST HERE A SPELL WITH A CAN OF PORK AND BEANS IF YOU DON'T MIND, MA'AM!

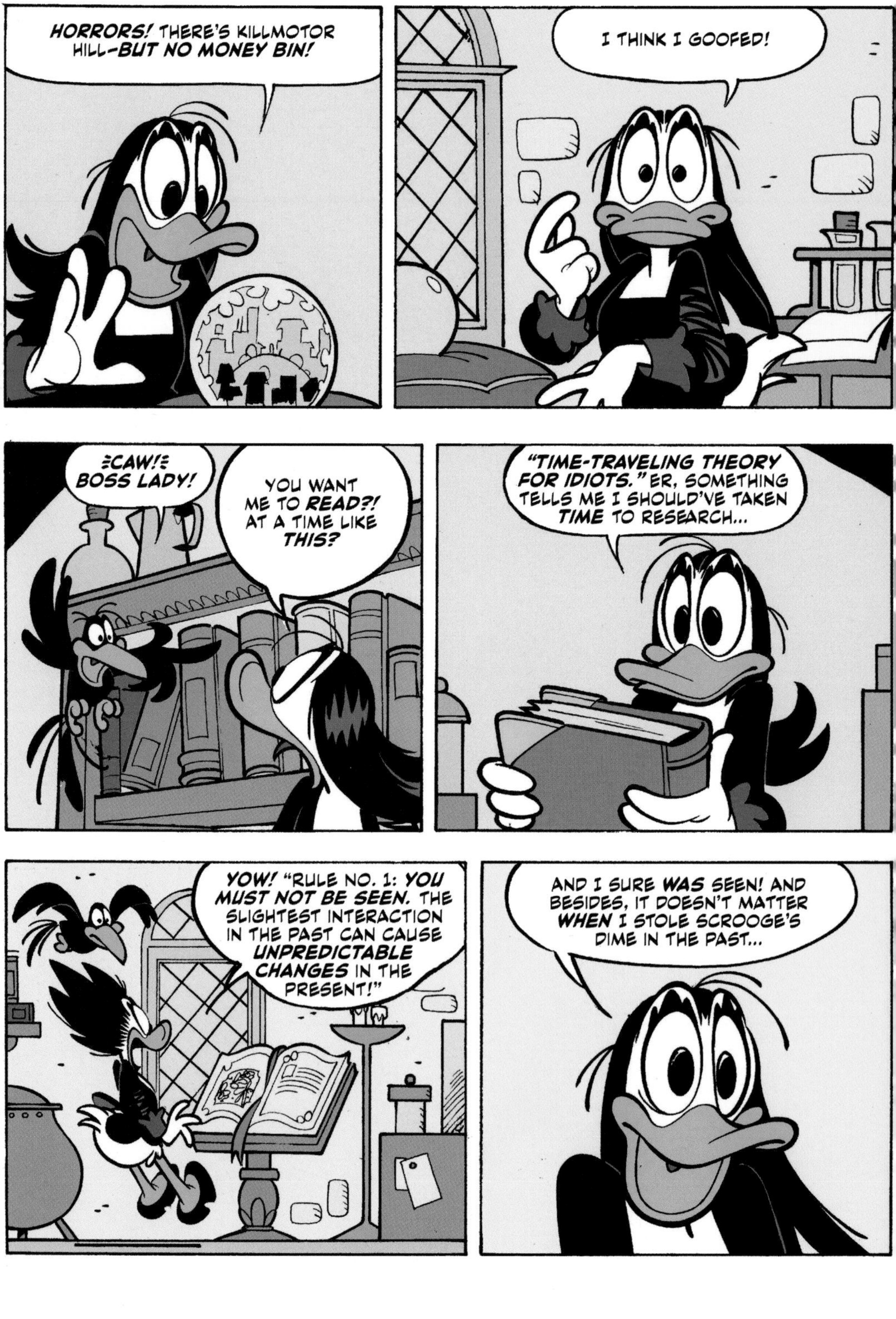
HORRORS! THERE'S KILLMOTOR HILL–BUT NO MONEY BIN!
I THINK I GOOFED!
CAW! BOSS LADY!
YOU WANT ME TO READ?! AT A TIME LIKE THIS?
"TIME-TRAVELING THEORY FOR IDIOTS." ER, SOMETHING TELLS ME I SHOULD'VE TAKEN TIME TO RESEARCH...
YOW! "RULE NO. 1: YOU MUST NOT BE SEEN. THE SLIGHTEST INTERACTION IN THE PAST CAN CAUSE UNPREDICTABLE CHANGES IN THE PRESENT!"
AND I SURE WAS SEEN! AND BESIDES, IT DOESN'T MATTER WHEN I STOLE SCROOGE'S DIME IN THE PAST...

...BECAUSE HE'S *ALWAYS* HAD IT IN THE *PRESENT!* EXCEPT *THIS* PRESENT...

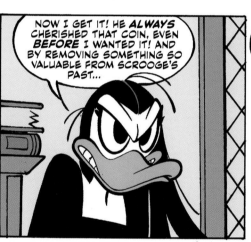

NOW I GET IT! HE *ALWAYS* CHERISHED THAT COIN, EVEN *BEFORE* I WANTED IT! AND BY REMOVING SOMETHING SO VALUABLE FROM SCROOGE'S PAST...

...*I'M* STUCK IN THIS ROTTEN PRESENT! *A THOUSAND CURSES ON THIS WORTHLESS DIME!*

PING

AS TRULY *SHAMEFUL* AN ACT AS THIS WILL BE...

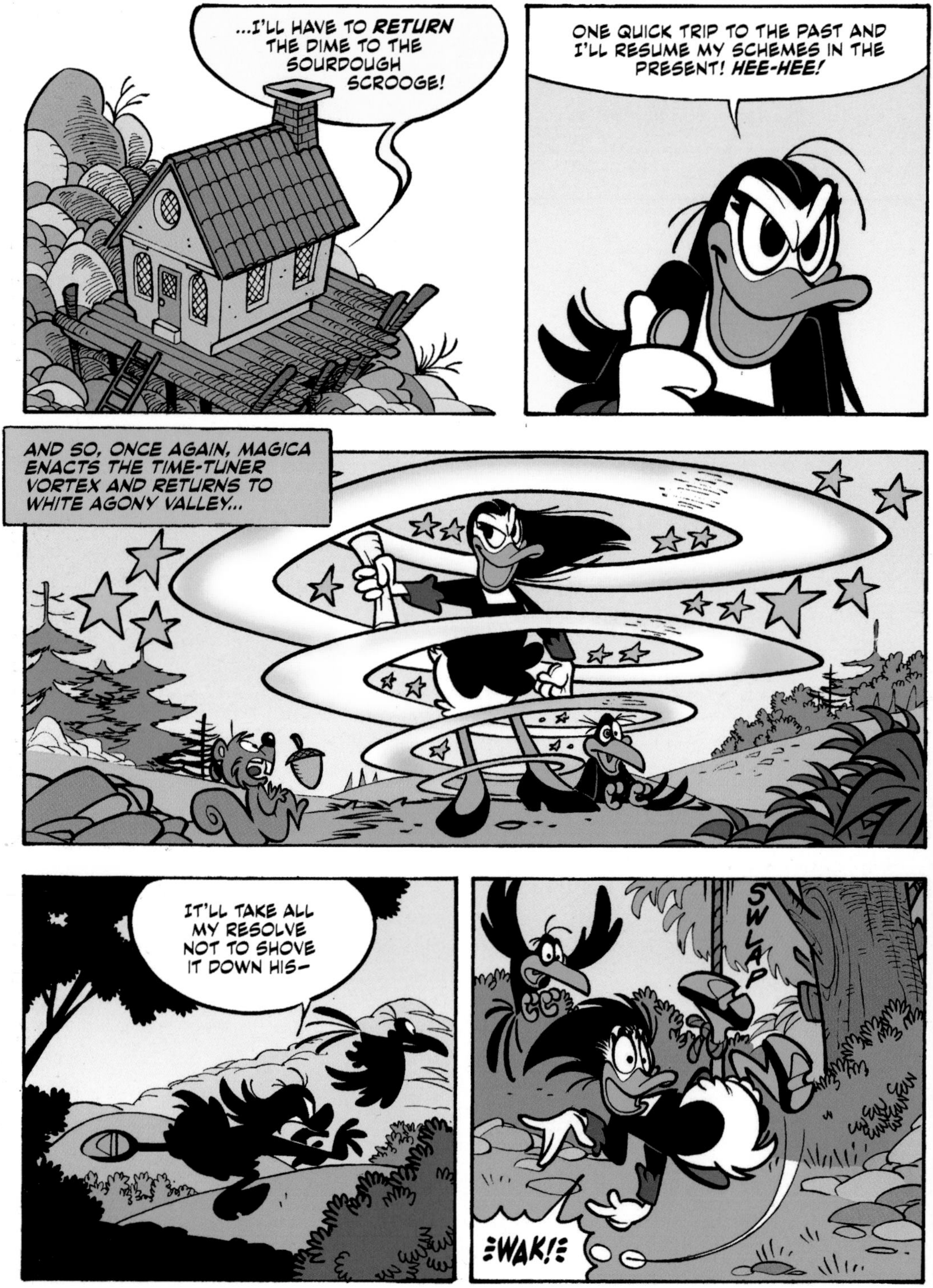
...I'LL HAVE TO ***RETURN*** THE DIME TO THE SOURDOUGH SCROOGE!
ONE QUICK TRIP TO THE PAST AND I'LL RESUME MY SCHEMES IN THE PRESENT! ***HEE-HEE!***
AND SO, ONCE AGAIN, MAGICA ENACTS THE TIME-TUNER VORTEX AND RETURNS TO WHITE AGONY VALLEY...
IT'LL TAKE ALL MY RESOLVE NOT TO SHOVE IT DOWN HIS–
SWLAP
WAK!

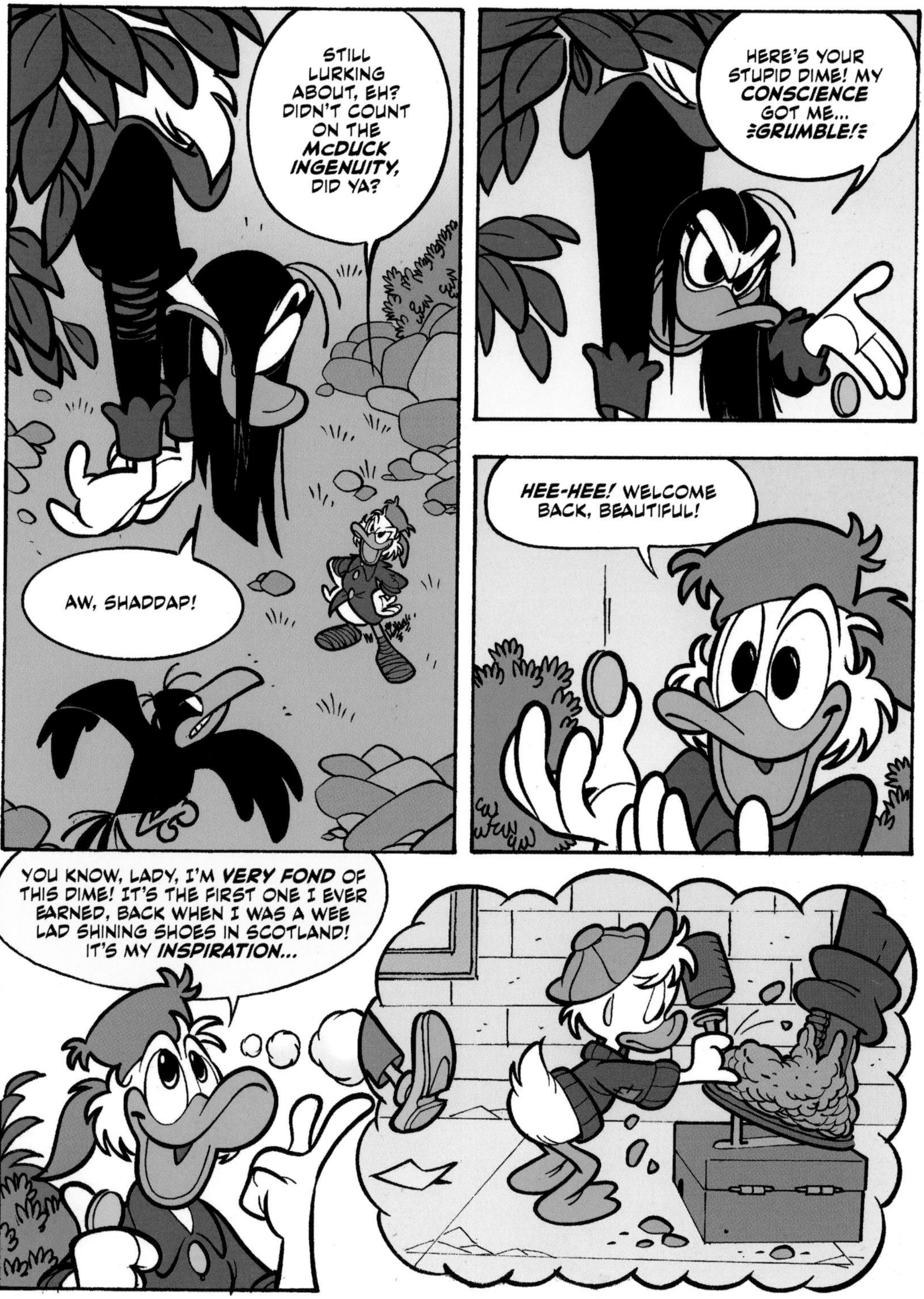

STILL LURKING ABOUT, EH? DIDN'T COUNT ON THE McDUCK INGENUITY, DID YA?
AW, SHADDAP!
HERE'S YOUR STUPID DIME! MY CONSCIENCE GOT ME... GRUMBLE!
HEE-HEE! WELCOME BACK, BEAUTIFUL!
YOU KNOW, LADY, I'M VERY FOND OF THIS DIME! IT'S THE FIRST ONE I EVER EARNED, BACK WHEN I WAS A WEE LAD SHINING SHOES IN SCOTLAND! IT'S MY INSPIRATION...

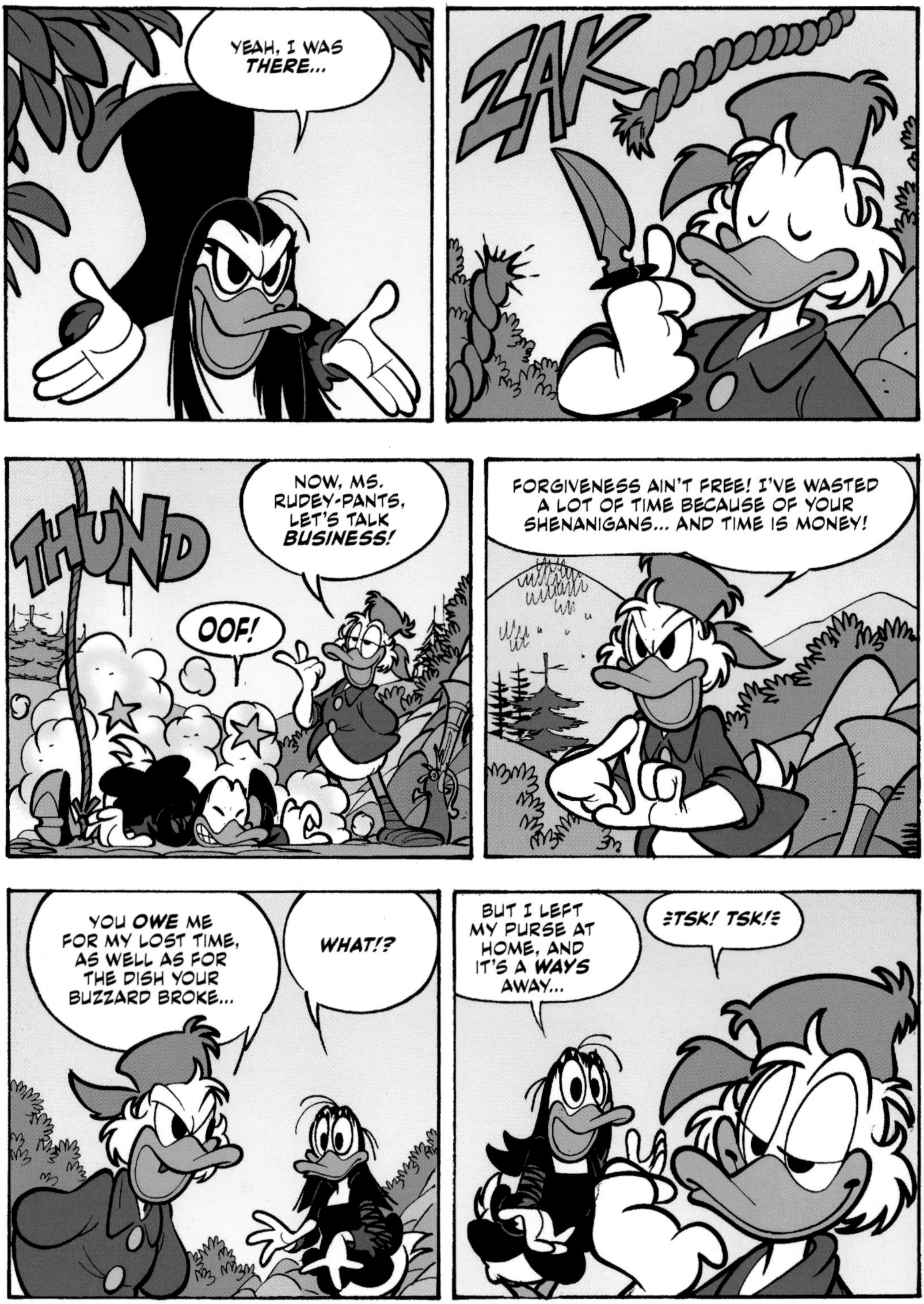
YEAH, I WAS THERE...
ZAK
THUND
NOW, MS. RUDEY-PANTS, LET'S TALK BUSINESS!
OOF!
FORGIVENESS AIN'T FREE! I'VE WASTED A LOT OF TIME BECAUSE OF YOUR SHENANIGANS... AND TIME IS MONEY!
YOU OWE ME FOR MY LOST TIME, AS WELL AS FOR THE DISH YOUR BUZZARD BROKE...
WHAT!?
BUT I LEFT MY PURSE AT HOME, AND IT'S A WAYS AWAY...
TSK! TSK!

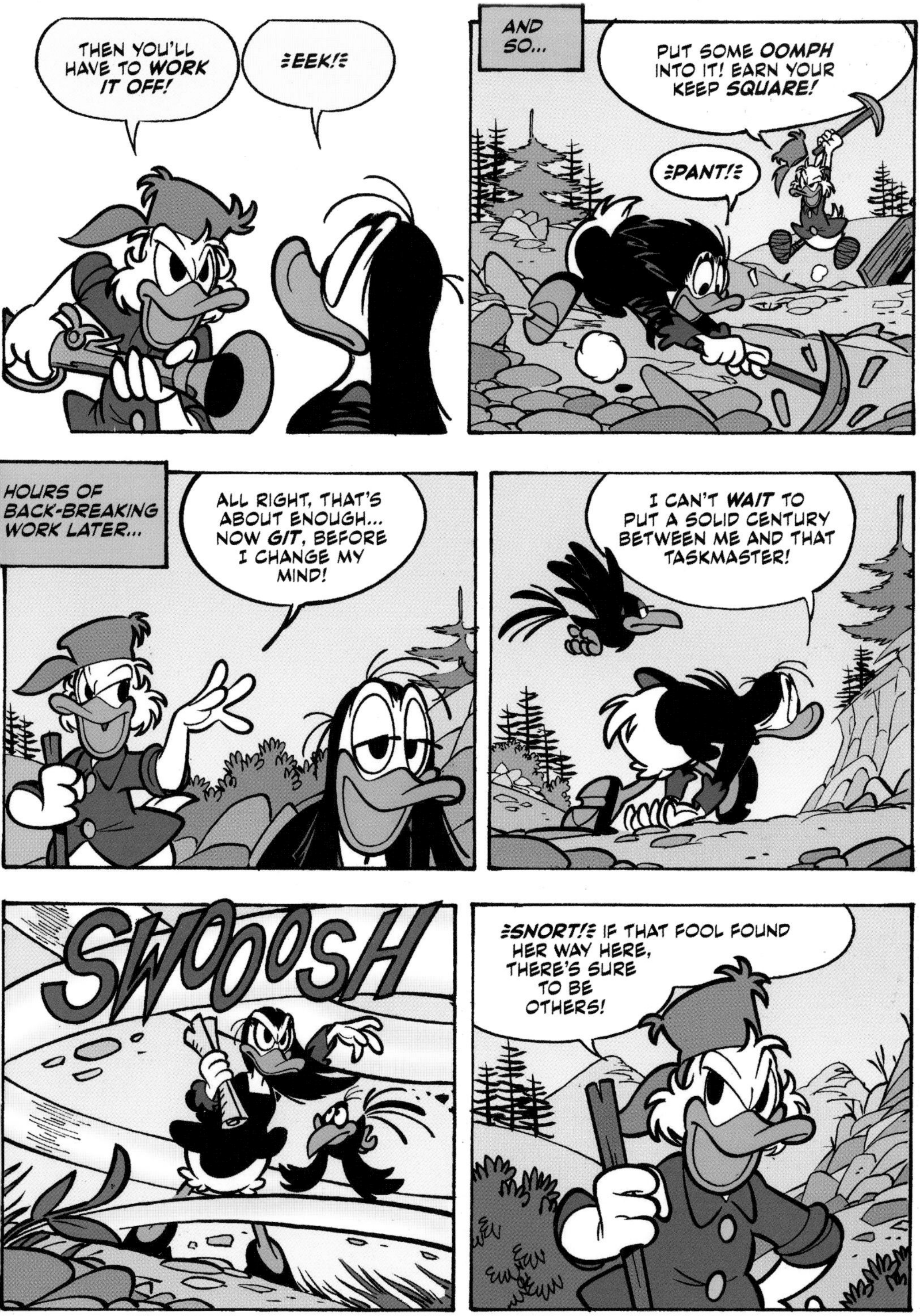
THEN YOU'LL HAVE TO WORK IT OFF!
≡EEK!≡
AND SO...
PUT SOME OOMPH INTO IT! EARN YOUR KEEP SQUARE!
≡PANT!≡
HOURS OF BACK-BREAKING WORK LATER...
ALL RIGHT, THAT'S ABOUT ENOUGH... NOW GIT, BEFORE I CHANGE MY MIND!
I CAN'T WAIT TO PUT A SOLID CENTURY BETWEEN ME AND THAT TASKMASTER!
SWOOOSH
≡SNORT!≡ IF THAT FOOL FOUND HER WAY HERE, THERE'S SURE TO BE OTHERS!

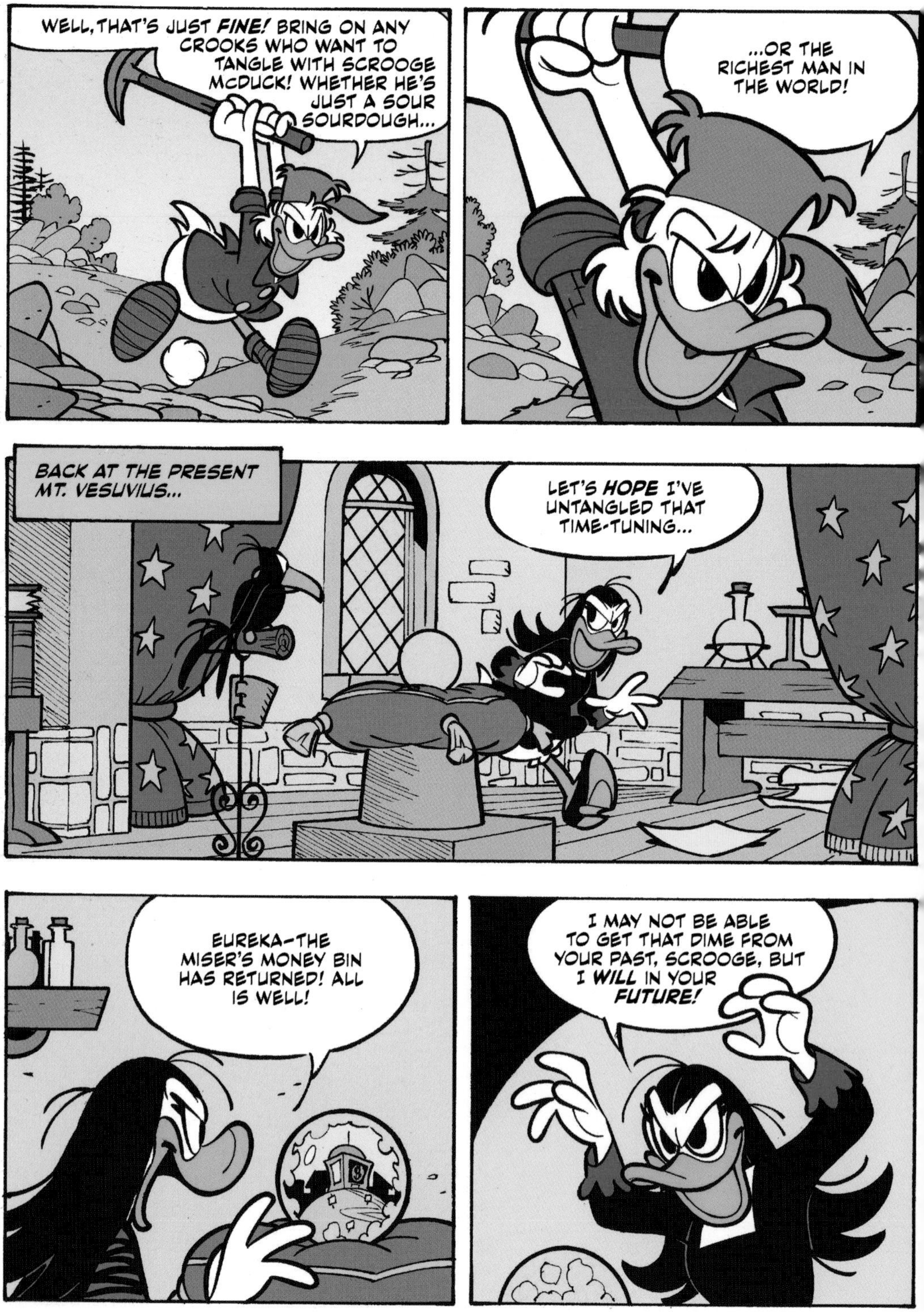
WELL, THAT'S JUST FINE! BRING ON ANY CROOKS WHO WANT TO TANGLE WITH SCROOGE McDUCK! WHETHER HE'S JUST A SOUR SOURDOUGH...
...OR THE RICHEST MAN IN THE WORLD!
BACK AT THE PRESENT MT. VESUVIUS...
LET'S HOPE I'VE UNTANGLED THAT TIME-TUNING...
EUREKA—THE MISER'S MONEY BIN HAS RETURNED! ALL IS WELL!
I MAY NOT BE ABLE TO GET THAT DIME FROM YOUR PAST, SCROOGE, BUT I WILL IN YOUR FUTURE!

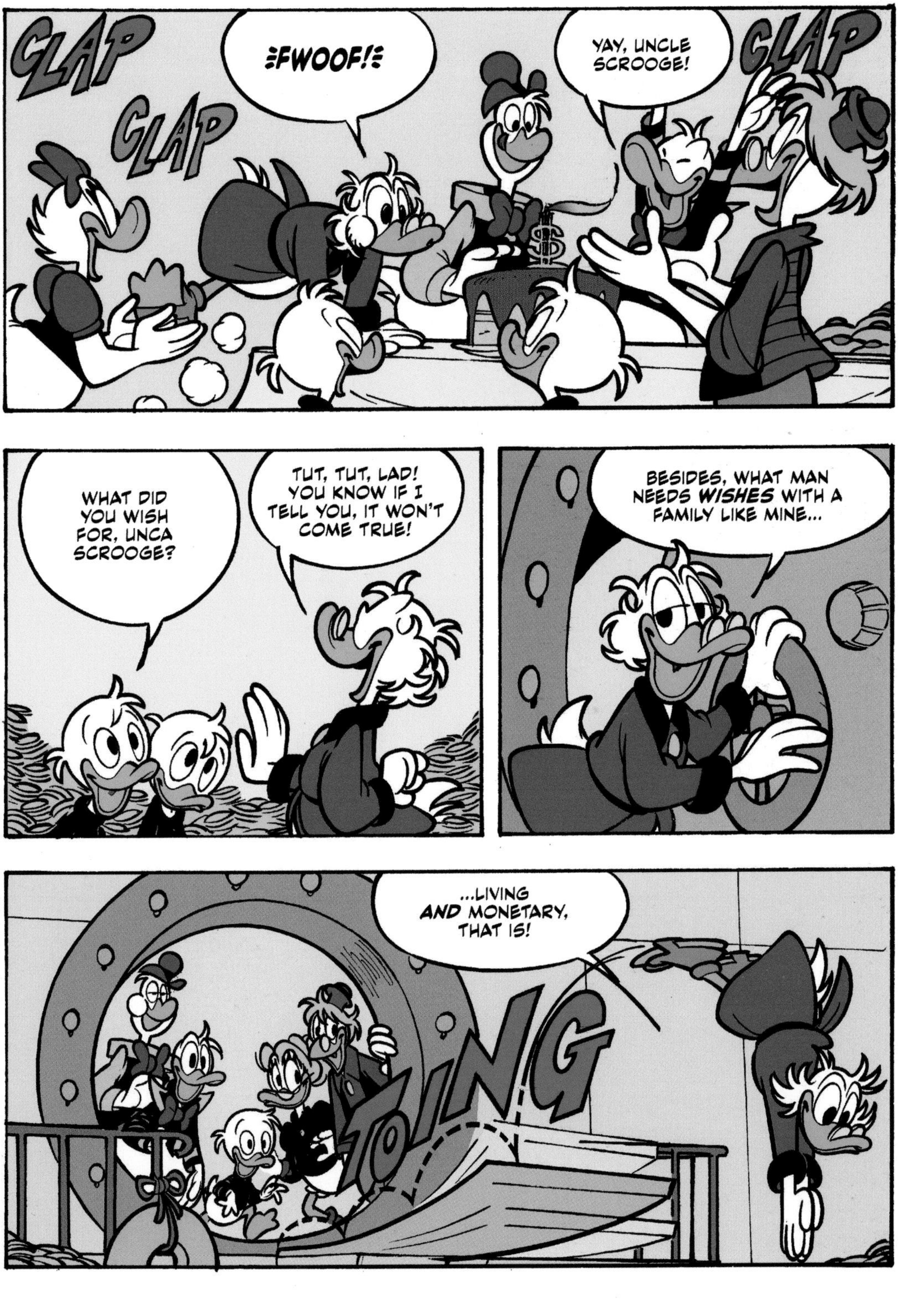
CLAP
CLAP
FWOOF!
YAY, UNCLE SCROOGE!
CLAP
WHAT DID YOU WISH FOR, UNCA SCROOGE?
TUT, TUT, LAD! YOU KNOW IF I TELL YOU, IT WON'T COME TRUE!
BESIDES, WHAT MAN NEEDS WISHES WITH A FAMILY LIKE MINE...
...LIVING AND MONETARY, THAT IS!
BOING

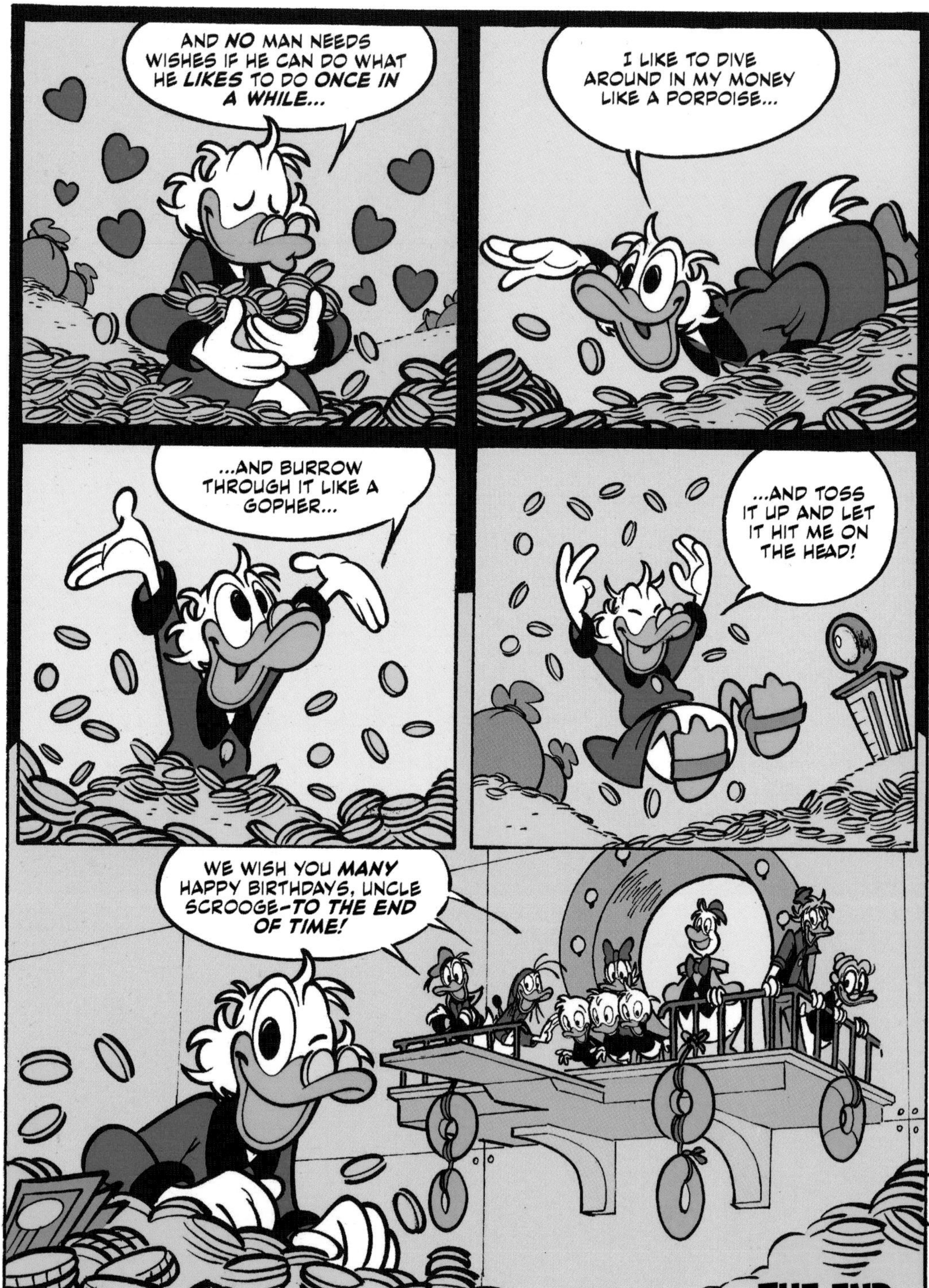
AND NO MAN NEEDS WISHES IF HE CAN DO WHAT HE LIKES TO DO ONCE IN A WHILE...
I LIKE TO DIVE AROUND IN MY MONEY LIKE A PORPOISE...
...AND BURROW THROUGH IT LIKE A GOPHER...
...AND TOSS IT UP AND LET IT HIT ME ON THE HEAD!
WE WISH YOU MANY HAPPY BIRTHDAYS, UNCLE SCROOGE—TO THE END OF TIME!
THE END

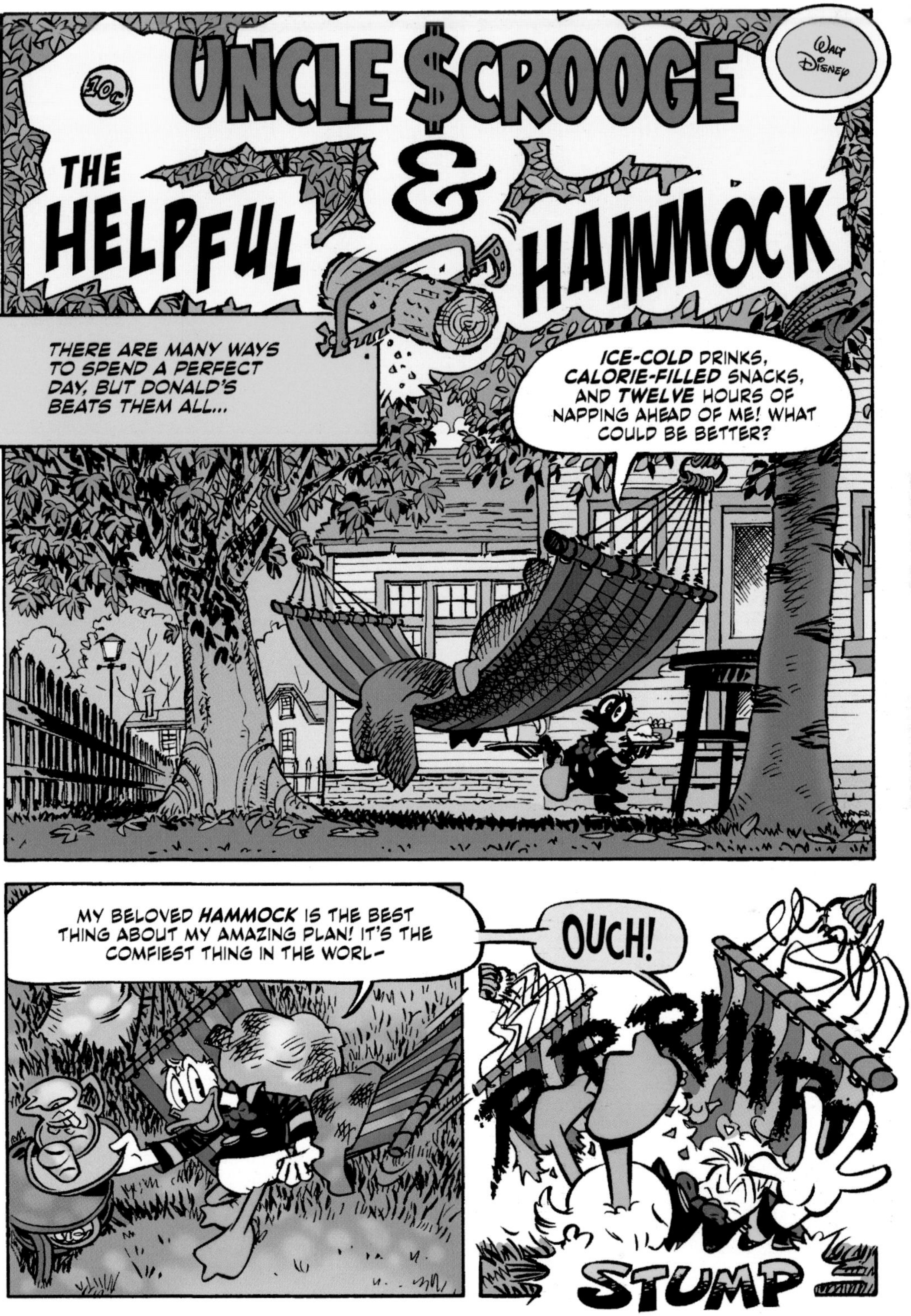
UNCLE $CROOGE
10¢
WALT DISNEY
THE HELPFUL & HAMMOCK
THERE ARE MANY WAYS TO SPEND A PERFECT DAY, BUT DONALD'S BEATS THEM ALL...
ICE-COLD DRINKS, CALORIE-FILLED SNACKS, AND TWELVE HOURS OF NAPPING AHEAD OF ME! WHAT COULD BE BETTER?
MY BELOVED HAMMOCK IS THE BEST THING ABOUT MY AMAZING PLAN! IT'S THE COMFIEST THING IN THE WORL—
OUCH!
RRRIIIP
STUMP

ORIGINALLY PUBLISHED IN TOPOLINO #3260 (ITALY, 2018) • FIRST USA PUBLICATION

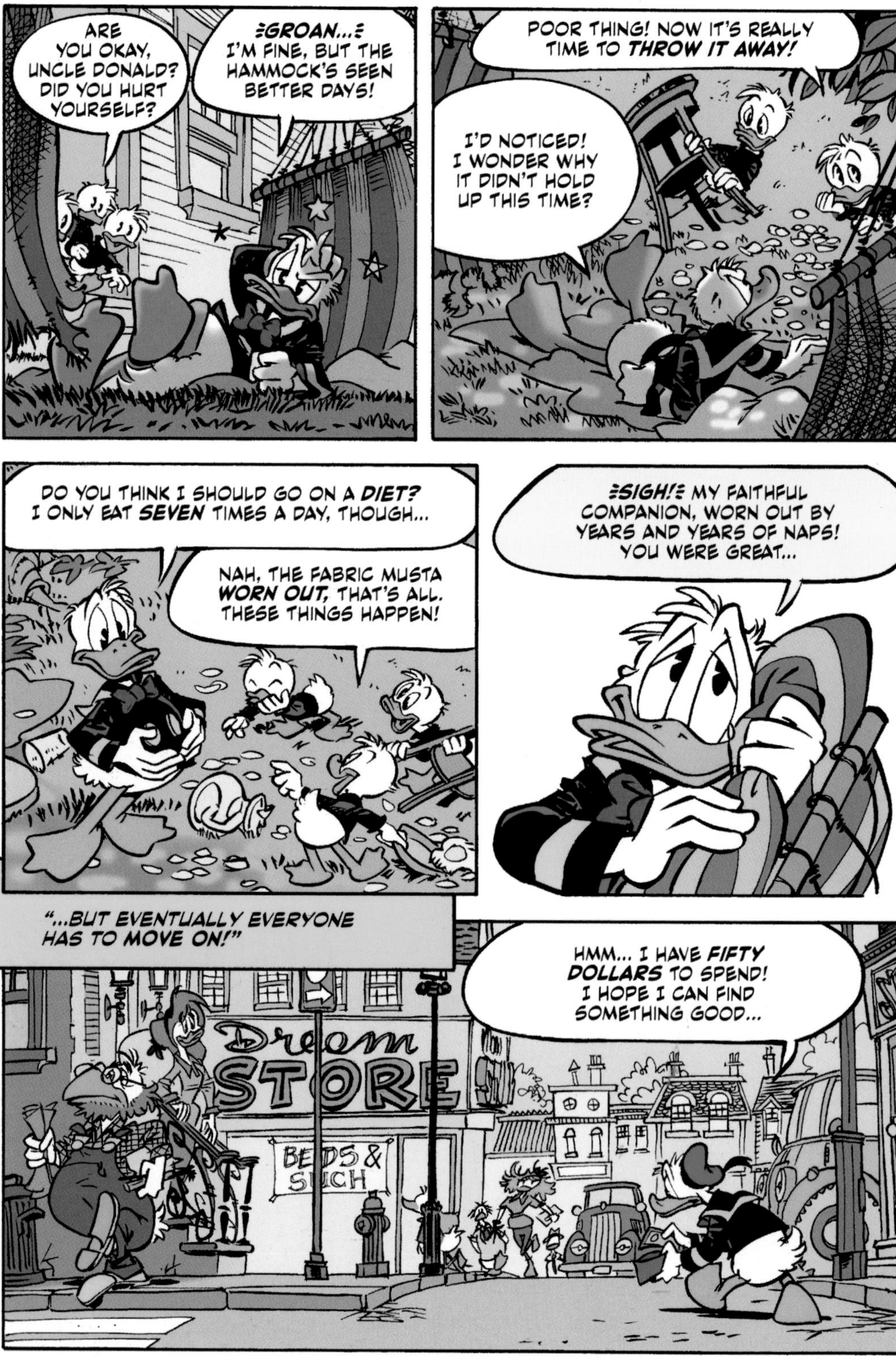

ARE YOU OKAY, UNCLE DONALD? DID YOU HURT YOURSELF?
GROAN... I'M FINE, BUT THE HAMMOCK'S SEEN BETTER DAYS!
POOR THING! NOW IT'S REALLY TIME TO THROW IT AWAY!
I'D NOTICED! I WONDER WHY IT DIDN'T HOLD UP THIS TIME?
DO YOU THINK I SHOULD GO ON A DIET? I ONLY EAT SEVEN TIMES A DAY, THOUGH...
NAH, THE FABRIC MUSTA WORN OUT, THAT'S ALL. THESE THINGS HAPPEN!
SIGH! MY FAITHFUL COMPANION, WORN OUT BY YEARS AND YEARS OF NAPS! YOU WERE GREAT...
"...BUT EVENTUALLY EVERYONE HAS TO MOVE ON!"
Dream STORE
BEDS & SUCH
HMM... I HAVE FIFTY DOLLARS TO SPEND! I HOPE I CAN FIND SOMETHING GOOD...

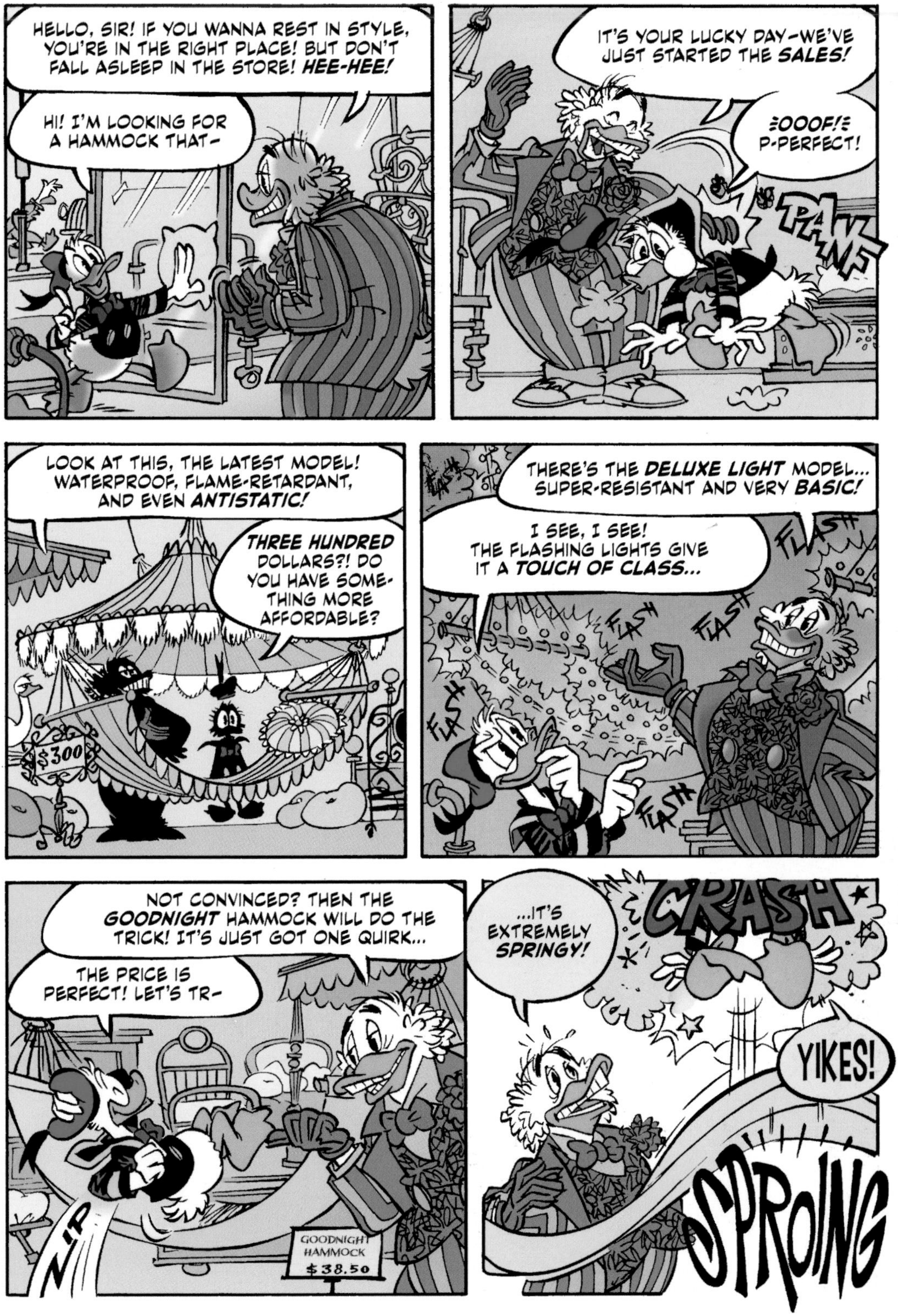
HELLO, SIR! IF YOU WANNA REST IN STYLE, YOU'RE IN THE RIGHT PLACE! BUT DON'T FALL ASLEEP IN THE STORE! HEE-HEE!
HI! I'M LOOKING FOR A HAMMOCK THAT-
IT'S YOUR LUCKY DAY-WE'VE JUST STARTED THE SALES!
OOOF! P-PERFECT!
PLANK
LOOK AT THIS, THE LATEST MODEL! WATERPROOF, FLAME-RETARDANT, AND EVEN ANTISTATIC!
THREE HUNDRED DOLLARS?! DO YOU HAVE SOMETHING MORE AFFORDABLE?
$300
THERE'S THE DELUXE LIGHT MODEL... SUPER-RESISTANT AND VERY BASIC!
I SEE, I SEE! THE FLASHING LIGHTS GIVE IT A TOUCH OF CLASS...
FLASH
FLASH
FLASH
FLASH
FLASH
FLASH
NOT CONVINCED? THEN THE GOODNIGHT HAMMOCK WILL DO THE TRICK! IT'S JUST GOT ONE QUIRK...
THE PRICE IS PERFECT! LET'S TR-
GOODNIGHT HAMMOCK $38.50
ZIP
...IT'S EXTREMELY SPRINGY!
CRASH
YIKES!
SPROING

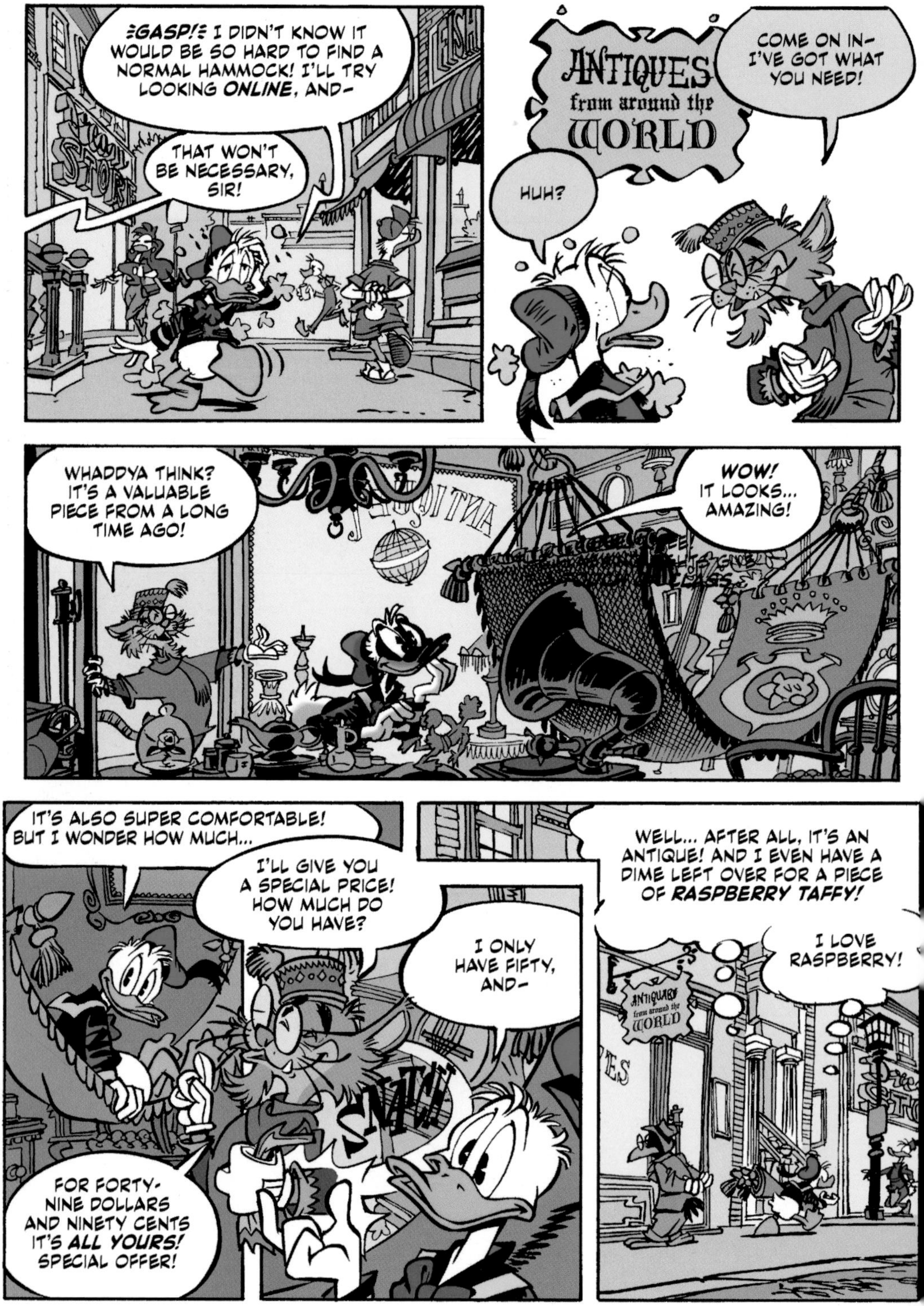
=GASP!= I DIDN'T KNOW IT WOULD BE SO HARD TO FIND A NORMAL HAMMOCK! I'LL TRY LOOKING **ONLINE**, AND–
THAT WON'T BE NECESSARY, SIR!
ANTIQUES from around the WORLD
COME ON IN– I'VE GOT WHAT YOU NEED!
HUH?
WHADDYA THINK? IT'S A VALUABLE PIECE FROM A LONG TIME AGO!
WOW! IT LOOKS... AMAZING!
IT'S ALSO SUPER COMFORTABLE! BUT I WONDER HOW MUCH...
I'LL GIVE YOU A SPECIAL PRICE! HOW MUCH DO YOU HAVE?
I ONLY HAVE FIFTY, AND–
SNATCH
FOR FORTY-NINE DOLLARS AND NINETY CENTS IT'S **ALL YOURS!** SPECIAL OFFER!
WELL... AFTER ALL, IT'S AN ANTIQUE! AND I EVEN HAVE A DIME LEFT OVER FOR A PIECE OF **RASPBERRY TAFFY!**
I LOVE RASPBERRY!

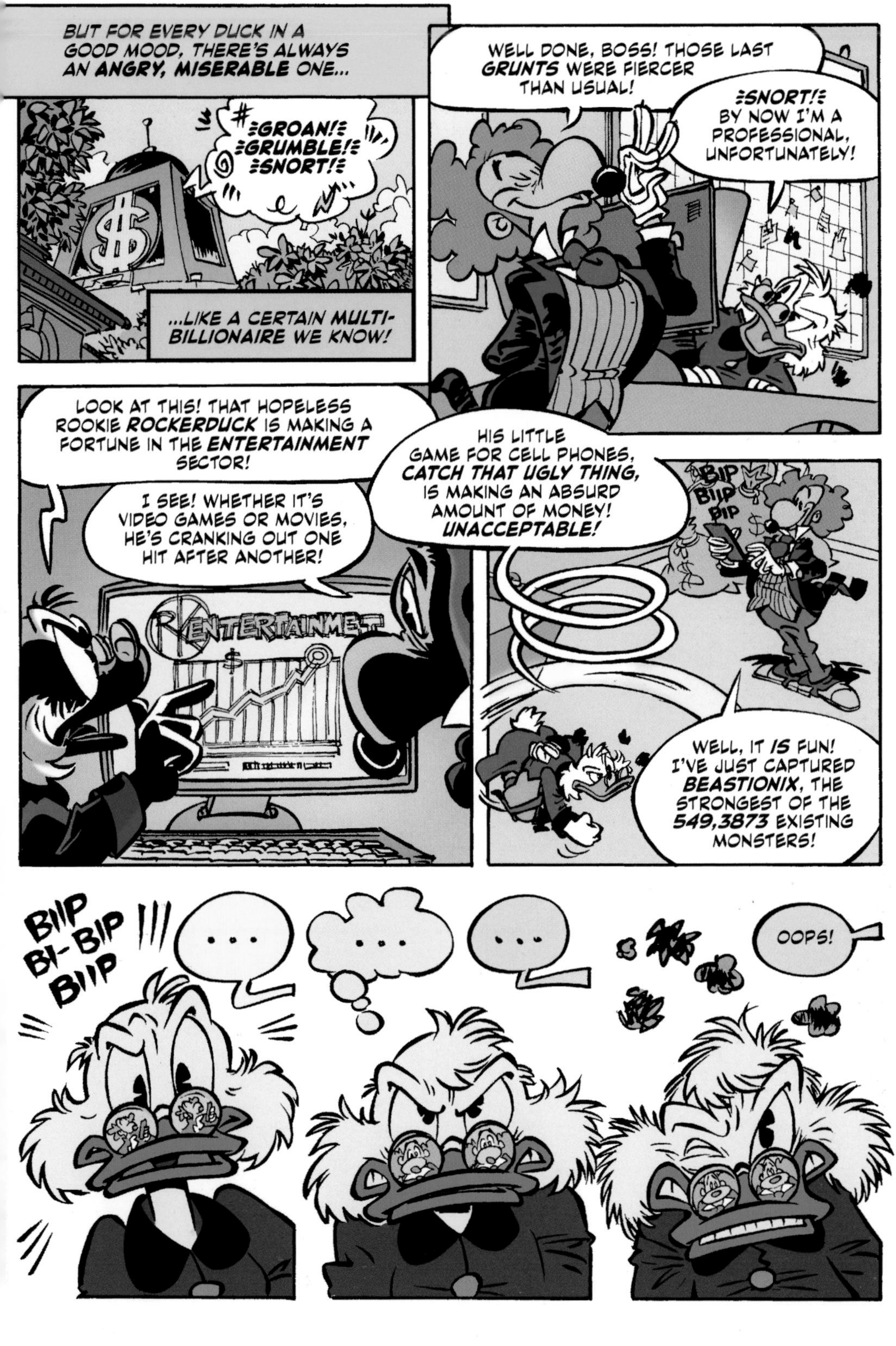
BUT FOR EVERY DUCK IN A GOOD MOOD, THERE'S ALWAYS AN ANGRY, MISERABLE ONE...
GROAN! GRUMBLE! SNORT!
...LIKE A CERTAIN MULTI-BILLIONAIRE WE KNOW!
WELL DONE, BOSS! THOSE LAST GRUNTS WERE FIERCER THAN USUAL!
SNORT! BY NOW I'M A PROFESSIONAL, UNFORTUNATELY!
LOOK AT THIS! THAT HOPELESS ROOKIE ROCKERDUCK IS MAKING A FORTUNE IN THE ENTERTAINMENT SECTOR!
I SEE! WHETHER IT'S VIDEO GAMES OR MOVIES, HE'S CRANKING OUT ONE HIT AFTER ANOTHER!
ENTERTAINMET
HIS LITTLE GAME FOR CELL PHONES, CATCH THAT UGLY THING, IS MAKING AN ABSURD AMOUNT OF MONEY! UNACCEPTABLE!
BIP BIIP BIP
WELL, IT IS FUN! I'VE JUST CAPTURED BEASTIONIX, THE STRONGEST OF THE 549,3873 EXISTING MONSTERS!
BIIP BI-BIP BIIP
...
...
...
OOPS!

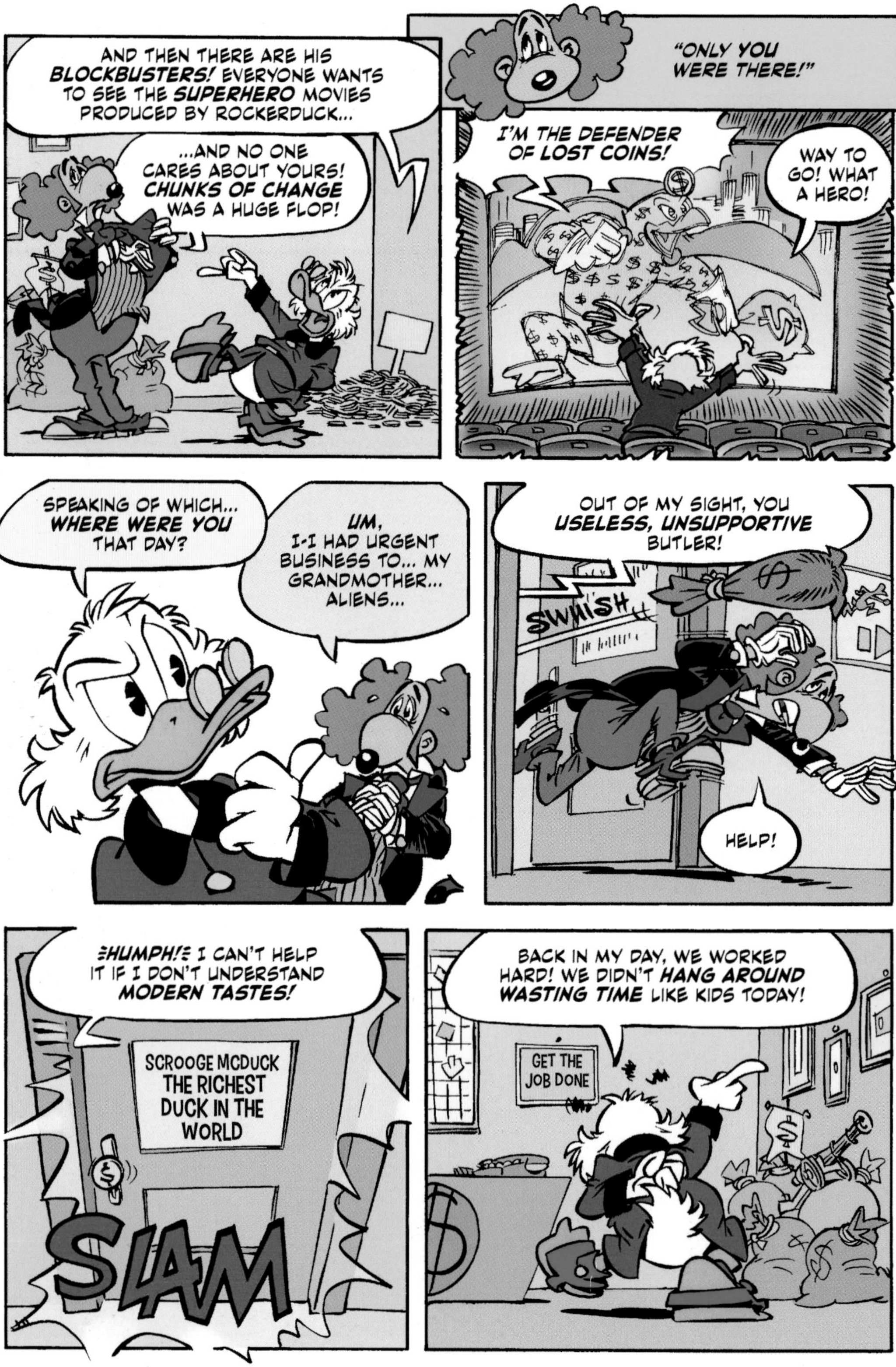
AND THEN THERE ARE HIS BLOCKBUSTERS! EVERYONE WANTS TO SEE THE SUPERHERO MOVIES PRODUCED BY ROCKERDUCK...
...AND NO ONE CARES ABOUT YOURS! CHUNKS OF CHANGE WAS A HUGE FLOP!
"ONLY YOU WERE THERE!"
I'M THE DEFENDER OF LOST COINS!
WAY TO GO! WHAT A HERO!
SPEAKING OF WHICH... WHERE WERE YOU THAT DAY?
UM, I-I HAD URGENT BUSINESS TO... MY GRANDMOTHER... ALIENS...
OUT OF MY SIGHT, YOU USELESS, UNSUPPORTIVE BUTLER!
SWHISH
HELP!
HUMPH! I CAN'T HELP IT IF I DON'T UNDERSTAND MODERN TASTES!
SCROOGE McDUCK THE RICHEST DUCK IN THE WORLD
SLAM
BACK IN MY DAY, WE WORKED HARD! WE DIDN'T HANG AROUND WASTING TIME LIKE KIDS TODAY!
GET THE JOB DONE

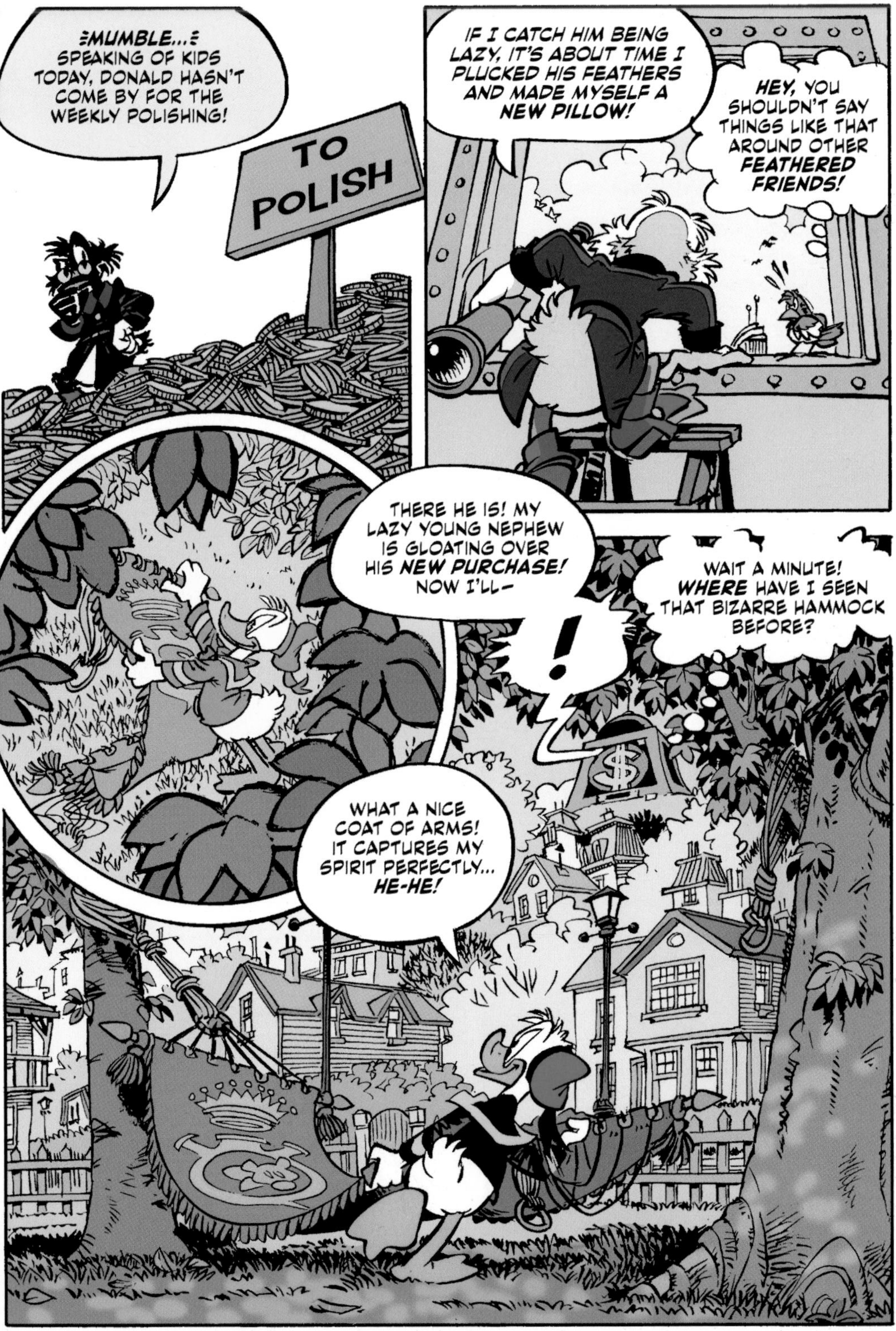

≡MUMBLE...≡ SPEAKING OF KIDS TODAY, DONALD HASN'T COME BY FOR THE WEEKLY POLISHING!
TO POLISH
IF I CATCH HIM BEING LAZY, IT'S ABOUT TIME I PLUCKED HIS FEATHERS AND MADE MYSELF A NEW PILLOW!
HEY, YOU SHOULDN'T SAY THINGS LIKE THAT AROUND OTHER FEATHERED FRIENDS!
THERE HE IS! MY LAZY YOUNG NEPHEW IS GLOATING OVER HIS NEW PURCHASE! NOW I'LL–
!
WAIT A MINUTE! WHERE HAVE I SEEN THAT BIZARRE HAMMOCK BEFORE?
WHAT A NICE COAT OF ARMS! IT CAPTURES MY SPIRIT PERFECTLY... HE-HE!

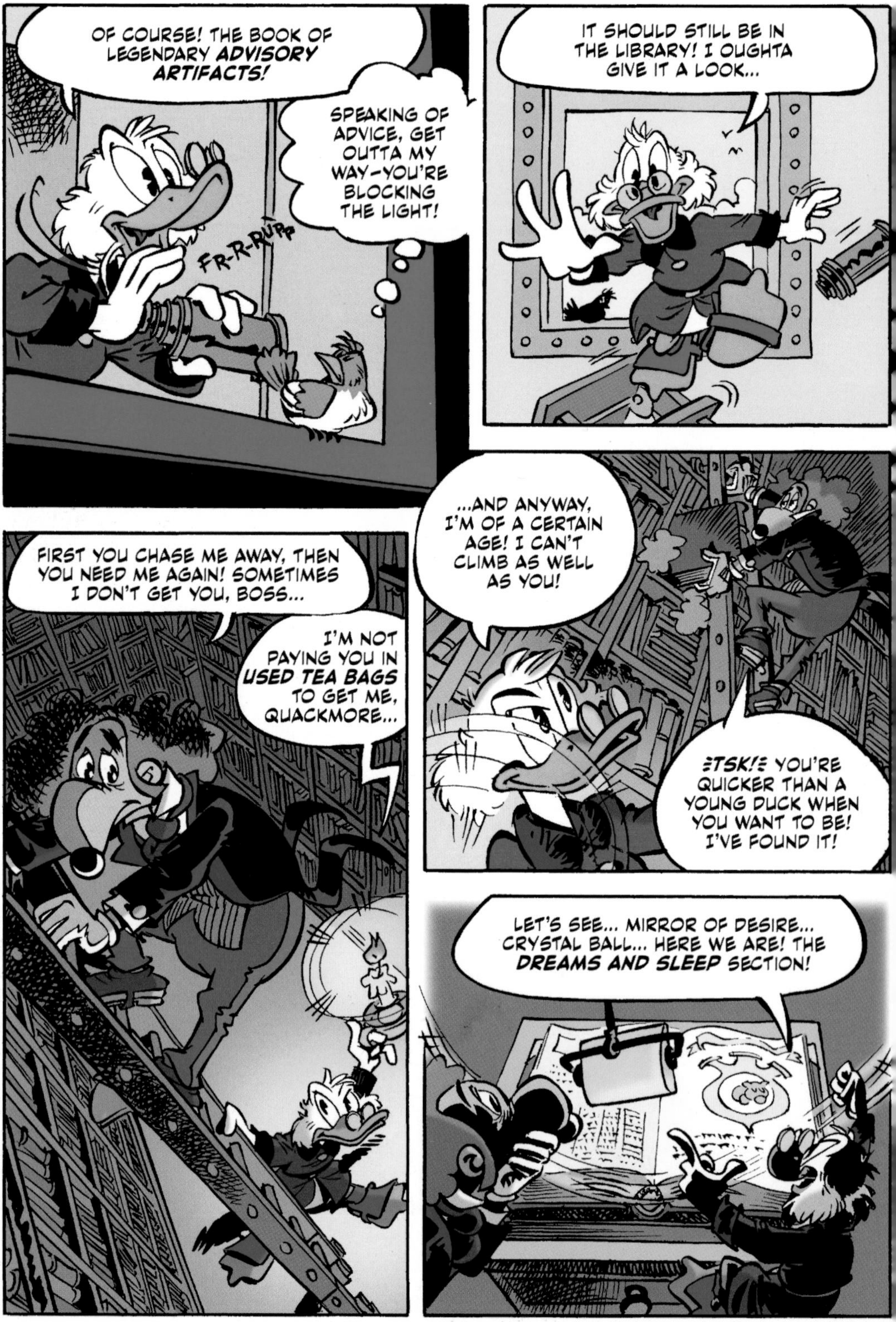
OF COURSE! THE BOOK OF LEGENDARY ADVISORY ARTIFACTS!
SPEAKING OF ADVICE, GET OUTTA MY WAY–YOU'RE BLOCKING THE LIGHT!
FR-R-RUPP
IT SHOULD STILL BE IN THE LIBRARY! I OUGHTA GIVE IT A LOOK...
FIRST YOU CHASE ME AWAY, THEN YOU NEED ME AGAIN! SOMETIMES I DON'T GET YOU, BOSS...
I'M NOT PAYING YOU IN USED TEA BAGS TO GET ME, QUACKMORE...
...AND ANYWAY, I'M OF A CERTAIN AGE! I CAN'T CLIMB AS WELL AS YOU!
TSK! YOU'RE QUICKER THAN A YOUNG DUCK WHEN YOU WANT TO BE! I'VE FOUND IT!
LET'S SEE... MIRROR OF DESIRE... CRYSTAL BALL... HERE WE ARE! THE DREAMS AND SLEEP SECTION!

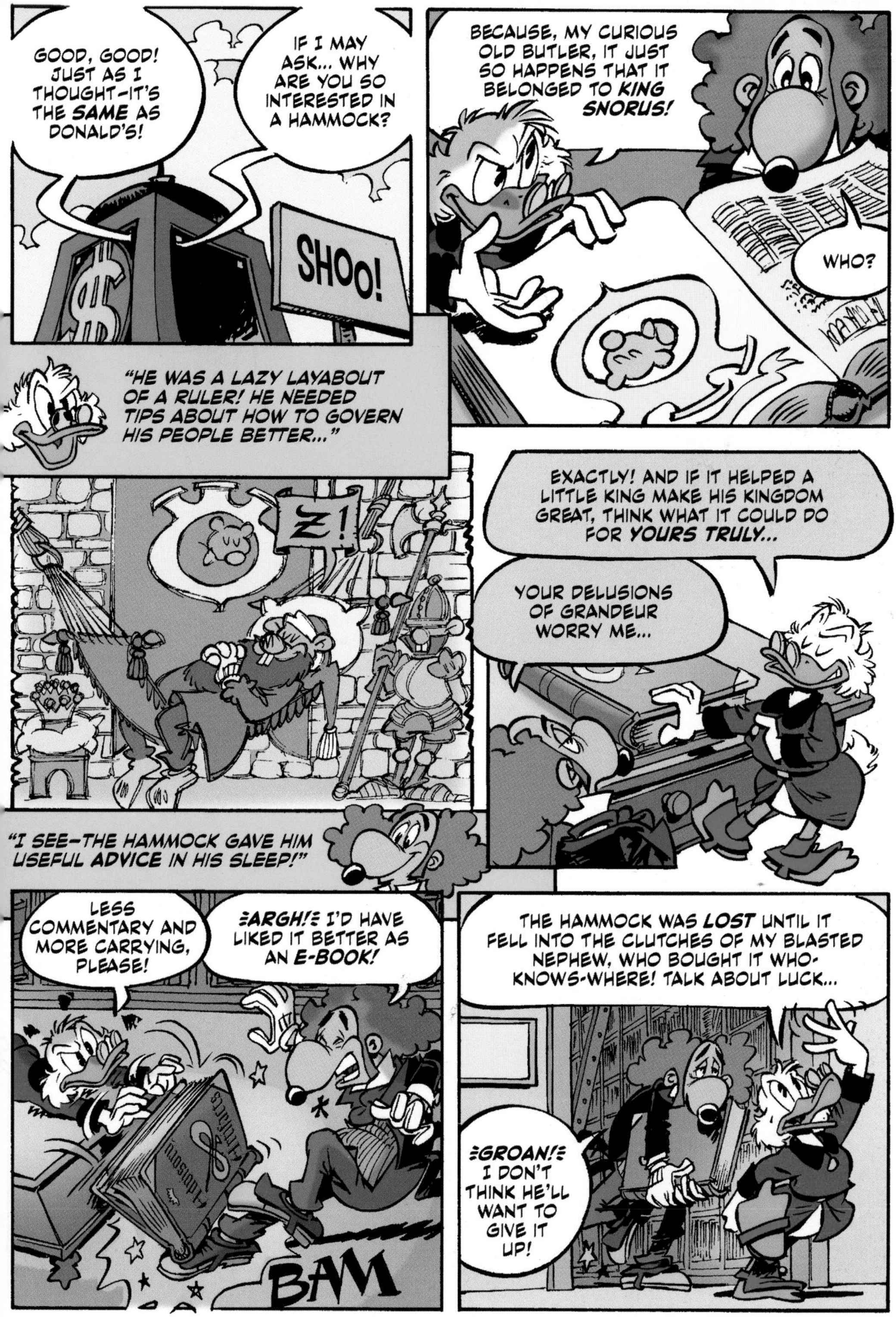
GOOD, GOOD! JUST AS I THOUGHT—IT'S THE SAME AS DONALD'S!
IF I MAY ASK... WHY ARE YOU SO INTERESTED IN A HAMMOCK?
SHOO!
BECAUSE, MY CURIOUS OLD BUTLER, IT JUST SO HAPPENS THAT IT BELONGED TO KING SNORUS!
WHO?
"HE WAS A LAZY LAYABOUT OF A RULER! HE NEEDED TIPS ABOUT HOW TO GOVERN HIS PEOPLE BETTER..."
Z!
"I SEE—THE HAMMOCK GAVE HIM USEFUL ADVICE IN HIS SLEEP!"
EXACTLY! AND IF IT HELPED A LITTLE KING MAKE HIS KINGDOM GREAT, THINK WHAT IT COULD DO FOR YOURS TRULY...
YOUR DELUSIONS OF GRANDEUR WORRY ME...
LESS COMMENTARY AND MORE CARRYING, PLEASE!
ARGH! I'D HAVE LIKED IT BETTER AS AN E-BOOK!
BAM
THE HAMMOCK WAS LOST UNTIL IT FELL INTO THE CLUTCHES OF MY BLASTED NEPHEW, WHO BOUGHT IT WHO-KNOWS-WHERE! TALK ABOUT LUCK...
GROAN! I DON'T THINK HE'LL WANT TO GIVE IT UP!

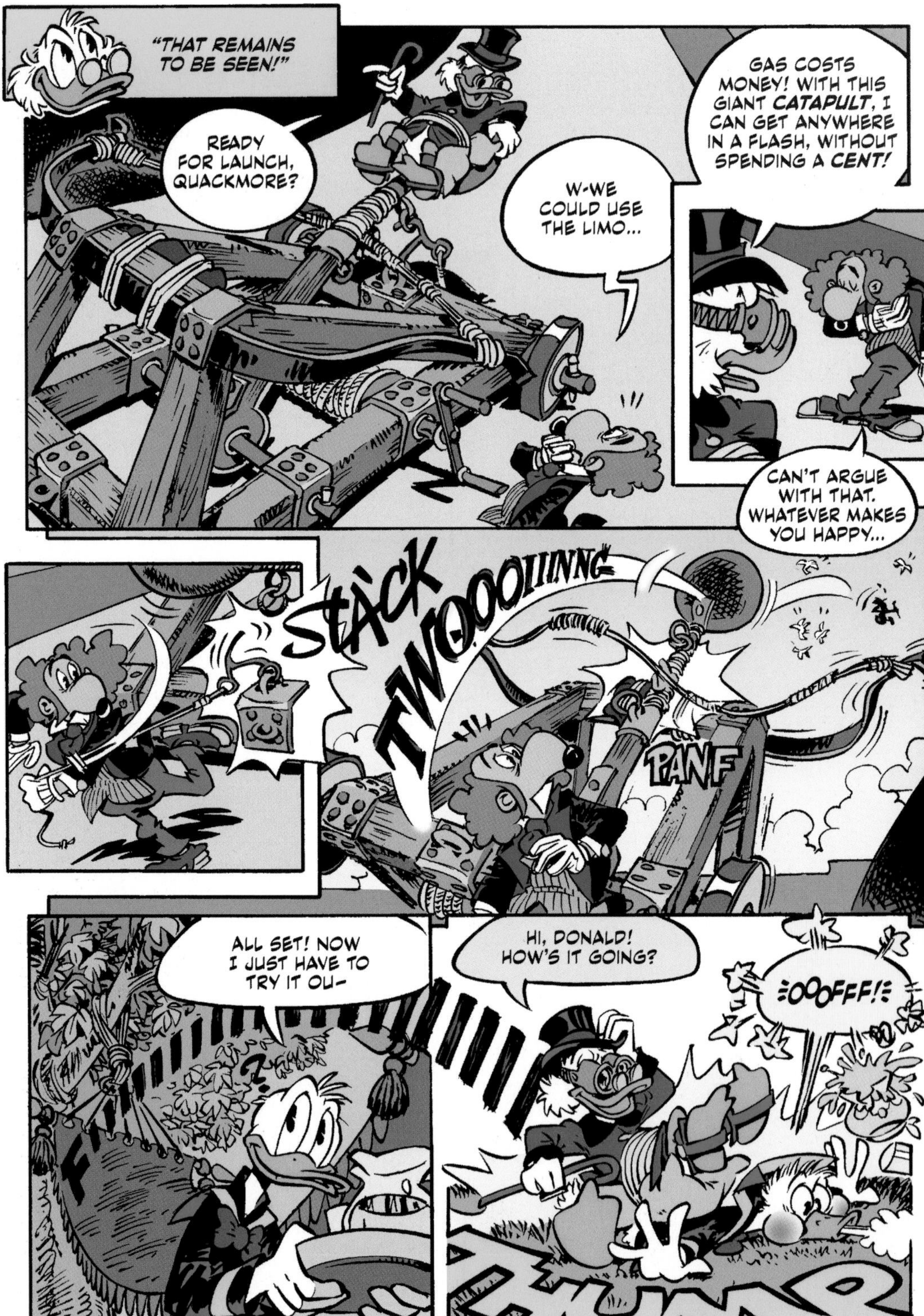
"THAT REMAINS TO BE SEEN!"
READY FOR LAUNCH, QUACKMORE?
W-WE COULD USE THE LIMO...
GAS COSTS MONEY! WITH THIS GIANT CATAPULT, I CAN GET ANYWHERE IN A FLASH, WITHOUT SPENDING A CENT!
CAN'T ARGUE WITH THAT. WHATEVER MAKES YOU HAPPY...
STACK
TWOOOIIINNG
PANF
ALL SET! NOW I JUST HAVE TO TRY IT OU–
HI, DONALD! HOW'S IT GOING?
OOOFFF!
THUMP

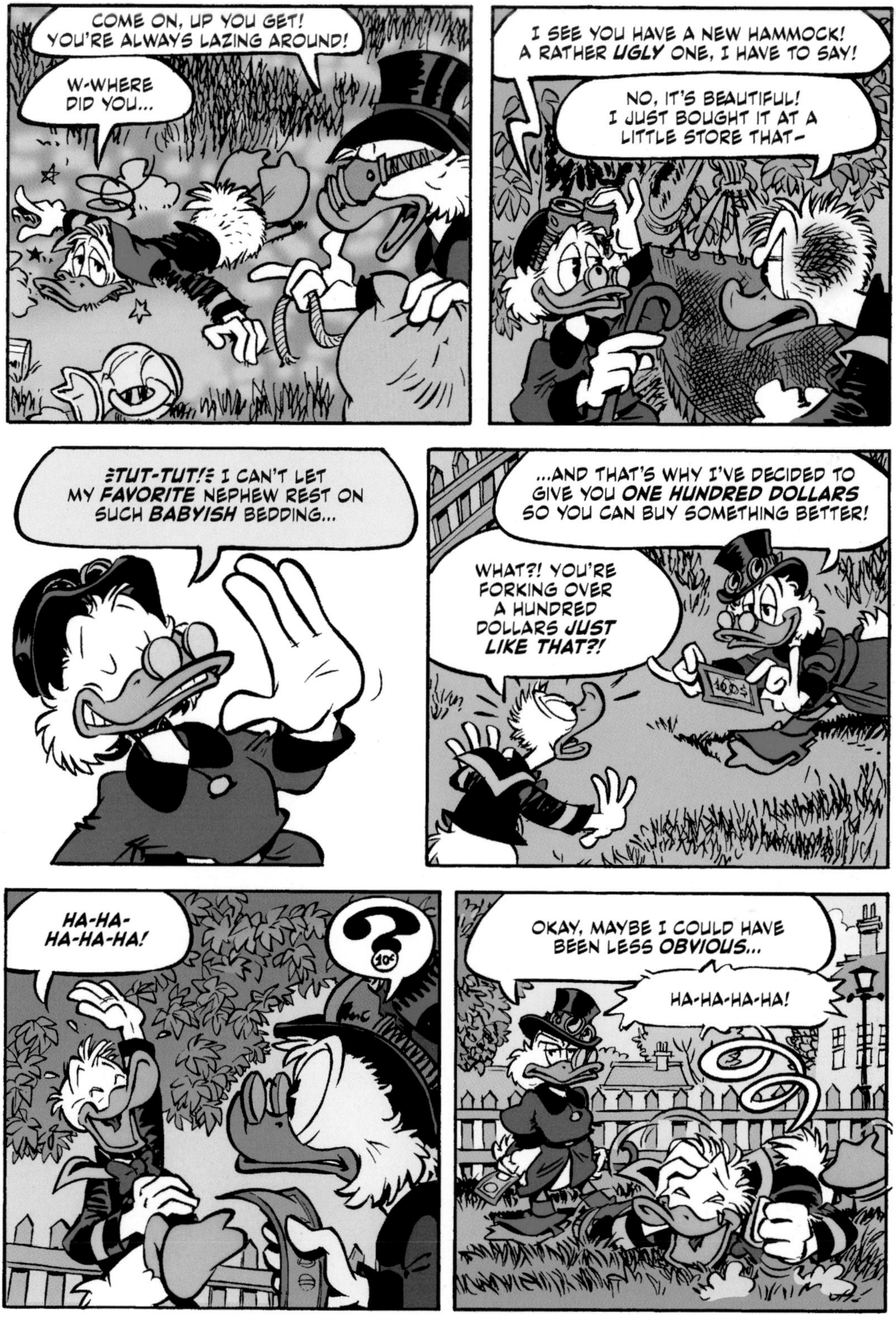
COME ON, UP YOU GET! YOU'RE ALWAYS LAZING AROUND!
W-WHERE DID YOU...
I SEE YOU HAVE A NEW HAMMOCK! A RATHER UGLY ONE, I HAVE TO SAY!
NO, IT'S BEAUTIFUL! I JUST BOUGHT IT AT A LITTLE STORE THAT–
≡TUT-TUT!≡ I CAN'T LET MY FAVORITE NEPHEW REST ON SUCH BABYISH BEDDING...
...AND THAT'S WHY I'VE DECIDED TO GIVE YOU ONE HUNDRED DOLLARS SO YOU CAN BUY SOMETHING BETTER!
WHAT?! YOU'RE FORKING OVER A HUNDRED DOLLARS JUST LIKE THAT?!
HA-HA-HA-HA-HA!
?
10¢
OKAY, MAYBE I COULD HAVE BEEN LESS OBVIOUS...
HA-HA-HA-HA!

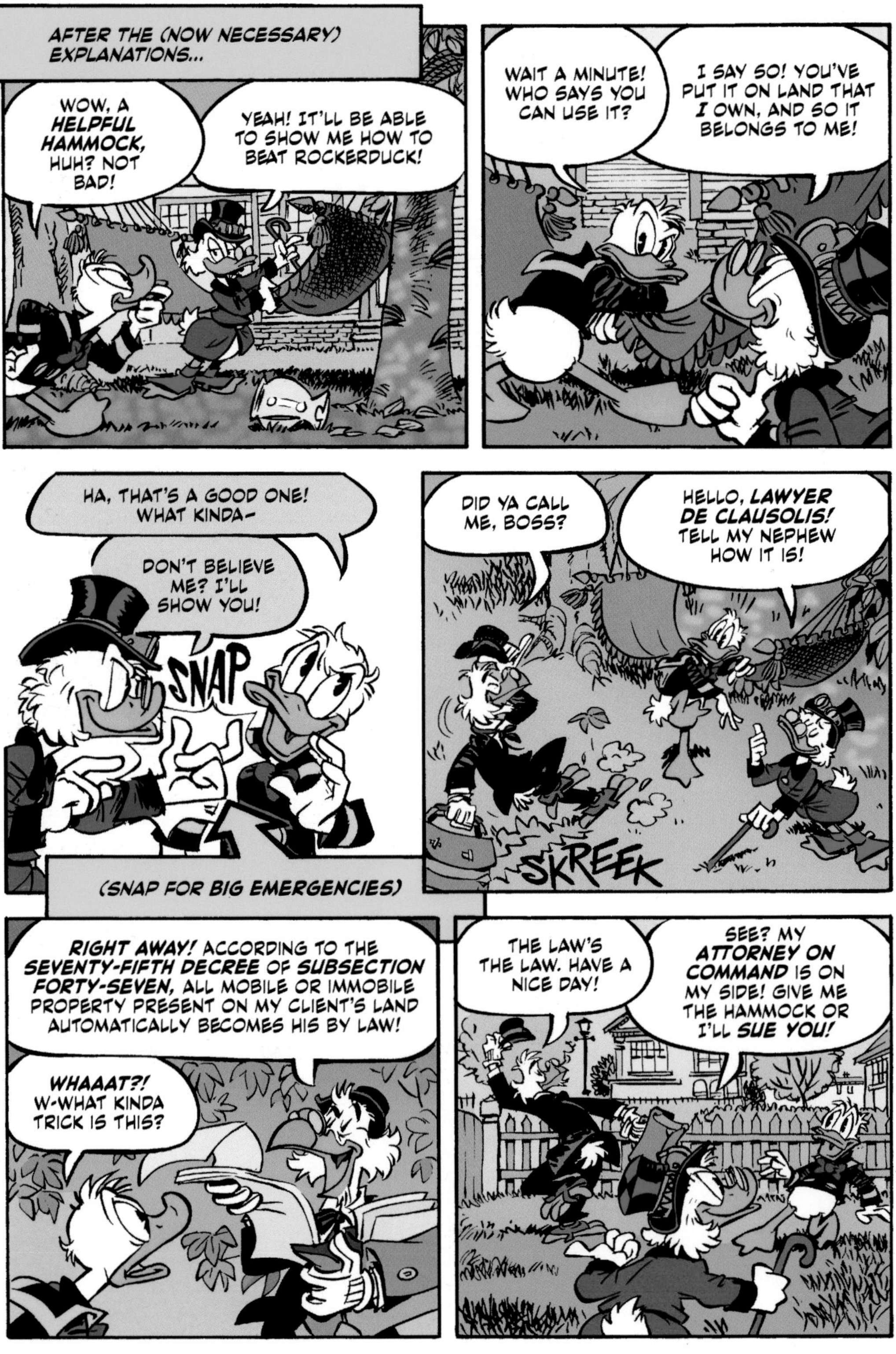
AFTER THE (NOW NECESSARY) EXPLANATIONS...
WOW, A HELPFUL HAMMOCK, HUH? NOT BAD!
YEAH! IT'LL BE ABLE TO SHOW ME HOW TO BEAT ROCKERDUCK!
WAIT A MINUTE! WHO SAYS YOU CAN USE IT?
I SAY SO! YOU'VE PUT IT ON LAND THAT I OWN, AND SO IT BELONGS TO ME!
HA, THAT'S A GOOD ONE! WHAT KINDA-
DON'T BELIEVE ME? I'LL SHOW YOU!
SNAP
(SNAP FOR BIG EMERGENCIES)
DID YA CALL ME, BOSS?
HELLO, LAWYER DE CLAUSOLIS! TELL MY NEPHEW HOW IT IS!
SKREEK
RIGHT AWAY! ACCORDING TO THE SEVENTY-FIFTH DECREE OF SUBSECTION FORTY-SEVEN, ALL MOBILE OR IMMOBILE PROPERTY PRESENT ON MY CLIENT'S LAND AUTOMATICALLY BECOMES HIS BY LAW!
WHAAAT?! W-WHAT KINDA TRICK IS THIS?
THE LAW'S THE LAW. HAVE A NICE DAY!
SEE? MY ATTORNEY ON COMMAND IS ON MY SIDE! GIVE ME THE HAMMOCK OR I'LL SUE YOU!

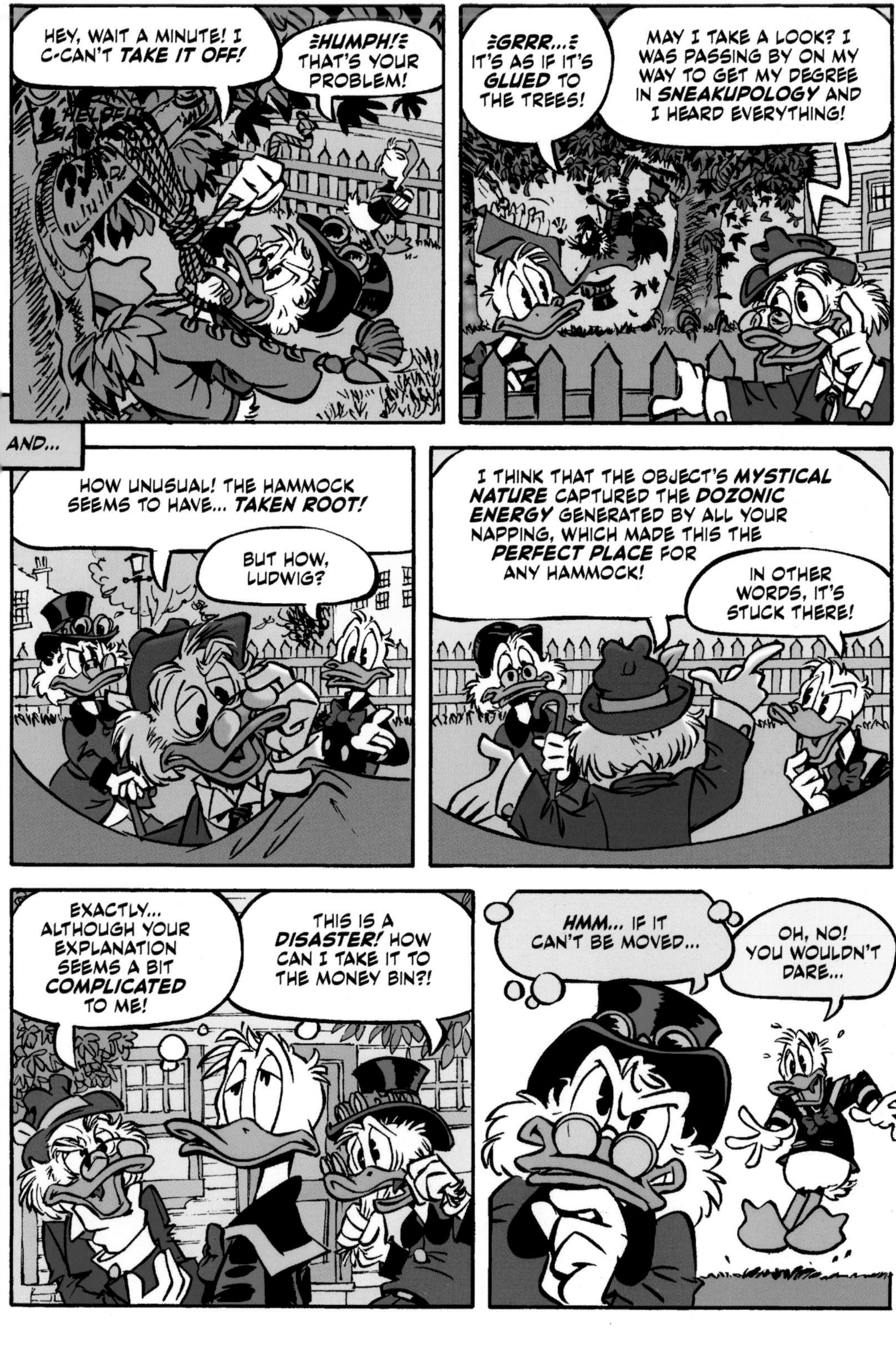
HEY, WAIT A MINUTE! I C-CAN'T *TAKE IT OFF!*
HUMPH! THAT'S YOUR PROBLEM!
GRRR... IT'S AS IF IT'S *GLUED* TO THE TREES!
MAY I TAKE A LOOK? I WAS PASSING BY ON MY WAY TO GET MY DEGREE IN *SNEAKUPOLOGY* AND I HEARD EVERYTHING!
AND...
HOW UNUSUAL! THE HAMMOCK SEEMS TO HAVE... *TAKEN ROOT!*
BUT HOW, LUDWIG?
I THINK THAT THE OBJECT'S *MYSTICAL NATURE* CAPTURED THE *DOZONIC ENERGY* GENERATED BY ALL YOUR NAPPING, WHICH MADE THIS THE *PERFECT PLACE* FOR ANY HAMMOCK!
IN OTHER WORDS, IT'S STUCK THERE!
EXACTLY... ALTHOUGH YOUR EXPLANATION SEEMS A BIT *COMPLICATED* TO ME!
THIS IS A *DISASTER!* HOW CAN I TAKE IT TO THE MONEY BIN?!
HMM... IF IT CAN'T BE MOVED...
OH, NO! YOU WOULDN'T DARE...

"OH, BUT I WOULD!"

GOOD MORNING, DUCKBURG! WHAT A *FANTASTIC* DAY!

HI, BOYS! WHAT'S FOR BREAKFAST?

PANCAKES WITH MAPLE SYRUP, AS YOU *SPECIFICALLY REQUESTED!*

YUM! OF COURSE, YOU COULD HAVE MADE A FEW MORE! BIT *STINGY,* AREN'T YOU?

HOW LONG IS THIS GONNA GO ON FOR?

REMEMBER, YOUR MOVE TO MY HOUSE IS JUST TEMPORARY!

ACTUALLY, THIS HOUSE IS *MY* PROPERTY, AND I'LL DO *WHAT I WANT!* BESIDES...

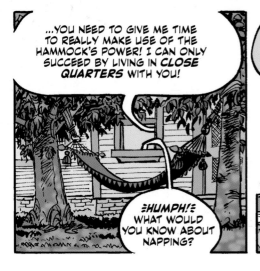

...YOU NEED TO GIVE ME TIME TO REALLY MAKE USE OF THE HAMMOCK'S POWER! I CAN ONLY SUCCEED BY LIVING IN *CLOSE QUARTERS* WITH YOU!

≥HUMPH!≤ WHAT WOULD YOU KNOW ABOUT NAPPING?

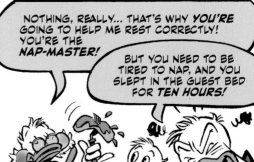

NOTHING, REALLY... THAT'S WHY *YOU'RE* GOING TO HELP ME REST CORRECTLY! YOU'RE THE *NAP-MASTER!*

BUT YOU NEED TO BE TIRED TO NAP, AND YOU SLEPT IN THE GUEST BED FOR *TEN HOURS!*

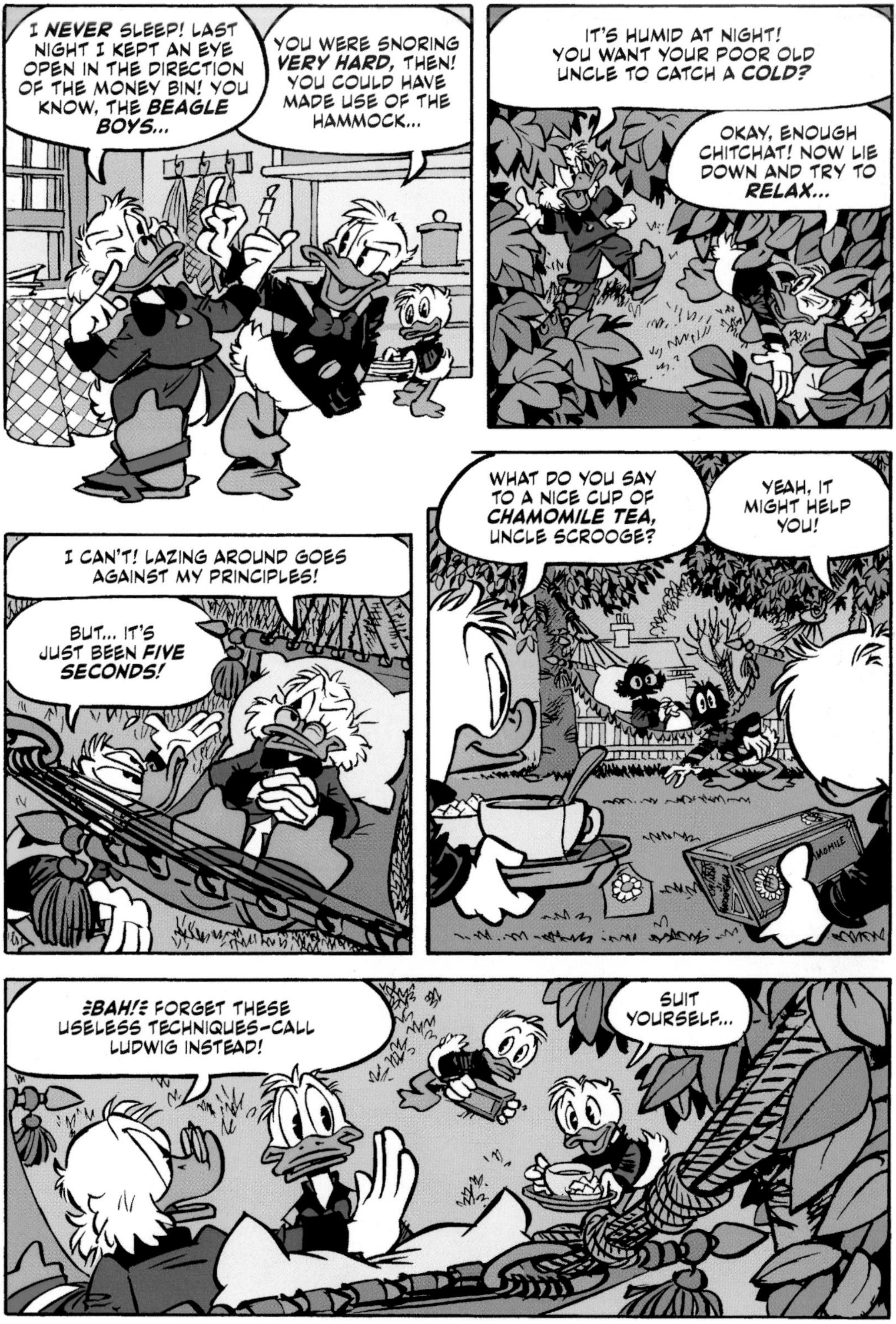
I NEVER SLEEP! LAST NIGHT I KEPT AN EYE OPEN IN THE DIRECTION OF THE MONEY BIN! YOU KNOW, THE BEAGLE BOYS...
YOU WERE SNORING VERY HARD, THEN! YOU COULD HAVE MADE USE OF THE HAMMOCK...
IT'S HUMID AT NIGHT! YOU WANT YOUR POOR OLD UNCLE TO CATCH A COLD?
OKAY, ENOUGH CHITCHAT! NOW LIE DOWN AND TRY TO RELAX...
I CAN'T! LAZING AROUND GOES AGAINST MY PRINCIPLES!
BUT... IT'S JUST BEEN FIVE SECONDS!
WHAT DO YOU SAY TO A NICE CUP OF CHAMOMILE TEA, UNCLE SCROOGE?
YEAH, IT MIGHT HELP YOU!
BAH! FORGET THESE USELESS TECHNIQUES—CALL LUDWIG INSTEAD!
SUIT YOURSELF...

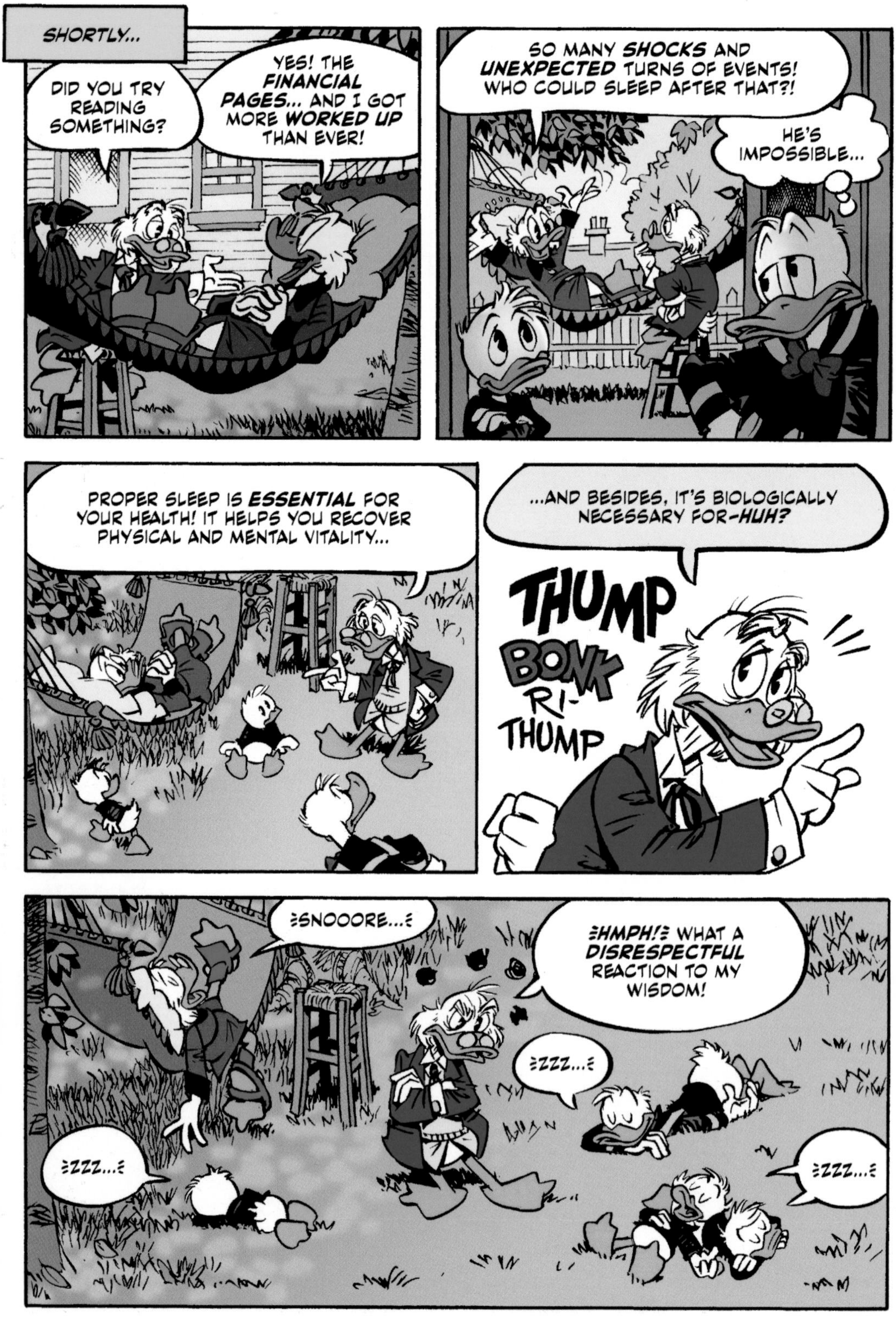

SHORTLY...
DID YOU TRY READING SOMETHING?
YES! THE FINANCIAL PAGES... AND I GOT MORE WORKED UP THAN EVER!
SO MANY SHOCKS AND UNEXPECTED TURNS OF EVENTS! WHO COULD SLEEP AFTER THAT?!
HE'S IMPOSSIBLE...
PROPER SLEEP IS ESSENTIAL FOR YOUR HEALTH! IT HELPS YOU RECOVER PHYSICAL AND MENTAL VITALITY...
...AND BESIDES, IT'S BIOLOGICALLY NECESSARY FOR-HUH?
THUMP
BONK
RI-THUMP
SNOOORE...
HMPH! WHAT A DISRESPECTFUL REACTION TO MY WISDOM!
ZZZ...
ZZZ...
ZZZ...

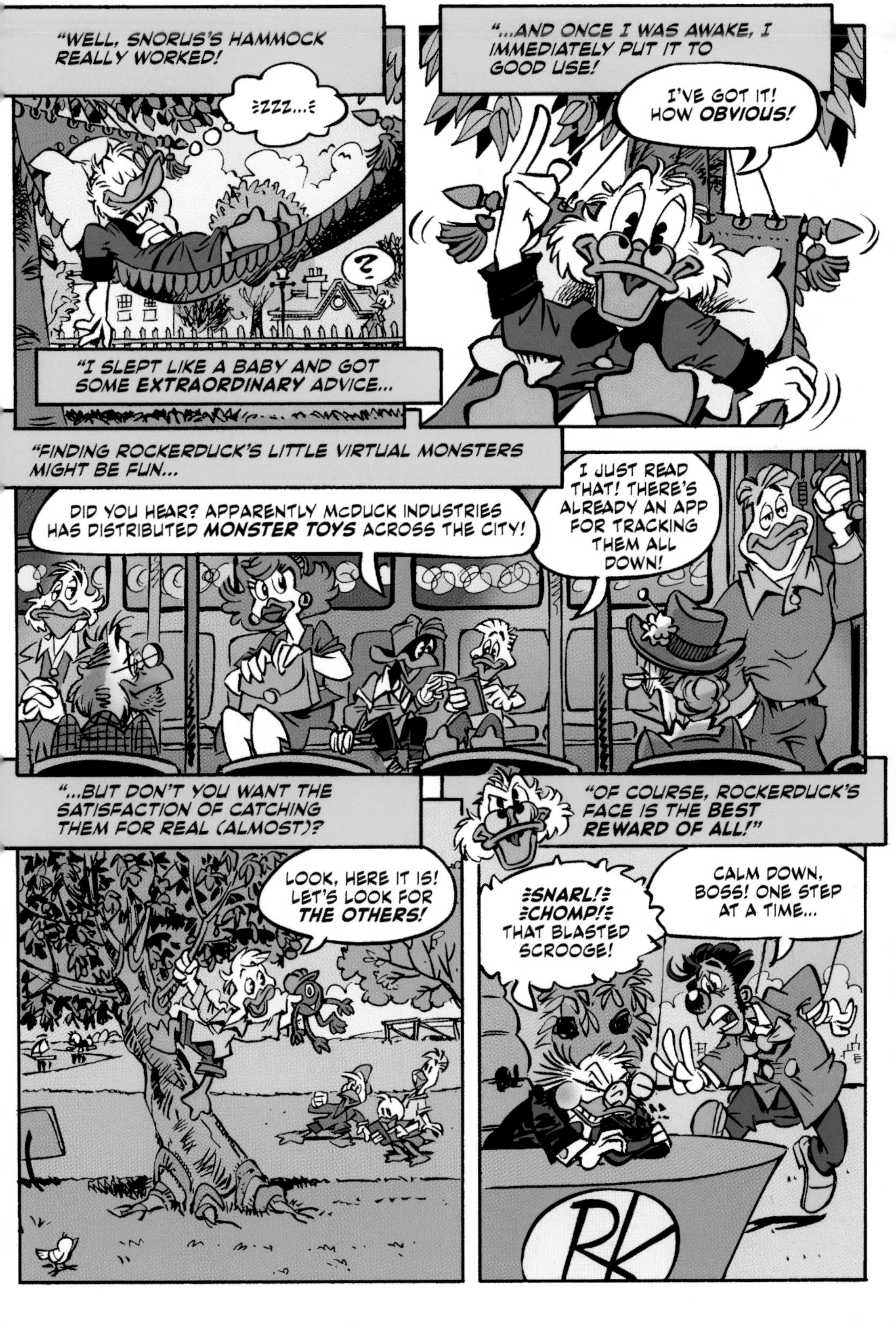
"WELL, SNORUS'S HAMMOCK REALLY WORKED!
ZZZ...
?
"I SLEPT LIKE A BABY AND GOT SOME EXTRAORDINARY ADVICE...
"...AND ONCE I WAS AWAKE, I IMMEDIATELY PUT IT TO GOOD USE!
I'VE GOT IT! HOW OBVIOUS!
"FINDING ROCKERDUCK'S LITTLE VIRTUAL MONSTERS MIGHT BE FUN...
DID YOU HEAR? APPARENTLY McDUCK INDUSTRIES HAS DISTRIBUTED MONSTER TOYS ACROSS THE CITY!
I JUST READ THAT! THERE'S ALREADY AN APP FOR TRACKING THEM ALL DOWN!
"...BUT DON'T YOU WANT THE SATISFACTION OF CATCHING THEM FOR REAL (ALMOST)?
LOOK, HERE IT IS! LET'S LOOK FOR THE OTHERS!
"OF COURSE, ROCKERDUCK'S FACE IS THE BEST REWARD OF ALL!"
SNARL! CHOMP! THAT BLASTED SCROOGE!
CALM DOWN, BOSS! ONE STEP AT A TIME...
RK

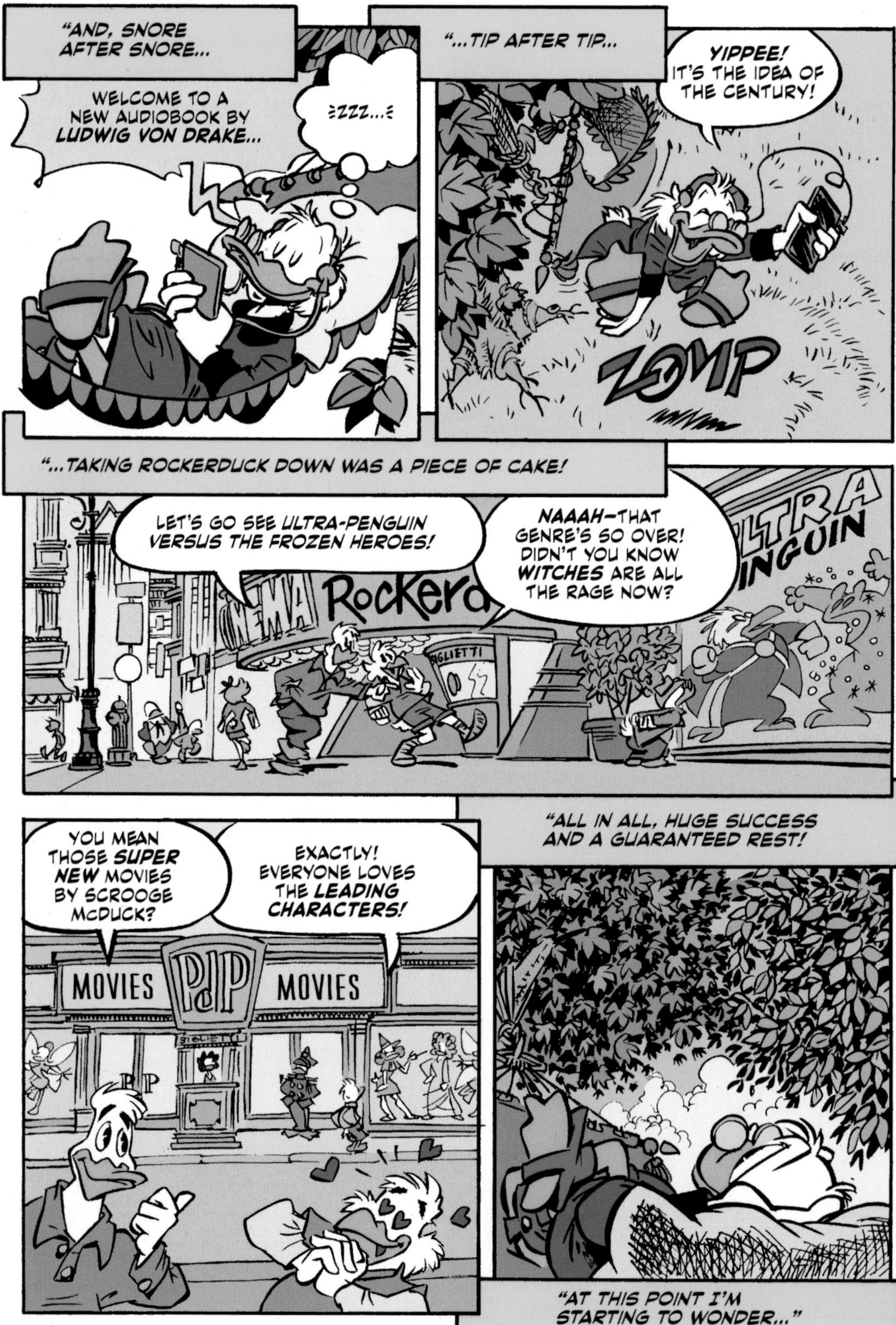
"AND, SNORE AFTER SNORE...
WELCOME TO A NEW AUDIOBOOK BY LUDWIG VON DRAKE...
ZZZ...
"...TIP AFTER TIP...
YIPPEE! IT'S THE IDEA OF THE CENTURY!
ZOMP
"...TAKING ROCKERDUCK DOWN WAS A PIECE OF CAKE!
LET'S GO SEE ULTRA-PENGUIN VERSUS THE FROZEN HEROES!
NAAAH—THAT GENRE'S SO OVER! DIDN'T YOU KNOW WITCHES ARE ALL THE RAGE NOW?
Rockerd
BIGLIETTI
ULTRA PENGUIN
YOU MEAN THOSE SUPER NEW MOVIES BY SCROOGE McDUCK?
EXACTLY! EVERYONE LOVES THE LEADING CHARACTERS!
MOVIES
PdP
MOVIES
"ALL IN ALL, HUGE SUCCESS AND A GUARANTEED REST!
"AT THIS POINT I'M STARTING TO WONDER..."

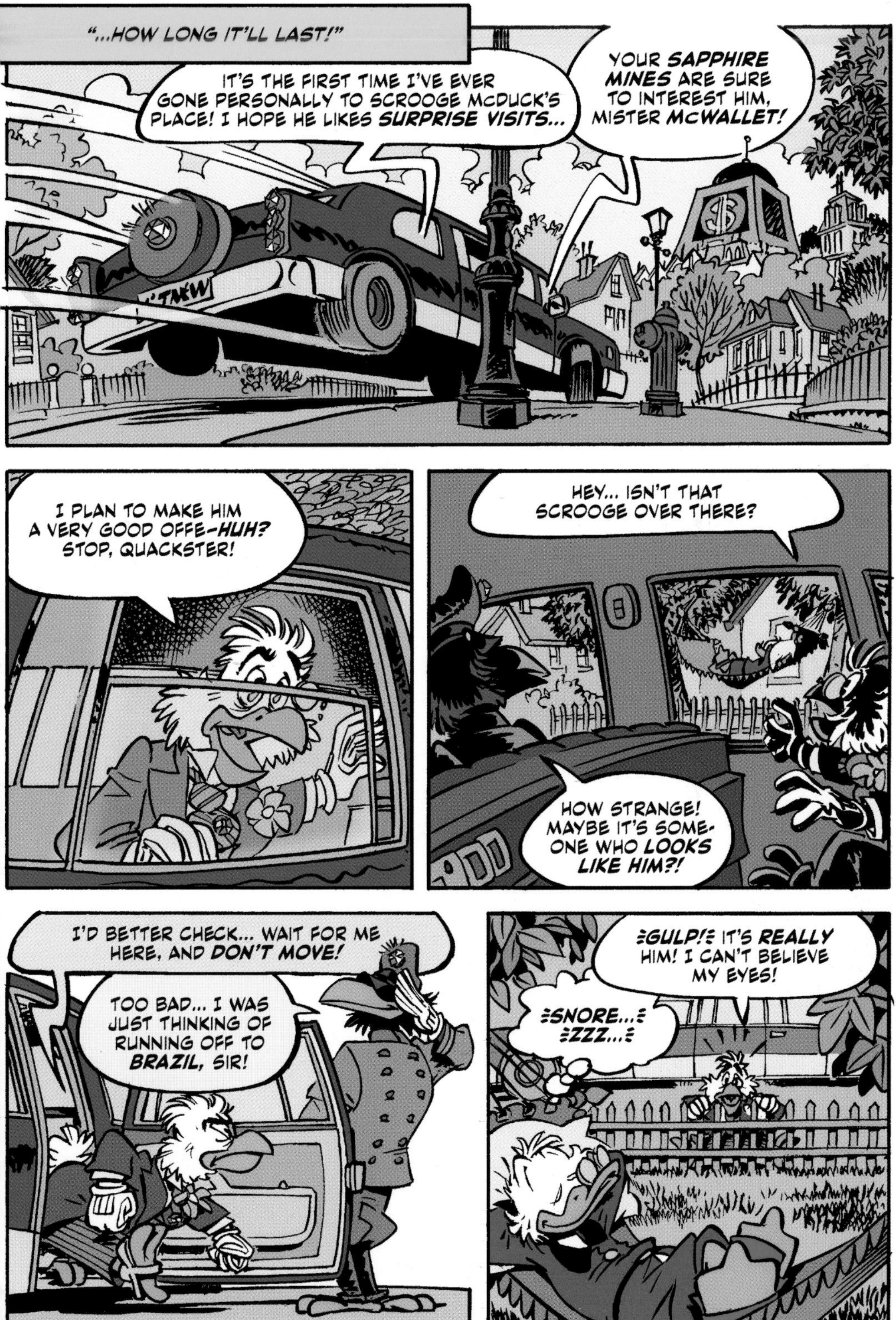
"...HOW LONG IT'LL LAST!"
IT'S THE FIRST TIME I'VE EVER GONE PERSONALLY TO SCROOGE McDUCK'S PLACE! I HOPE HE LIKES SURPRISE VISITS...
YOUR SAPPHIRE MINES ARE SURE TO INTEREST HIM, MISTER McWALLET!
I PLAN TO MAKE HIM A VERY GOOD OFFE-HUH? STOP, QUACKSTER!
HEY... ISN'T THAT SCROOGE OVER THERE?
HOW STRANGE! MAYBE IT'S SOME-ONE WHO LOOKS LIKE HIM?!
I'D BETTER CHECK... WAIT FOR ME HERE, AND DON'T MOVE!
TOO BAD... I WAS JUST THINKING OF RUNNING OFF TO BRAZIL, SIR!
GULP! IT'S REALLY HIM! I CAN'T BELIEVE MY EYES!
SNORE... ZZZ...

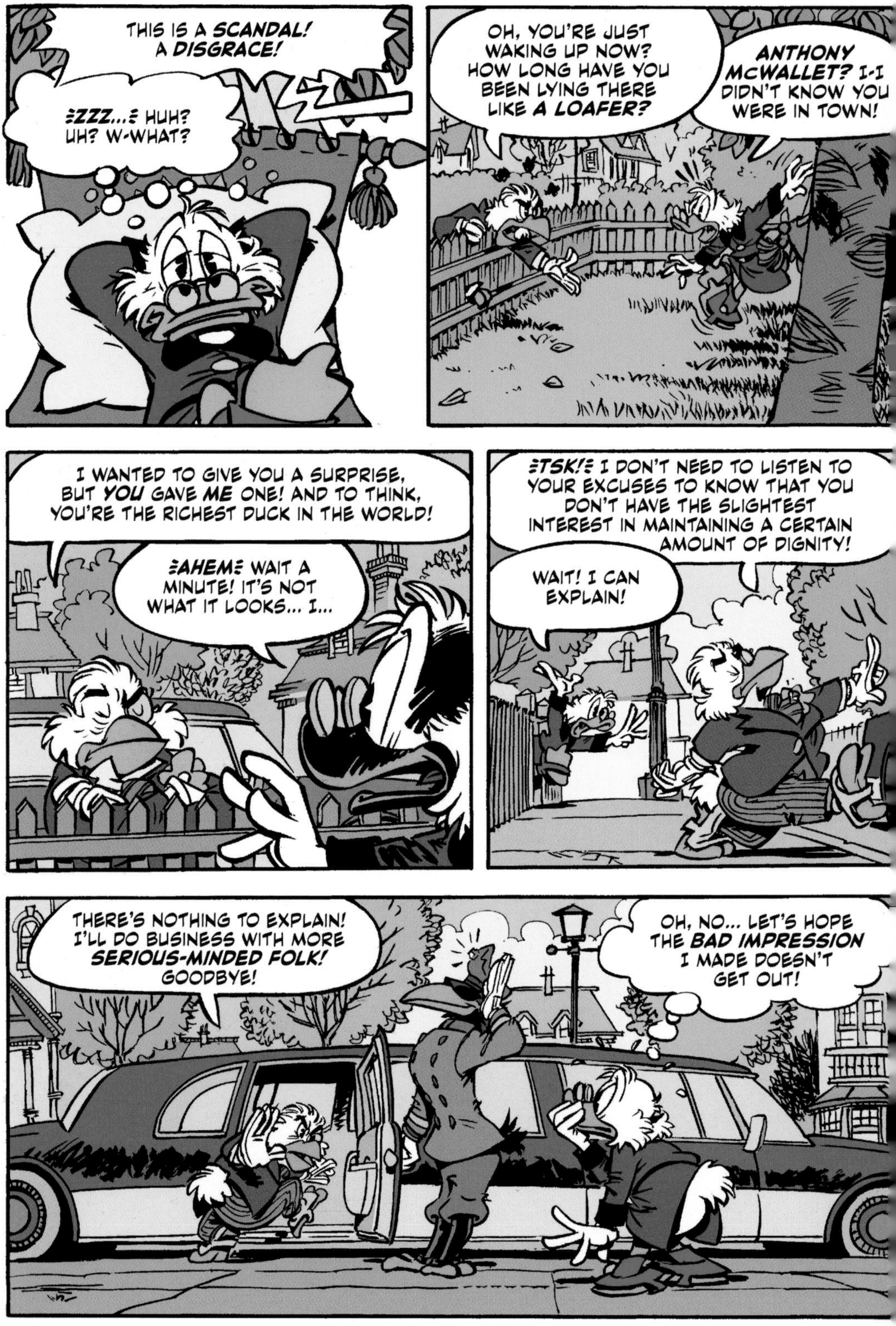
THIS IS A SCANDAL! A DISGRACE!
ZZZ... HUH? UH? W-WHAT?
OH, YOU'RE JUST WAKING UP NOW? HOW LONG HAVE YOU BEEN LYING THERE LIKE A LOAFER?
ANTHONY MCWALLET? I-I DIDN'T KNOW YOU WERE IN TOWN!
I WANTED TO GIVE YOU A SURPRISE, BUT YOU GAVE ME ONE! AND TO THINK, YOU'RE THE RICHEST DUCK IN THE WORLD!
AHEM WAIT A MINUTE! IT'S NOT WHAT IT LOOKS... I...
TSK! I DON'T NEED TO LISTEN TO YOUR EXCUSES TO KNOW THAT YOU DON'T HAVE THE SLIGHTEST INTEREST IN MAINTAINING A CERTAIN AMOUNT OF DIGNITY!
WAIT! I CAN EXPLAIN!
THERE'S NOTHING TO EXPLAIN! I'LL DO BUSINESS WITH MORE SERIOUS-MINDED FOLK! GOODBYE!
OH, NO... LET'S HOPE THE BAD IMPRESSION I MADE DOESN'T GET OUT!

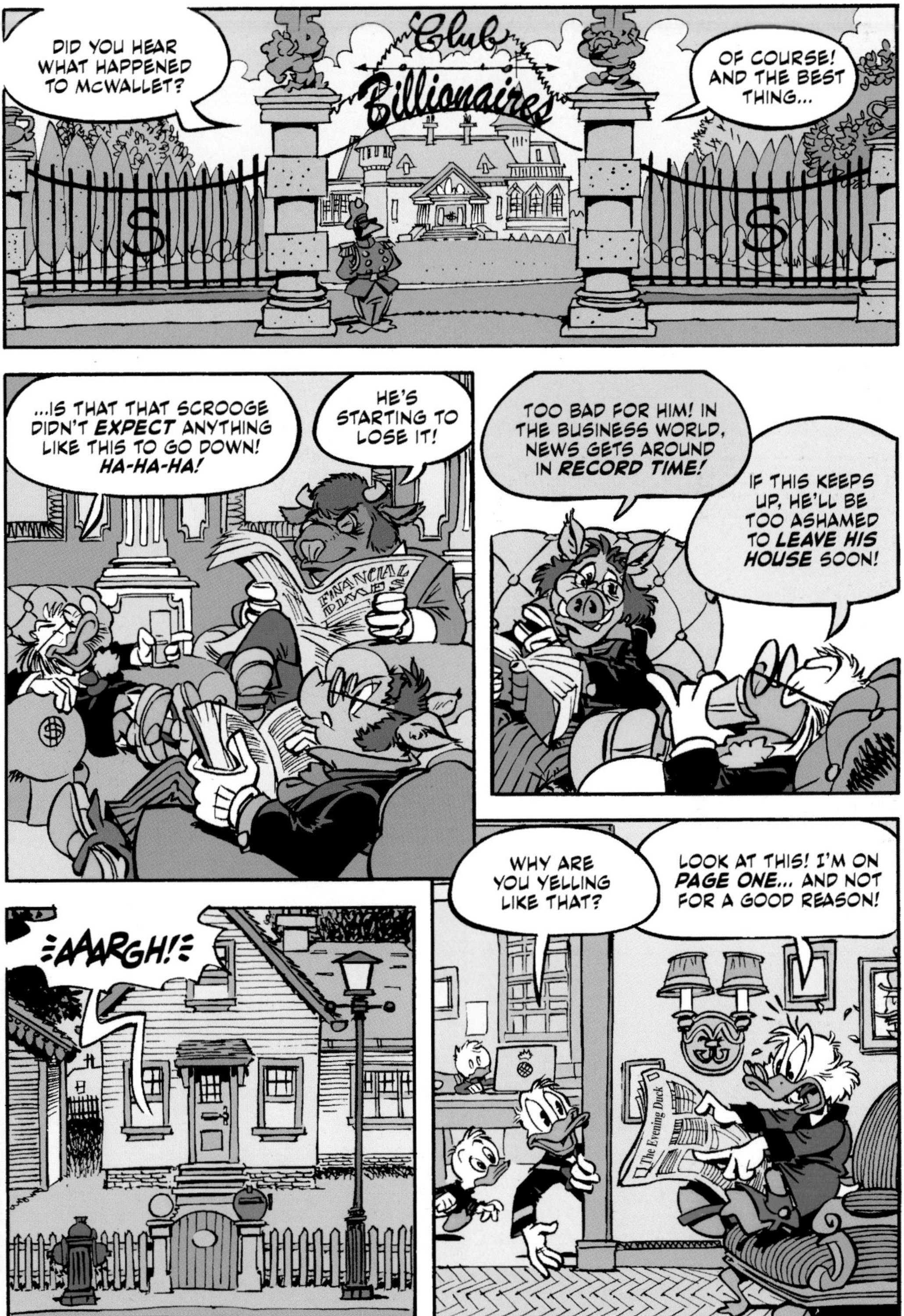
Club Billionaires
DID YOU HEAR WHAT HAPPENED TO McWALLET?
OF COURSE! AND THE BEST THING...
...IS THAT THAT SCROOGE DIDN'T EXPECT ANYTHING LIKE THIS TO GO DOWN! HA-HA-HA!
HE'S STARTING TO LOSE IT!
TOO BAD FOR HIM! IN THE BUSINESS WORLD, NEWS GETS AROUND IN RECORD TIME!
IF THIS KEEPS UP, HE'LL BE TOO ASHAMED TO LEAVE HIS HOUSE SOON!
AAARGH!
WHY ARE YOU YELLING LIKE THAT?
LOOK AT THIS! I'M ON PAGE ONE... AND NOT FOR A GOOD REASON!
The Evening Duck

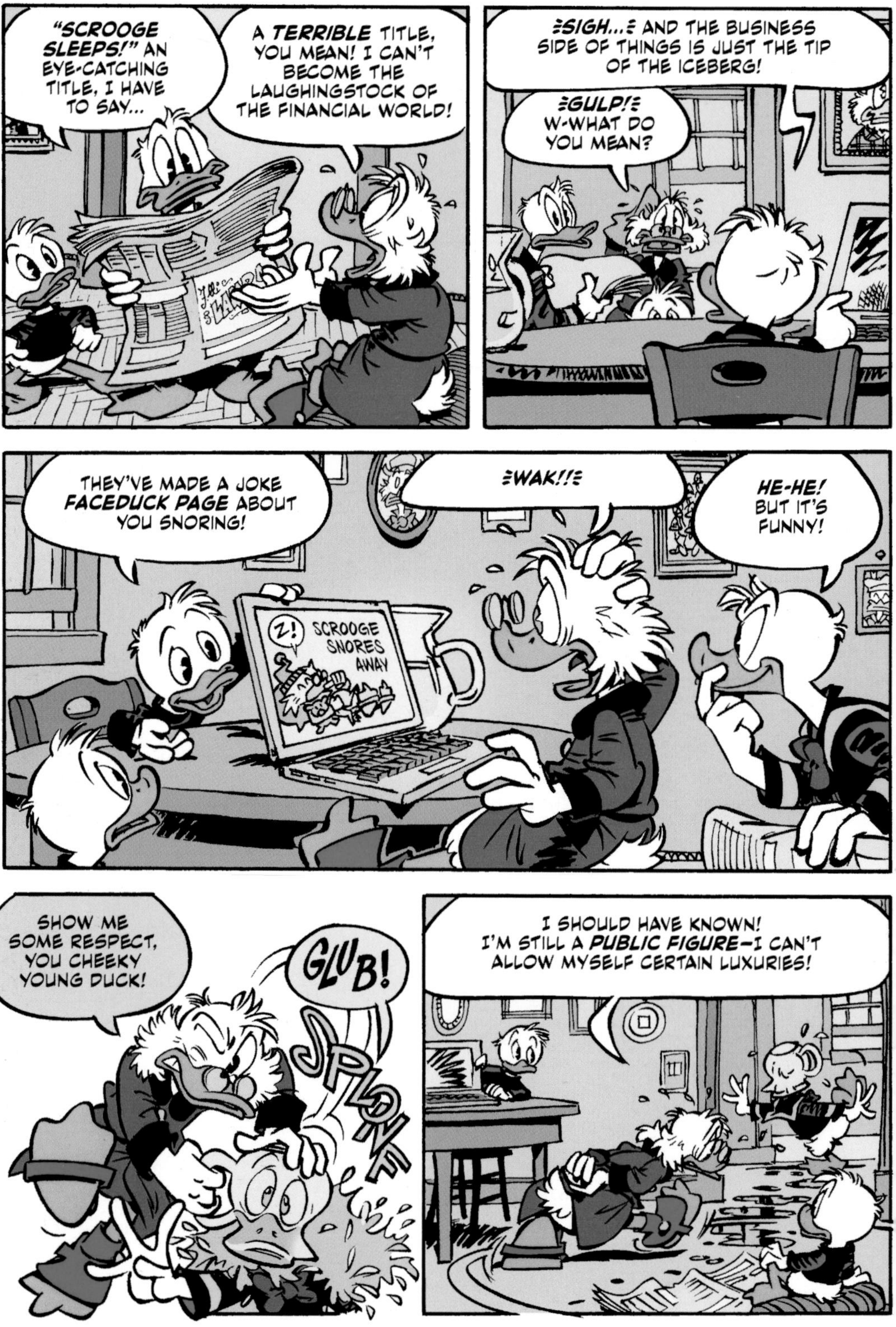
"SCROOGE SLEEPS!" AN EYE-CATCHING TITLE, I HAVE TO SAY...
A TERRIBLE TITLE, YOU MEAN! I CAN'T BECOME THE LAUGHINGSTOCK OF THE FINANCIAL WORLD!
SIGH... AND THE BUSINESS SIDE OF THINGS IS JUST THE TIP OF THE ICEBERG!
GULP! W-WHAT DO YOU MEAN?
THEY'VE MADE A JOKE FACEDUCK PAGE ABOUT YOU SNORING!
Z!
SCROOGE SNORES AWAY
WAK!!
HE-HE! BUT IT'S FUNNY!
SHOW ME SOME RESPECT, YOU CHEEKY YOUNG DUCK!
GLUB!
SPLOSH
I SHOULD HAVE KNOWN! I'M STILL A PUBLIC FIGURE—I CAN'T ALLOW MYSELF CERTAIN LUXURIES!

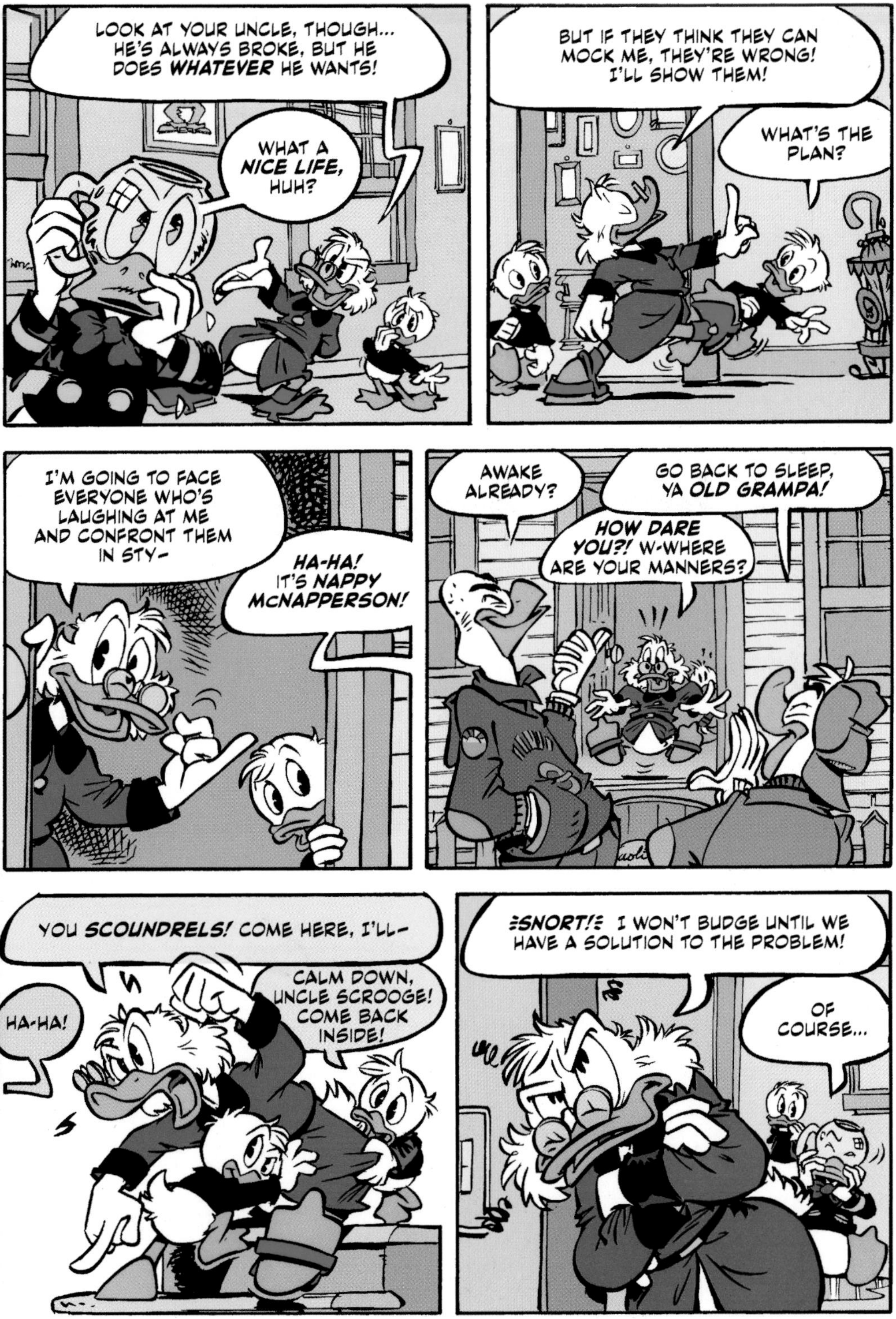
LOOK AT YOUR UNCLE, THOUGH... HE'S ALWAYS BROKE, BUT HE DOES WHATEVER HE WANTS!
WHAT A NICE LIFE, HUH?
BUT IF THEY THINK THEY CAN MOCK ME, THEY'RE WRONG! I'LL SHOW THEM!
WHAT'S THE PLAN?
I'M GOING TO FACE EVERYONE WHO'S LAUGHING AT ME AND CONFRONT THEM IN STY–
HA-HA! IT'S NAPPY McNAPPERSON!
AWAKE ALREADY?
GO BACK TO SLEEP, YA OLD GRAMPA!
HOW DARE YOU?! W-WHERE ARE YOUR MANNERS?
YOU SCOUNDRELS! COME HERE, I'LL–
HA-HA!
CALM DOWN, UNCLE SCROOGE! COME BACK INSIDE!
SNORT! I WON'T BUDGE UNTIL WE HAVE A SOLUTION TO THE PROBLEM!
OF COURSE...

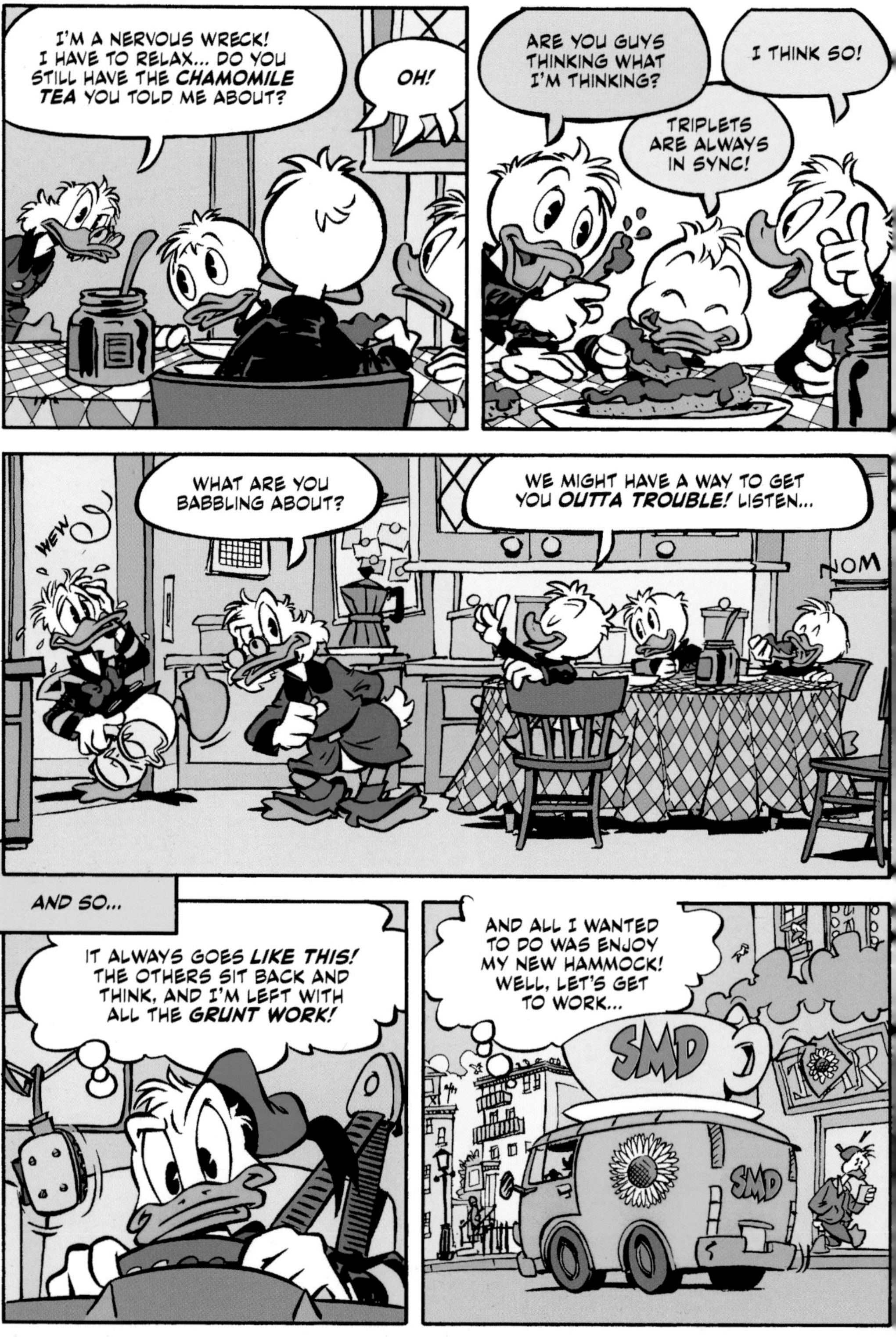
I'M A NERVOUS WRECK! I HAVE TO RELAX... DO YOU STILL HAVE THE CHAMOMILE TEA YOU TOLD ME ABOUT?
OH!
ARE YOU GUYS THINKING WHAT I'M THINKING?
TRIPLETS ARE ALWAYS IN SYNC!
I THINK SO!
WEW
WHAT ARE YOU BABBLING ABOUT?
WE MIGHT HAVE A WAY TO GET YOU OUTTA TROUBLE! LISTEN...
NOM
AND SO...
IT ALWAYS GOES LIKE THIS! THE OTHERS SIT BACK AND THINK, AND I'M LEFT WITH ALL THE GRUNT WORK!
AND ALL I WANTED TO DO WAS ENJOY MY NEW HAMMOCK! WELL, LET'S GET TO WORK...
SMD
SMD

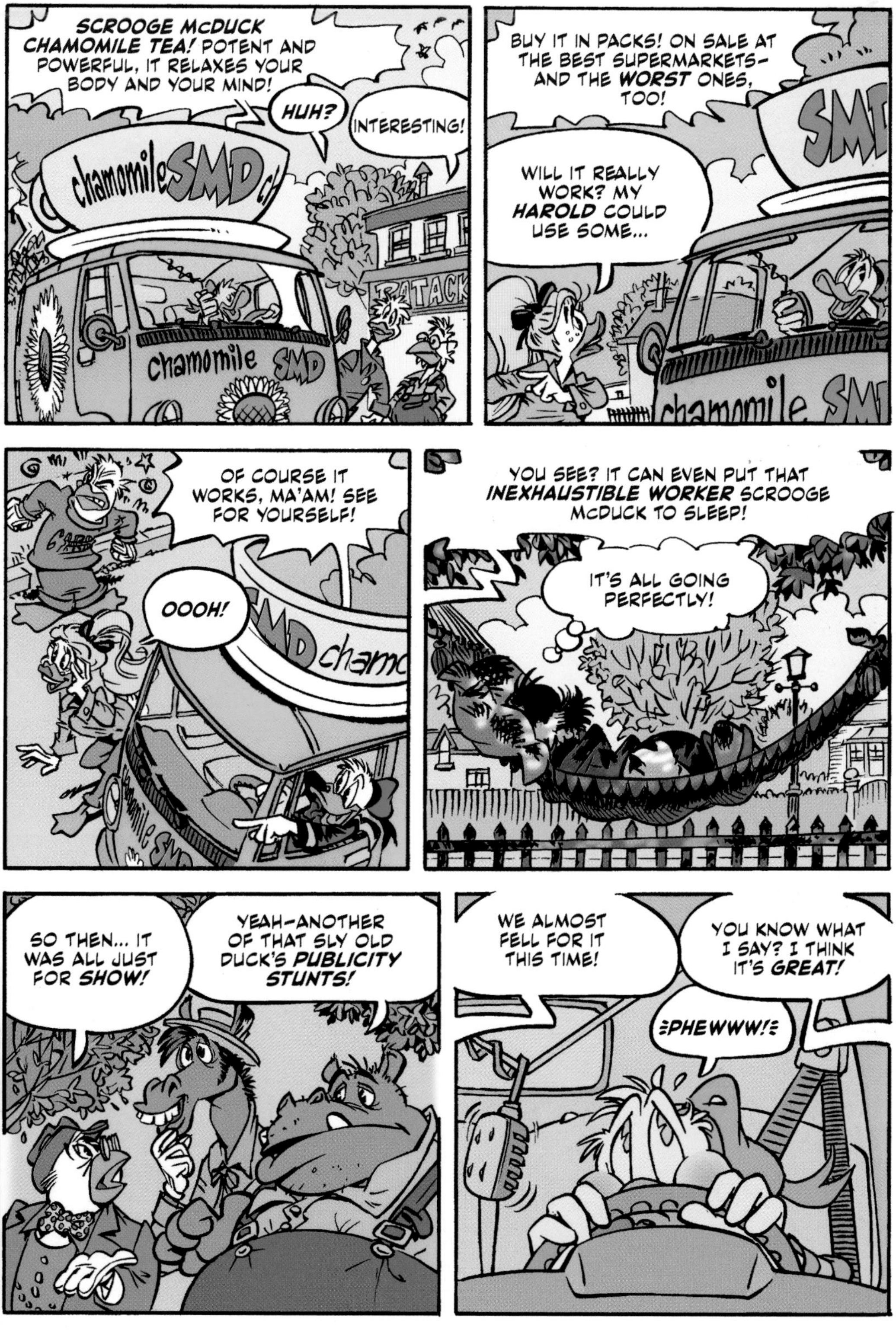

SCROOGE McDUCK CHAMOMILE TEA! POTENT AND POWERFUL, IT RELAXES YOUR BODY AND YOUR MIND!
HUH?
INTERESTING!
chamomile SMD
PATACK
chamomile SMD
BUY IT IN PACKS! ON SALE AT THE BEST SUPERMARKETS– AND THE WORST ONES, TOO!
WILL IT REALLY WORK? MY HAROLD COULD USE SOME...
OF COURSE IT WORKS, MA'AM! SEE FOR YOURSELF!
OOOH!
YOU SEE? IT CAN EVEN PUT THAT INEXHAUSTIBLE WORKER SCROOGE McDUCK TO SLEEP!
IT'S ALL GOING PERFECTLY!
SO THEN... IT WAS ALL JUST FOR SHOW!
YEAH–ANOTHER OF THAT SLY OLD DUCK'S PUBLICITY STUNTS!
WE ALMOST FELL FOR IT THIS TIME!
YOU KNOW WHAT I SAY? I THINK IT'S GREAT!
PHEWWW!

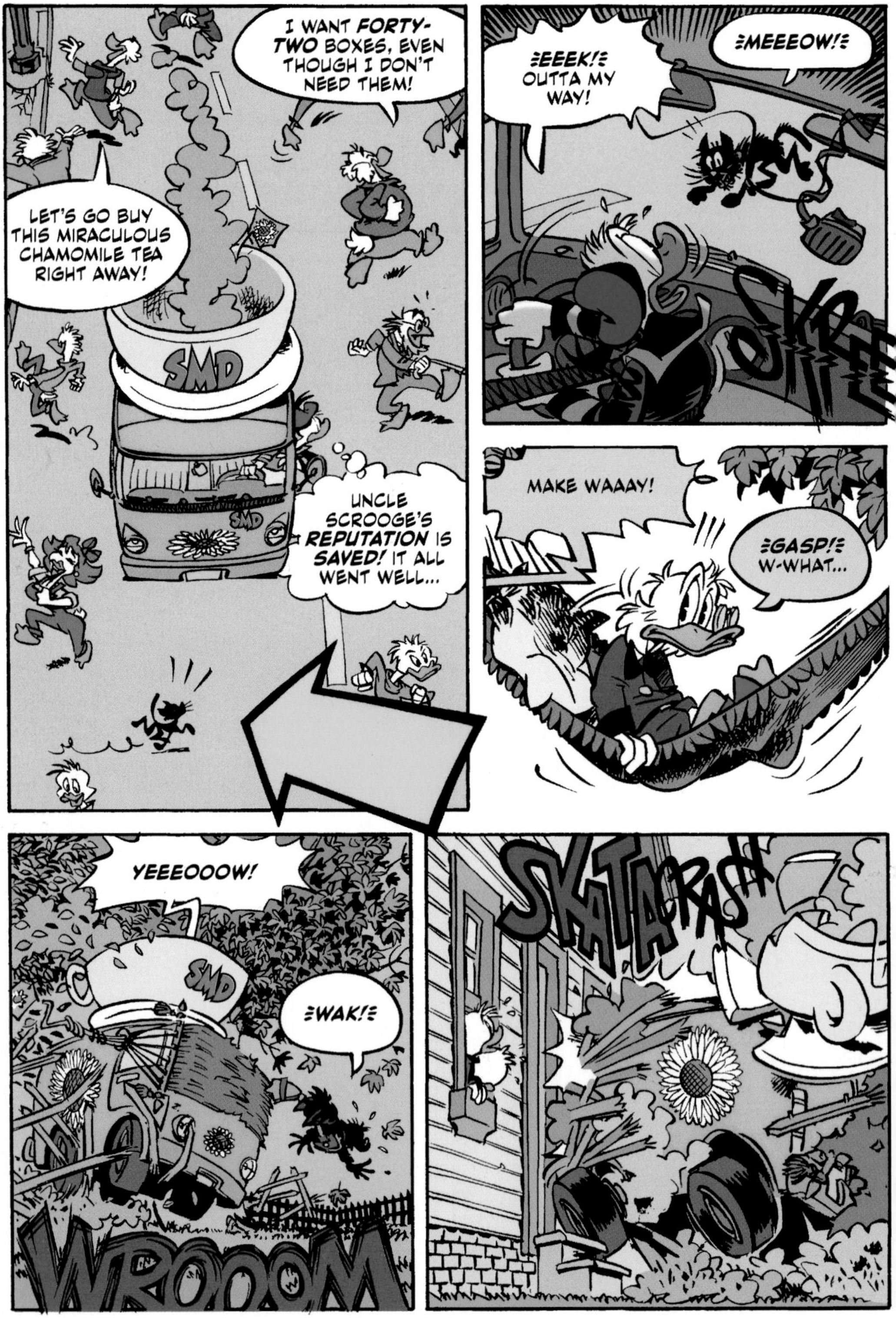
I WANT FORTY-TWO BOXES, EVEN THOUGH I DON'T NEED THEM!
LET'S GO BUY THIS MIRACULOUS CHAMOMILE TEA RIGHT AWAY!
SMD
SMD
UNCLE SCROOGE'S REPUTATION IS SAVED! IT ALL WENT WELL...
EEEK! OUTTA MY WAY!
MEEEOW!
SKREE
MAKE WAAAY!
GASP! W-WHAT...
YEEEOOOW!
SMD
WAK!
WROOOM
SKATACRASH

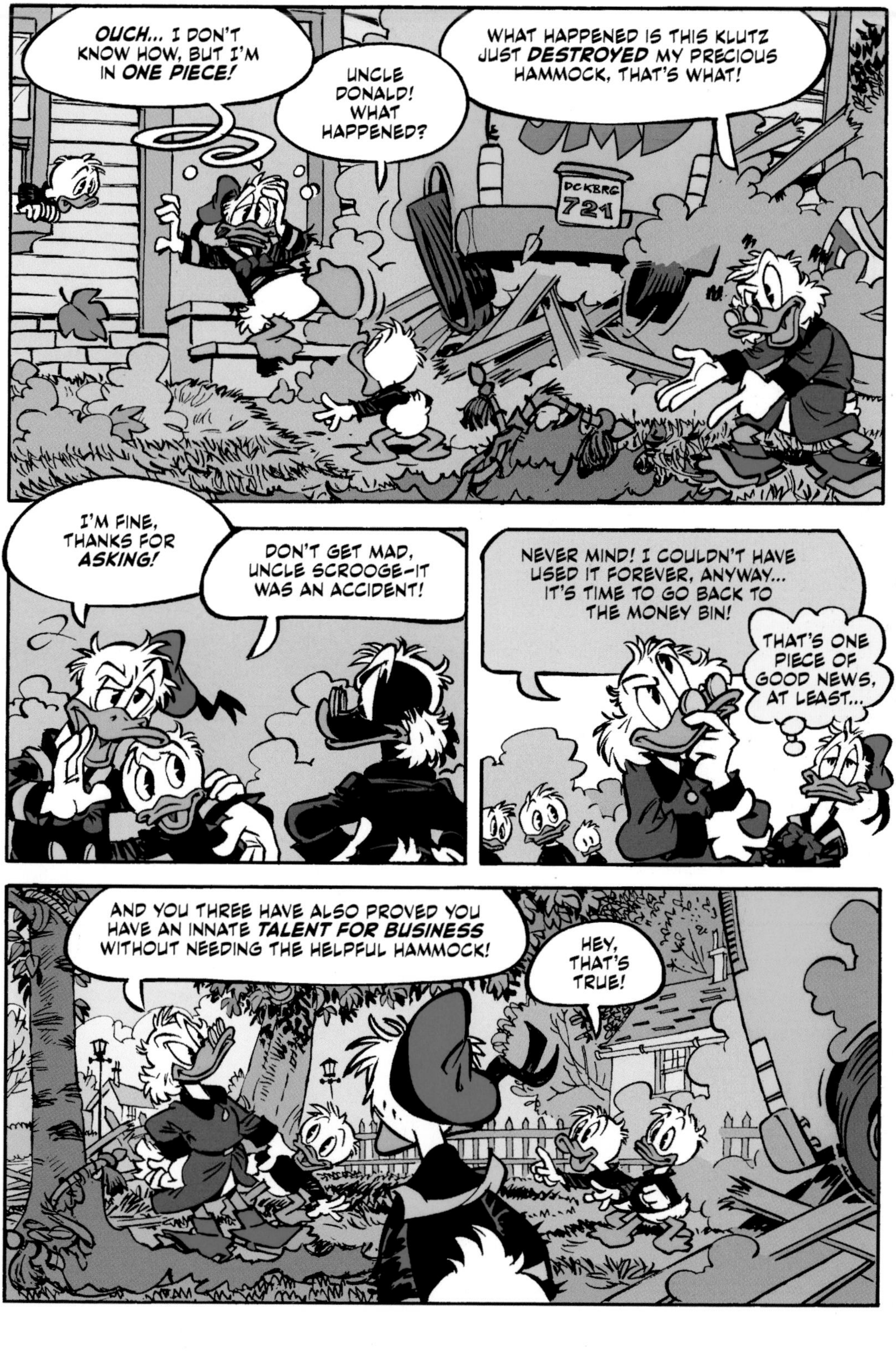
OUCH... I DON'T KNOW HOW, BUT I'M IN ONE PIECE!
UNCLE DONALD! WHAT HAPPENED?
WHAT HAPPENED IS THIS KLUTZ JUST DESTROYED MY PRECIOUS HAMMOCK, THAT'S WHAT!
DCKBRG 721
I'M FINE, THANKS FOR ASKING!
DON'T GET MAD, UNCLE SCROOGE—IT WAS AN ACCIDENT!
NEVER MIND! I COULDN'T HAVE USED IT FOREVER, ANYWAY... IT'S TIME TO GO BACK TO THE MONEY BIN!
THAT'S ONE PIECE OF GOOD NEWS, AT LEAST...
AND YOU THREE HAVE ALSO PROVED YOU HAVE AN INNATE TALENT FOR BUSINESS WITHOUT NEEDING THE HELPFUL HAMMOCK!
HEY, THAT'S TRUE!

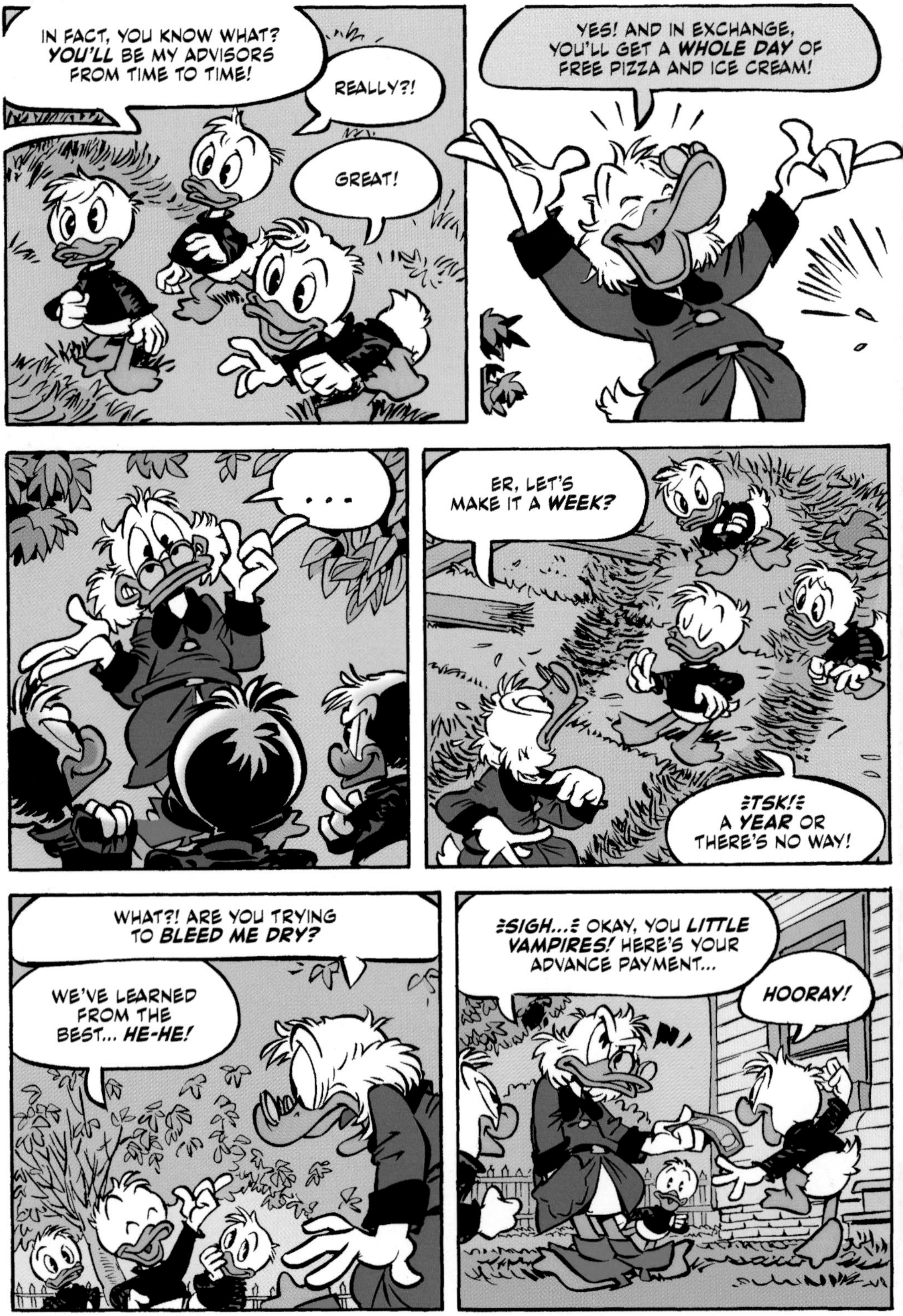
IN FACT, YOU KNOW WHAT? YOU'LL BE MY ADVISORS FROM TIME TO TIME!
REALLY?!
GREAT!
YES! AND IN EXCHANGE, YOU'LL GET A WHOLE DAY OF FREE PIZZA AND ICE CREAM!
. . .
ER, LET'S MAKE IT A WEEK?
TSK! A YEAR OR THERE'S NO WAY!
WHAT?! ARE YOU TRYING TO BLEED ME DRY?
WE'VE LEARNED FROM THE BEST... HE-HE!
SIGH... OKAY, YOU LITTLE VAMPIRES! HERE'S YOUR ADVANCE PAYMENT...
HOORAY!

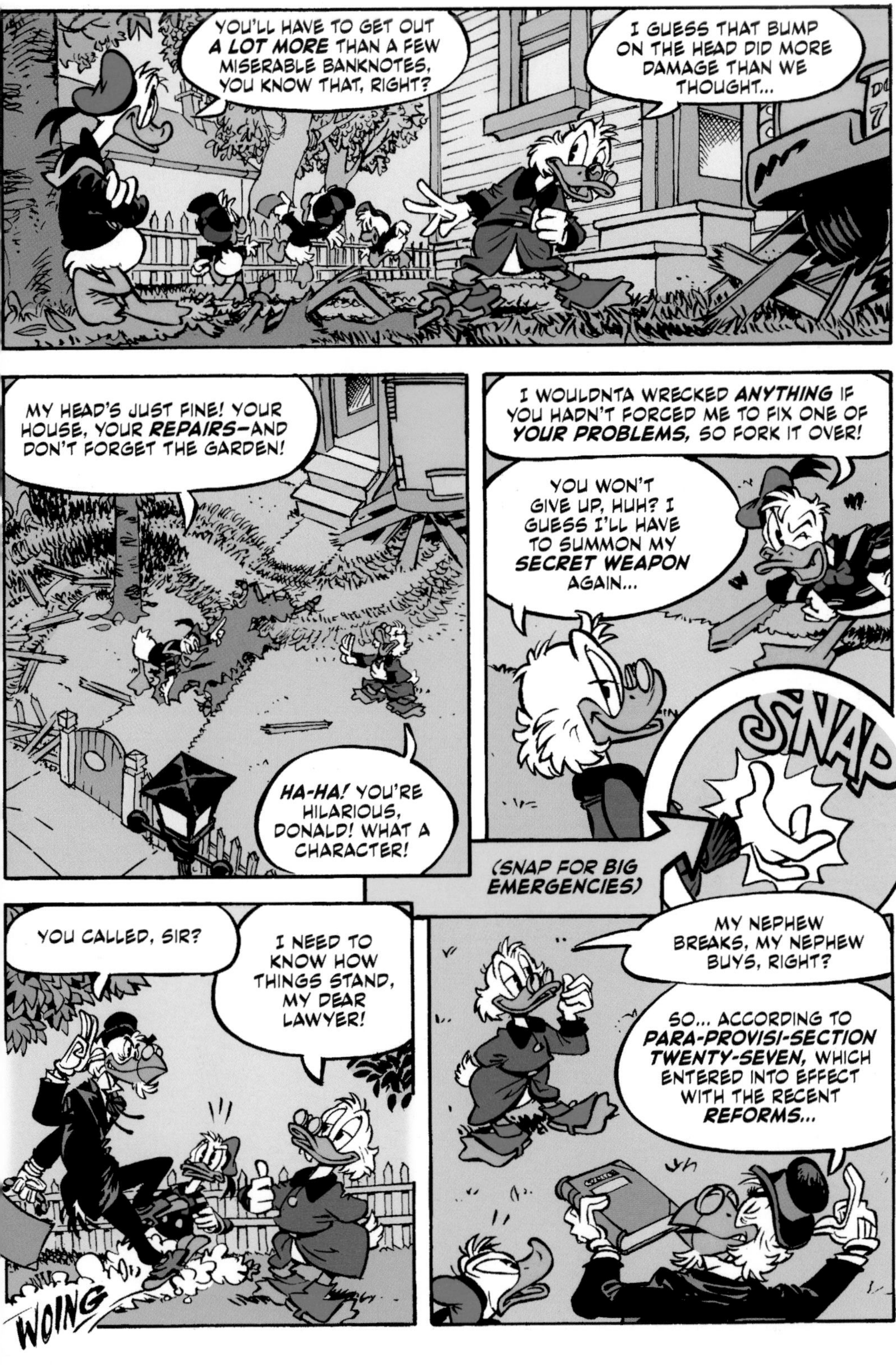
YOU'LL HAVE TO GET OUT A LOT MORE THAN A FEW MISERABLE BANKNOTES, YOU KNOW THAT, RIGHT?
I GUESS THAT BUMP ON THE HEAD DID MORE DAMAGE THAN WE THOUGHT...
MY HEAD'S JUST FINE! YOUR HOUSE, YOUR REPAIRS—AND DON'T FORGET THE GARDEN!
HA-HA! YOU'RE HILARIOUS, DONALD! WHAT A CHARACTER!
I WOULDNTA WRECKED ANYTHING IF YOU HADN'T FORCED ME TO FIX ONE OF YOUR PROBLEMS, SO FORK IT OVER!
YOU WON'T GIVE UP, HUH? I GUESS I'LL HAVE TO SUMMON MY SECRET WEAPON AGAIN...
SNAP
(SNAP FOR BIG EMERGENCIES)
YOU CALLED, SIR?
I NEED TO KNOW HOW THINGS STAND, MY DEAR LAWYER!
WOING
MY NEPHEW BREAKS, MY NEPHEW BUYS, RIGHT?
SO... ACCORDING TO PARA-PROVISI-SECTION TWENTY-SEVEN, WHICH ENTERED INTO EFFECT WITH THE RECENT REFORMS...

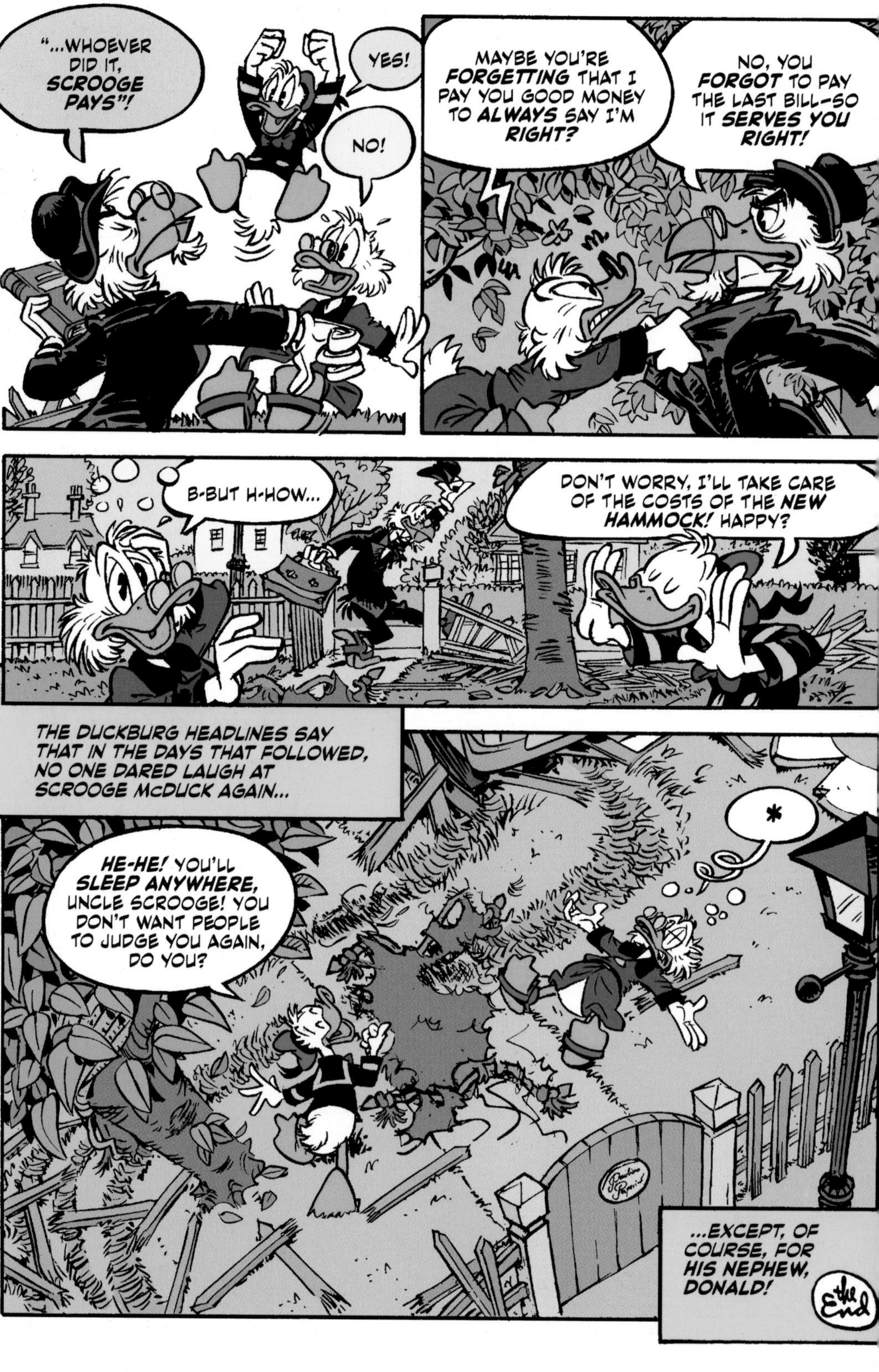
"...WHOEVER DID IT, SCROOGE PAYS"!
YES!
NO!
MAYBE YOU'RE FORGETTING THAT I PAY YOU GOOD MONEY TO ALWAYS SAY I'M RIGHT?
NO, YOU FORGOT TO PAY THE LAST BILL—SO IT SERVES YOU RIGHT!
B-BUT H-HOW...
DON'T WORRY, I'LL TAKE CARE OF THE COSTS OF THE NEW HAMMOCK! HAPPY?
THE DUCKBURG HEADLINES SAY THAT IN THE DAYS THAT FOLLOWED, NO ONE DARED LAUGH AT SCROOGE McDUCK AGAIN...
HE-HE! YOU'LL SLEEP ANYWHERE, UNCLE SCROOGE! YOU DON'T WANT PEOPLE TO JUDGE YOU AGAIN, DO YOU?
*
...EXCEPT, OF COURSE, FOR HIS NEPHEW, DONALD!
The End

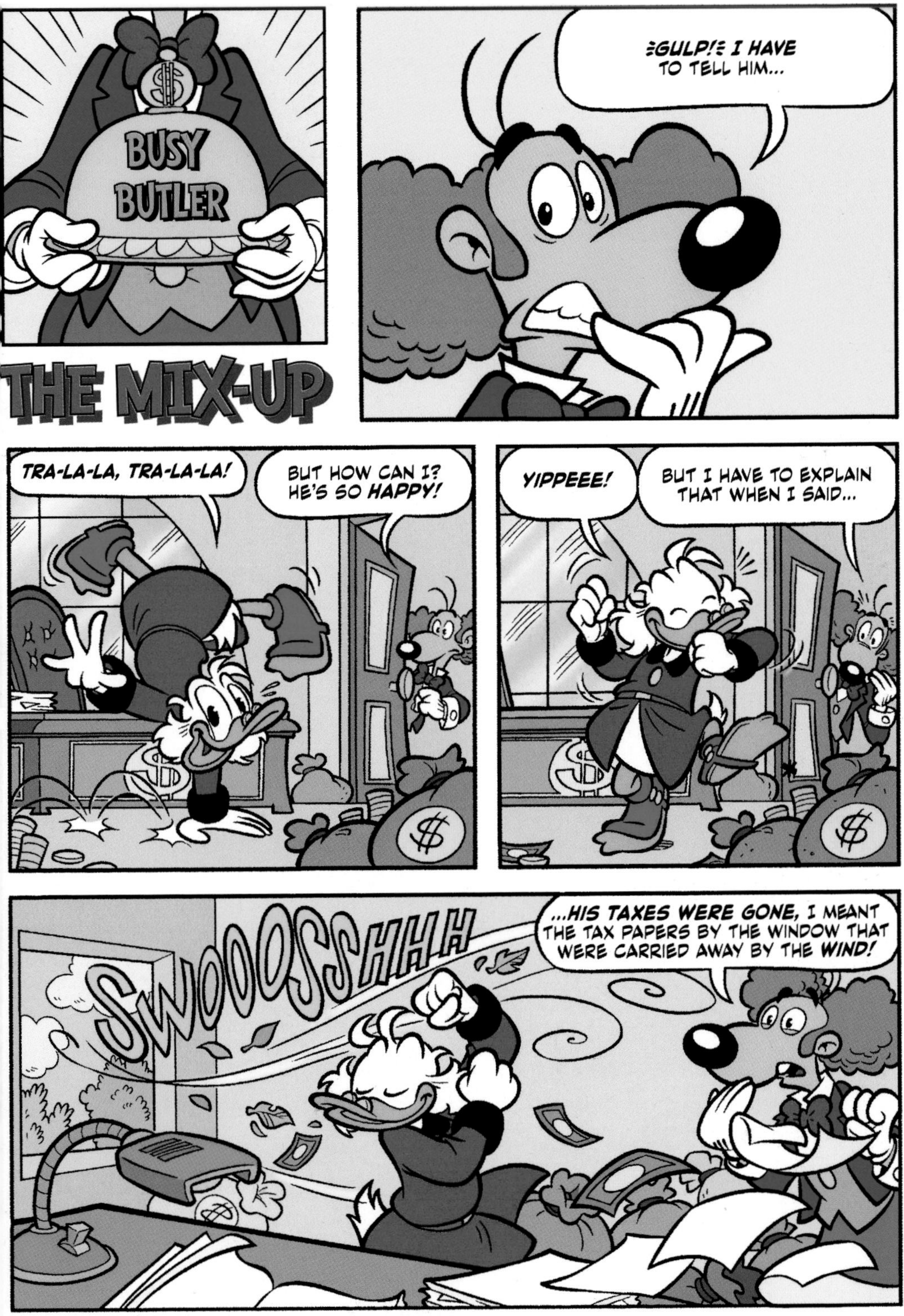
BUSY BUTLER
THE MIX-UP
≡GULP!≡ I HAVE TO TELL HIM...
TRA-LA-LA, TRA-LA-LA!
BUT HOW CAN I? HE'S SO HAPPY!
YIPPEEE!
BUT I HAVE TO EXPLAIN THAT WHEN I SAID...
SWOOOSSHHH
...HIS TAXES WERE GONE, I MEANT THE TAX PAPERS BY THE WINDOW THAT WERE CARRIED AWAY BY THE WIND!

ORIGINALLY PUBLISHED IN **TOPOLINO #3222** (ITALY, 2017) • **FIRST USA PUBLICATION**

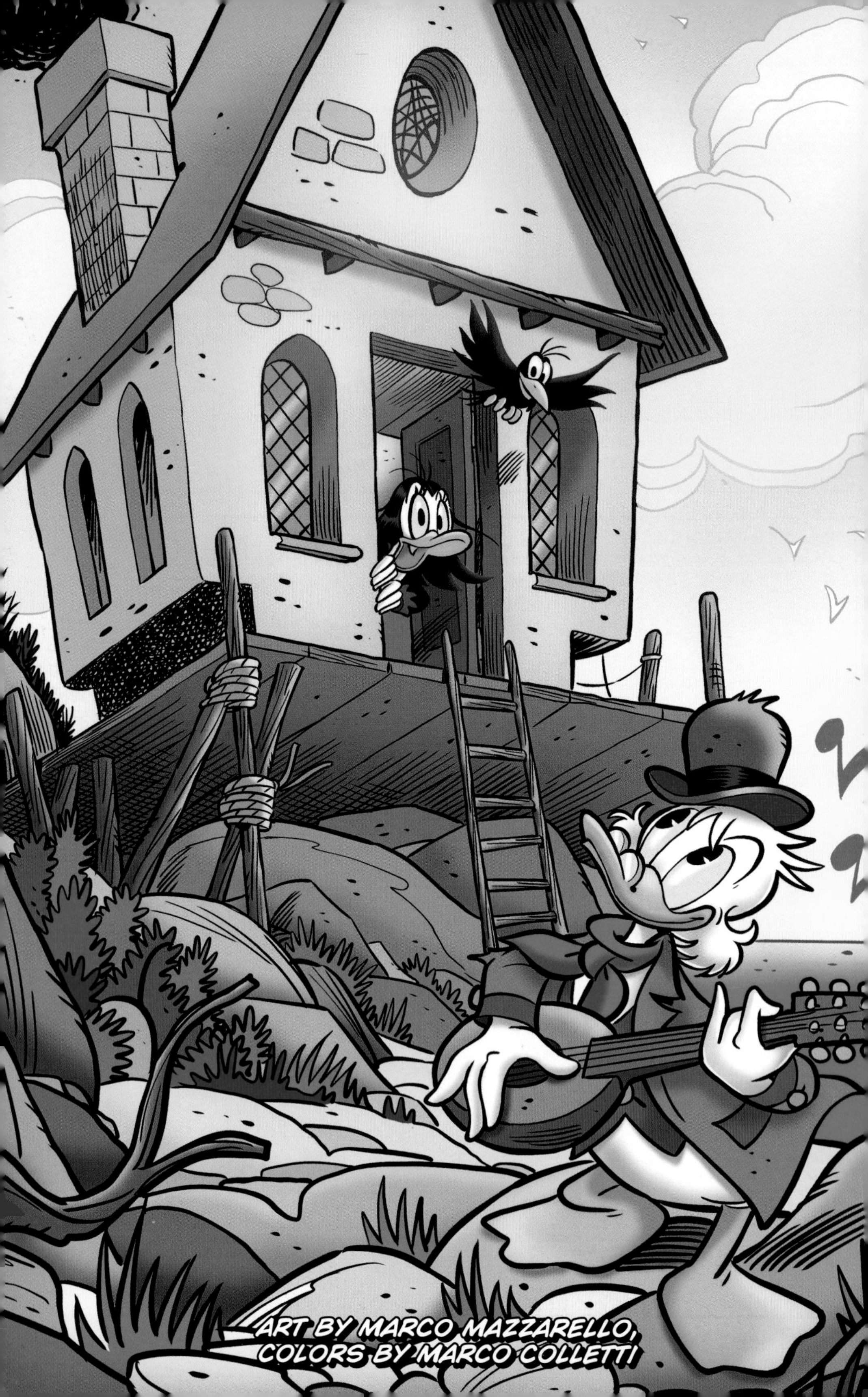
ART BY MARCO MAZZARELLO,
COLORS BY MARCO COLLETTI

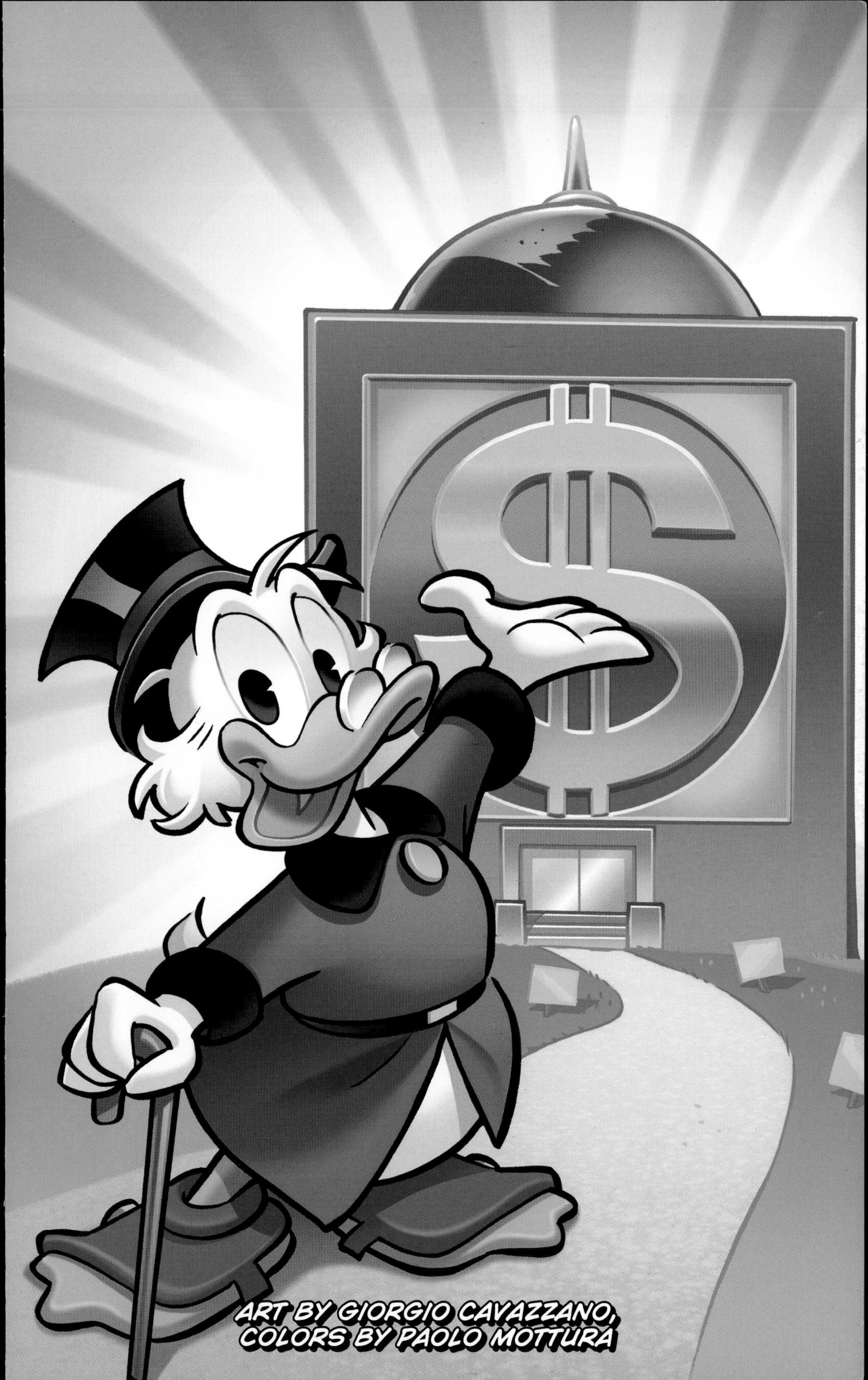

ART BY GIORGIO CAVAZZANO,
COLORS BY PAOLO MOTTURA

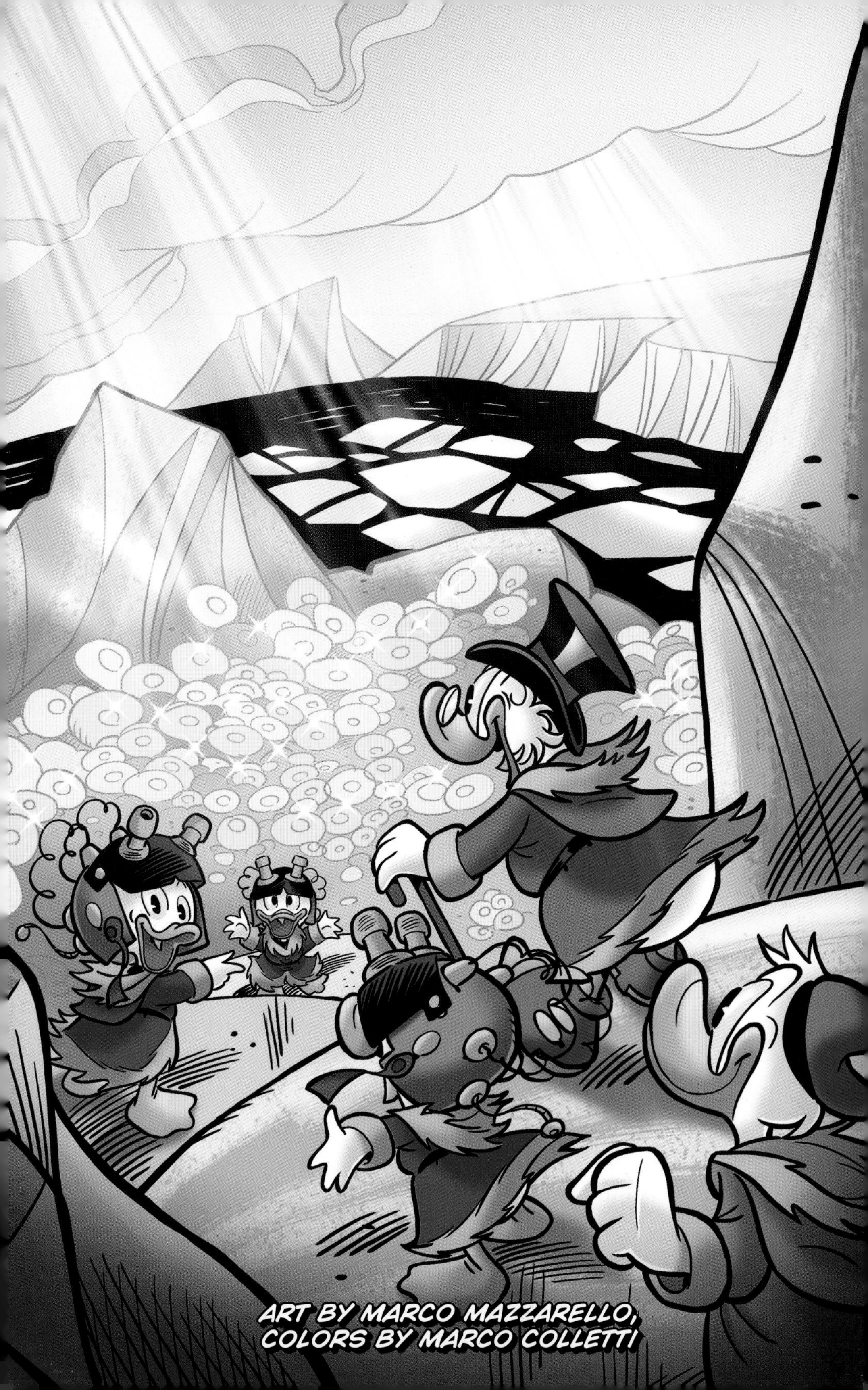
ART BY MARCO MAZZARELLO,
COLORS BY MARCO COLLETTI

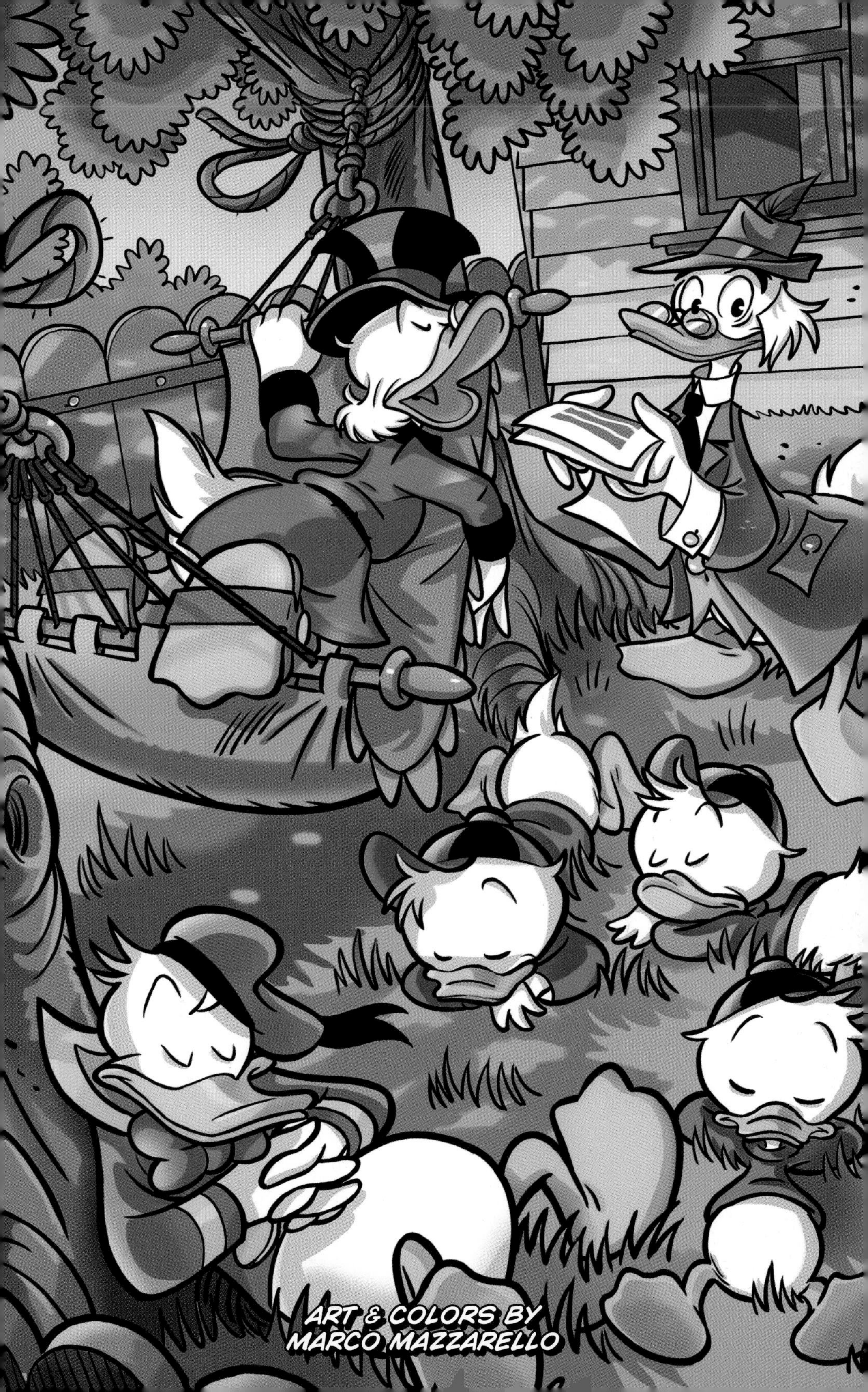
ART & COLORS BY
MARCO MAZZARELLO

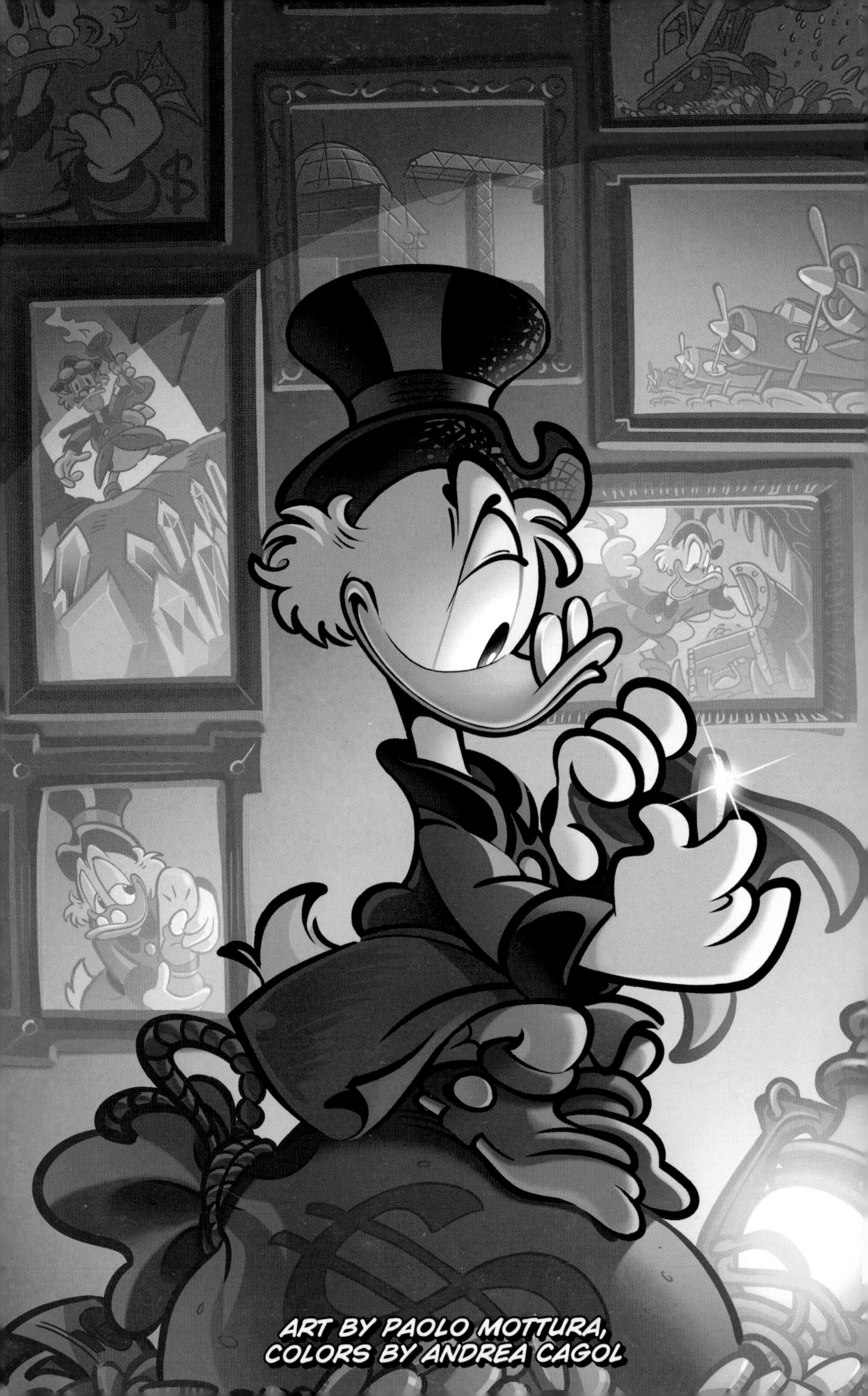

ART BY PAOLO MOTTURA,
COLORS BY ANDREA CAGOL